Penguin Crime Fiction
The Coconut Killings

Patricia Moyes was born in Dublin in 1923. Besides
writing novels, she has had an interesting variety of
jobs. In 1940 she joined the Women's Royal Air Force
and was then a technical adviser at a film studio, a
secretary to Peter Ustinov, a journalist on *Vogue* and
a translator of plays from the French.

Patricia Moyes is the pseudonym of Mrs Haszard,
who now lives in Washington. She first started writing
on a skiing holiday, when she had dislocated her foot.
Her first book was called, perhaps appropriately,
Dead Men Don't Ski. Among her other novels are
Who Saw Her Die? (which won the Edgar Allan Poe
Award from the Mystery Writers of America), *Season
of Snows and Sins*, *Murder à la Mode*, *Falling Star*,
Death and the Dutch Uncle (1969), *The Curious Affair
of the Third Dog* (1973), *Black Widower* (1977) and *How
to Talk to Your Cat* (1978).

Patricia Moyes

The Coconut Killings

Penguin Books

Penguin Books Ltd, Harmondsworth,
Middlesex, England
Penguin Books, 625 Madison Avenue,
New York, New York 10022, U.S.A.
Penguin Books Australia Ltd, Ringwood,
Victoria, Australia
Penguin Books Canada Ltd, 2801 John Street,
Markham, Ontario, Canada L3R 1B4
Penguin Books (N.Z.) Ltd, 182–190 Wairau Road,
Auckland 10, New Zealand

First published in Great Britain, under the title
To Kill a Coconut, by William Collins Sons &
Company Ltd in their Crime Club 1977
First published in the United States of America by
Holt, Rinehart and Winston 1977. This edition
published in the United States of America by
arrangement with Holt, Rinehart and Winston

Published in Penguin Books 1979

Copyright © Patricia Moyes, 1977
All rights reserved

Made and printed in Great Britain by
Cox & Wyman Ltd, London, Reading and Fakenham
Set in Linotype Plantin

This book is for Rocky

Chapter 1

Correspondence from Margaret Colville to Emmy Tibbett
2919 Mulberry Place
Washington DC
USA
November 30th

My dear Emmy,

This is to let you know that John and I finally succumbed to your propaganda and went to the Caribbean for a holiday. In fact, we're just back after spending Thanksgiving on your favourite island of Tampica.

It was wonderful, and we can quite see why you and Henry love it so much – but with all the new hotels opening up, it's beginning to get a bit crowded. Splendid for the island's economy, of course, but not so good for unsociable vacationers like us. However, we took a day trip to St Matthew's, which is one of the British Seaward Islands (I believe there was some talk of St Matthew's joining with Tampica at the time of Independence, but the islanders voted to stay British). We have quite lost our hearts to St Matthew's, which is just as you described Tampica before the big tourist boom. I have a feeling we shall be going back there.

How is London? It seems a long time since we left, and we are becoming quite Americanized. John still enjoys his job with the World Bank here, and of course we love living in Georgetown – but already we're beginning to think about retirement. It may sound a bit premature, but we both like the idea of doing something quite new and different while we're still young enough. John says this is a depressing era for economists. Have you ever known one that wasn't?

We both send our love to both of you,

Margaret

7

The Anchorage Inn
St Matthew's
British Seaward Islands
March 15th

Isn't this a pretty little inn? Having a wonderful time, wish you were here. Why do they make cards so small? Will write later. Love, M.

2919 Mulberry Place
Washington DC
April 5th

My dear Emmy,

At last, the promised letter. As you'll have gathered from my postcard, we had a marvellous holiday on St Matthew's. It's a smaller island than Tampica, but much the same when it comes to scenery – a mountainous centre covered in rain forest, miles of coral beaches and palm trees, and of course the incredible crystal-clear Caribbean.

You remember the luxury hotel on Tampica, where you and Henry stayed – Pirate's Cave? Well, I can only tell you that St Matthew's has an establishment which makes Pirate's Cave look like a holiday camp. It's called St Matthew's Golf Club, and the golf course is the main attraction. Quite apart from the huge daily rate for staying there, the annual subscription is . . . well, I won't even tell you, because you'd faint. Having thus ensured that only the very, very rich can afford to go there, the members take advantage of the fact that it's a club, and blackball any of the very rich whom they consider undesirable.

Needless to say, John and I are NOT members. However, we found a delightful little inn, run very much like an English pub, called the Anchorage. The rates are quite reasonable, the rooms are simple but attractive, and it's close to beautiful beaches. The owners are a pleasant couple (British) – but they are moving back to England before the end of the year, so we don't know what will become of the Anchorage. Anyway we have booked to go there again in August.

Give our love to Chelsea. We saw Henry's name in the English papers on St Matthew's – something about Chief Superintendent Tibbett making a statement on a murder case. He does lead an exciting life. John says economics is getting a duller and more discouraging profession every day.

Love,
Margaret

The Anchorage Inn
St Matthew's
British Seaward Islands
August 21st

My dear Emmy,

I'm afraid this is rather a sad letter, in spite of the fact that St Matthew's is just as lovely as ever. Ann and Harry (the owners of the Anchorage) are definitely retiring in October, and so far they haven't found a buyer for the pub – that is, other than the Golf Club, who want to turn it into staff quarters. So it looks as though this will be our last visit to our beautiful and special island. Still – we are making the most of it. The snorkelling in Cedar Valley Bay is fantastic – I saw a parrot fish this afternoon, about a foot long and all colours of the rainbow and not a bit scared – I could have touched him. John has been doing a lot of horseback riding and sailing. I think he hates the idea of going back to Washington even more than I do. He's talking a lot about early retirement, so perhaps you'll see us back in London sooner than you expect!

Love,
Margaret

Printed matter. Postmark, St Matthew's, BSI, 30 October
John and Margaret Colville are delighted to inform their friends, both old and new, that they are taking over the Anchorage Inn, St Matthew's, BSI, on the retirement of Harry and Ann Parsons. The Anchorage is at present closed for redecoration, but will open for the Christmas season on December 15th. Bookings accepted now. Looking forward to seeing you!

The Anchorage Inn
St Matthew's
January 10th

My dear Emmy,

Bless you for your Christmas card and your sweet letter. I'm sorry about the nasty little printed announcement, but, as you can imagine, life has been hectic.

It all happened in such a hurry. By one of those unbelievable coincidences, John heard all within a week that a) he had inherited a legacy which would just cover the down payment on the Anchorage, and b) that he was eligible for an early-retirement scheme, with a good pension. You may have gathered from my letters that this idea has been simmering in our minds for some time – but it seemed just like a pipe dream.

In fact, it was rather like a scene in an old-time melodrama where the hero is about to face the firing-squad when a messenger gallops up shouting, 'Don't shoot! He's reprieved!' We called Ann and Harry to discuss the situation at leisure, only to hear that they were due to sign a contract with the Golf Club the very next day! We took the night flight down, and by lunch-time the deal was fixed, we'd paid our deposit, and Major Chatsworth (that's the Secretary of the Golf Club) was miffed as all hell. Actually, he's a nice person and we're good friends now. I don't think his wife has quite forgiven us yet – she's something of a character.

We've never worked so hard in our lives, but we love it. I never thought we'd get the redecoration done in time for our December 15th opening – but somehow everything got done, mostly thanks to Sandy. He's our barman, right hand and general factotum, a native-born Mathusian and a tower of strength, both literally and figuratively. He's only twenty-three, but he's got brains as well as brawn, and I just don't know what we'd do without him.

Anyhow, we had a couple of guests booked in from the very first day, and for Christmas every room was full – all six of them! It was hectic but we managed, and I think they all had a good time. In fact, two couples booked in for next Christmas before they left! Major Chatsworth and the other people from the Golf Club are being very friendly and helpful – that's what we like so much about this island. Everybody is pleasant and welcoming, and as far as we can see there's absolutely no racial tension – which is more than you can say for a lot of places around here. There's a small group of young men – out-islanders who have come here to find work – who tend to congregate in one of the bars and breathe fire at the fat cats up at the Golf Club: but Sandy says it's just a lot of hot air and there are no real Mathusians involved. He says they knew very well what they were doing when they refused to 'go independent' along with Tampica, and they're perfectly happy as a Crown Colony.

By the way, we were honoured last week by a visit from His Excellency the Governor of the British Seawards, doing the rounds of his parish (the seat of government is on St Mark's, about twenty miles away). He stayed at the Golf Club, of course, but Major Chatsworth brought him over here one evening for a drink. He's a nice old boy – name of Sir Geoffrey Patterson. Quite bright, I think. Has some good ideas about the future of the islands – getting some source of income going aside from just tourism.

I need hardly say that John and I would adore to welcome you and Henry as our guests – but of course I know it's a horribly long way from England. Still, do think about it.

Love to you both,

Margaret

From The Times, *London, 21 March*
US Senator Murdered
The wave of racial violence which has been sweeping the Caribbean now appears to have reached the small British island of St Matthew's in the British Seawards. US Senator Brett Olsen was found dead yesterday on the links of the exclusive St Matthew's Golf Club, where he was spending a holiday. Victim of an apparently senseless and motiveless crime, the Senator had been savagely attacked and mutilated with a machete, or native knife.

The crime follows the pattern of similar incidents on other islands, in which young black men have attacked and killed total strangers, who are always both white and wealthy. Up until now, however, St Matthew's has been known for its exceptionally smooth race relations. Sir Geoffrey Patterson, the Governor of the British Seaward Islands, has expressed profound shock and regret at the murder. Sanderson Robbins, 23, a native of St Matthew's, has been arrested and charged with the crime.

Senator Olsen will best be remembered for his work on the so-called Olsen Committee, which has done much to encourage and stabilize the cotton industry of the United States.

The Anchorage Inn
St Matthew's
March 21st

Oh, Emmy, the most terrible thing has happened and we are distraught and Henry is the only person we can think of to help us. A very important American Senator was found dead on the golf course on Tuesday, and the police have arrested *Sandy*, of all people, and charged him with murder!!! They've got what seems on the surface to be a very good case against him, with a witness and everything, and I know Sandy's story sounds thin, but you've got to believe me, Emmy, Sandy is *innocent*. He just simply couldn't and wouldn't have done such an awful thing – he's the kindest, sweetest person on earth, and he'd only met this Olsen character a couple of times, in the bar here. He had absolutely no reason to attack him and carve him up with a machete – if it wasn't tragic it would be ridiculous even to think of it. What's more, the whole island is furious and upset at Sandy's arrest, and that little gang of out-islanders I told you about is all set to make trouble, you mark my words. Now, of course, people are saying that Sandy was one of them, but he *wasn't*.

Emmy, I may be just silly, but I can't help remembering how Henry cleared up that affair at the Tampican Embassy in Washington, and I know that if anybody can help poor Sandy, it's him – Henry, I mean. Please please, won't you both fly out here *as soon as possible* and stay with us and see what can be done? John and I will pay your fares, if that's a difficulty. We'd do anything for Sandy's sake – and for the sake of St Matthew's come to that. Tourists are leaving the Golf Club in droves, nobody dares go on to the links any more, and we've had three cancellations since the news broke yesterday in the American press. Somebody really horrible and frightening must have set out to do this to the island – and to poor Sandy – and it just must NOT be allowed to happen. We know Henry can help us, and we beg him to. Please cable your answer as soon as possible. You get here from England via Antigua and St Mark's by air, then take a boat. Please help us . . .

Margaret

(In a different hand)

Henry, old man, I realize that Margaret is somewhat incoherent, but the situation is grave, both on personal and political levels. If there is any way you could co-operate, we'd really appreciate it.

John

From The Times, *London, 23 March*

Unrest on Caribbean Island

Further racial unrest appears to be breaking out on the Caribbean island of St Matthew's, where US Senator Brett Olsen was murdered last Tuesday. Reports reaching Tampica tell of a small band of young blacks roaming the streets, overturning and burning a white-owned car and breaking several windows. The Governor of the BSI, Sir Geoffrey Patterson, visited St Matthew's yesterday, but so far no official comment on the disturbances has been issued.

Inter-office Memo. Dated 26 March

From: Assistant Commissioner's Office

To: Chief Superintendent Tibbett, Room 508, C Division

The Assistant Commissioner would like to see Chief Superintendent Tibbett in his office at 9.00 a.m. tomorrow, March 27th, in connection with a special assignment overseas.

(Signed) Indecipherable
For Assistant Commissioner

'Ah, good morning, Tibbett. Sit down.'

'Thank you, sir.'

'Well, I've got what you might call a little plum of a job in mind for you, Tibbett – although it may turn out to be tricky. You know the Caribbean, I believe?'

'I've been there once, sir. To Tampica. In connection with the Ironmonger case – '

'That's right. You know the area. You have connections with the Tampican Government.'

'I've met the Prime Minister, yes, sir. I wouldn't say the connection was very close.'

'Never mind. It's a connection, which is more than any of my other senior officers have. You've seen the papers? This affair on St Matthew's, in the Seawards?'

'Yes, sir.'

'I've had the High Commissioner on to me. The situation is in hand, but it could turn ugly. There seems to be no doubt that the young man they've arrested is guilty, but apparently he's a popular character, and unfortunately the Chief of Police is a white man. This has paved the way for all sorts of fire-raising rumours about racial influence and political bias and heaven knows what else. As I understand the situation, Tibbett, the trouble-makers are just a small group of itinerant workmen, not people from St Matthew's at all. The islanders themselves voted to remain British, and have been perfectly happy – until now. However, this is just the sort of incident that could lead to inflamed passions and . . . well . . .'

'If I might say so, sir – '

'The High Commissioner has been in touch with the Governor, who is currently on St Matthew's, and they both agree that the only way to avert a dangerous situation is to put the investigation of the crime into entirely neutral hands. In other words, they've asked us to help.'

'Sir, I must tell you that – '

'Let me finish, please, Tibbett. My plan is that you and Sergeant Reynolds should fly out to St Matthew's and take charge of the investigation. You will report to Inspector Montague, the island's Chief of Police, who made the arrest. He will give you all the details. As I said – '

'But, sir – '

'As I said, it's apparently an open-and-shut case, but it will make all the difference if the local people realize that it is in the hands of a completely impartial and expert detective from London. You will also keep in close touch with the Governor, Sir Geoffrey Patterson – '

'Sir, I – '

'You will stay at the Golf Club, of which you will become a temporary member, and Sergeant Reynolds at a small establishment known as the Anchorage Inn. Transportation is being arranged for tomorrow – my office has all the details. I shall expect you to report frequently to me. You must realize that this is not just another murder investigation, Tibbett. It is also a diplomatic mission of some delicacy. Well – any questions?'

'Yes, sir.'

'Oh. Really? Well?'

'I'm afraid I can't undertake the assignment, sir.'

'You're . . . what?'

'I have to disqualify myself, sir. I wouldn't be an impartial investigator.'

'This is ridiculous, Tibbett. Explain yourself.'

'I've been trying to, sir. You see, my wife and I are old friends of the Colvilles – the couple who run the Anchorage Inn. The suspect under arrest is their barman. In fact, my wife had a letter from Mrs Colville only this morning – ironically enough, asking if I couldn't go over there and try to sort the case out. She's considerably worked up about it.'

'H'm. That's not so good, Tibbett, I agree. These Colville people are white, I presume?'

'Yes, sir. A retired economist and his wife. They only took over the pub last Christmas.'

'I see. It certainly wouldn't do if it were known that you were a friend of these white people, who must be eager to see this fellow . . . what's his name? . . . this Sanderson Robbins convicted and sentenced as soon as – '

'Oh no, sir. You misunderstand me. The Colvilles are passionately convinced that Sandy . . . that Robbins is innocent. That's why they asked for my help – to try to clear him. They know him well, you see, and obviously they like him very much. They think he's been framed in some way.'

'They do, do they? Now this is interesting, Tibbett. This puts a different complexion on things. Do the islanders in general know that these Colvilles are rooting for Robbins?'

'I should think they must, sir. Margaret and John are both pretty outspoken people, and the letter made it plain how strongly they felt.'

'Well, now, Tibbett ... this could be to our advantage. If it were known that you and your wife were friends of these people ... that you could be presumed to have a bias in Robbins's favour, if anything ... then your eventual conclusion that he was guilty could not possibly be suspect. Yes – the more I think of it, the more I think that a leaning in *that* direction would be positively helpful. I suggest that Mrs Tibbett should travel with you, and that you should both stay at the Anchorage Inn. That does raise a small problem, however. You will need the assistance of Sergeant Reynolds, and you know our policy of accommodation for officers of different ranks – '

'Why shouldn't Sergeant Reynolds stay at the Golf Club, sir? It'll be useful to have somebody there, and I believe his handicap is coming down nicely. I don't play golf myself, so it would be a very suitable arrangement.'

'You know what sort of a place it is?'

'Yes, sir. Gold-plated and ultra-snobbish. British-owned, but patronized almost entirely by Americans.'

'You think they'd accept Reynolds as a temporary member?'

'They'd have to, wouldn't they, sir?'

'Yes, in the circumstances, I suppose they would. Might do 'em a bit of good. Cheer the place up a bit.'

'That's what I thought, sir. And another thing – I assume that my presence on the island will get a fair bit of publicity, but there's no need for anybody to know who Reynolds is, is there?'

'I suppose the Secretary will have to know.'

'All right, just the Secretary. Nobody else. It will give him much more freedom to operate.'

'A good idea, Tibbett. A very good idea.'

Chapter 2

The traveller wishing to get from England to St Matthew's must first of all take a jet plane from London to Antigua, which represents more than ninety-nine per cent of the journey in terms of mileage, and is accomplished comfortably in a matter of a few hours. After that, things become more complicated and take longer.

The quickest way should be to fly in a small two-engined Heron to the island of St Mark's, and from there ride on an open launch over the transparent blue waters of the Caribbean, in the company of assorted merchandise. Unfortunately, however, the launch runs only once a day, and is carefully timed to leave St Mark's just ten minutes before the flight from Antigua arrives. For some time now, the authorities on St Mark's and St Matthew's have had a lurking feeling that this schedule could be improved upon, but things move at a leisurely pace in the Caribbean, and nobody has yet got around to doing anything about it.

In practice, the most painless way to make the journey is to spend the day in Antigua, and in the evening board the ferry boat called the *Island Queen*. You will wake up the following morning in the sparkling little harbour of Priest Town on the southern coast of St Matthew's (there is controversy locally as to whether the village owes its name to an association with missionaries, or whether it is a corruption of Preston – the northern English textile town from which early settlers were said to have emigrated).

In any case, the question of convenient transportation from Europe hardly arises on St Matthew's, because less than one per cent of the visitors arrive from across the Atlantic. The life-blood of the island is the stream of wealthy Americans who patronize the Golf Club, and they are carefully catered for. Smooth, swift jet-liners fly from New York, Washington and Miami to the American island of St Boniface, where smartly-uniformed Golf Club staff are waiting to escort members to the club's own luxury motor launch for the last lap of the voyage. Mere travellers who are not members of the Club must undertake a complicated journey by way of the independent island of Tampica – a journey so exhausting and inconvenient that they seldom try it a second time. It is also possible to hire a local boat to St Matthew's, but this fact is kept very quiet. The committee and members of St Matthew's Golf Club are anxious to discourage ordinary tourism on the island. Several times, suggestions have been made in St Mark's that St Matthew's should build a small airstrip – but the Golf Club owns the only stretch of land flat enough for such a project, and has no intention of selling. After all, the rich, beautiful and important people of the world must have *some* place where they can enjoy a little privacy.

Henry and Emmy Tibbett, arriving from London, travelled by an even more roundabout route than usual, because Henry wanted to break his journey on Tampica and visit an old friend there. So, while Sergeant Reynolds went sightseeing on Antigua before embarking on the *Island Queen*, Henry and Emmy took the Heron to St Mark's, and from there climbed into a tiny six-seater Piper Aztec, and were soon craning their necks to catch a first glimpse of the familiar shape of Tampica, with its harbour-side town, golden crescents of beach and hilly green centre.

'Good Lord,' Henry said suddenly. 'Look at that.'

'Look at what?' Emmy raised her voice against the thrumming of the engine.

'Down there. Barracuda Bay.'

The few years since the Tibbetts' last visit had transformed the island. Where previously there had been just one harbour-side hotel and one luxury resort-complex, now huge high-rise concrete buildings ringed the sandy bays, gleaming whitely in the brilliant sunshine. An enormous construction site boasted a sign, clearly legible from the air, announcing the imminent completion of the Tampica Hilton. The sheltered anchorage of Barracuda Bay currently harboured no less than five big cruise liners, brave with fluttering bunting, and motor launches traced foaming white curves on the sapphire water as they ferried passengers ashore. Inland, developments of holiday homes looked like a sprawl of nursery building bricks on the deep green carpet of the hillside – uniform little boxes in orderly rows, some brightly painted, some still the drab grey of unfinished breeze-block.

'Margaret didn't tell us the half of it,' said Emmy. 'Oh, well, I suppose it's good for the economy. But I do hope everything hasn't changed.'

She was soon reassured. The airstrip was still a short length of dirt road, and the terminal building a small concrete hut – although the presence of bulldozers and a gang of men in hard hats showed that a billboard promising 'Tampica International Airport, opening soon' was making no idle boast. However, the sunshine and the sweet scent of frangipani on the warm breeze were the same as ever, and so was the big burly figure of Barney, the local garage-man-cum-bar-owner, waving a huge black hand in welcome beside the mini-moke which they had ordered to meet them at the airstrip.

'Good to see you folks again,' Barney said. 'Where you stayin'? Pirate's Cave, or one of the new places?'

'I'm afraid we're not staying anywhere,' Henry answered. 'Just passing through. We're catching the afternoon boat to St Matthew's.'

Barney's normally merry face clouded. 'Bad business, that killing on St Matthew's,' he said. 'Wouldn't never have happened if they'd gone come independent with us, like we wanted. Now they see how fine we doin', they're jealous, man. That's the root of it. Jealous.' He shook his head. 'Ah, well, no trouble of that sort here on Tampica, thank the Lord. You'll be off to see Miss Lucy, then?'

'How did you know?' Emmy asked.

Barney grinned. 'Ain't nobody who bin to Tampica before, comes just for a day and hires a moke and isn't headed for Sugar Mill Bay.'

'How's the road over the hill?' Henry asked.

'Got it tarred 'bout a mile beyond the Lodge and a parapet wall on the sea side going down to Sugar Mill.'

'Thank heaven for that,' Emmy remarked.

'Wall's not a foot high, wouldn't stop you goin' over,' Barney added cheerfully. 'It makes the visitors feel safer, that's all. Well, here's your keys. Don't forget to drive on the left, now.'

'We're from England,' Henry reminded him. 'We always drive on the left.'

'Sure, sure. Sorry ... I just say it automatic whenever I rent a car. Have a good trip now, man.'

'Want a lift back to the garage, Barney?' Henry asked.

'No, thanks a lot. Got a couple more mokes waiting for the St Thomas flight.'

As the little wagon wound its way from the airstrip along the coast road, Emmy said, 'Well, Barney hasn't changed.'

'No,' said Henry, 'but his establishment has. Look.'

When the Tibbetts had last seen Barney's garage, it had been a fenced-off area resembling an untidy junk yard, with a ramshackle open shed as repair shop. Across the road, Barney's Bar had been a little concrete box of a house, painted pistachio green and surrounded by scarlet hibiscus and pink oleanders. Now, as they rounded the bend in the road, a row of gleaming petrol pumps stood like sentinels on the concrete apron, under an illuminated sign reading 'Tampica Traction and Taxi Co'. Behind the pumps, a modern and well-equipped workshop was alive with activity, as mechanics worked in the inspection pits and operated sophisticated repair machinery. Over the way, the little green house was no more than a small annexe to the long, low, hacienda-type building, with terrace tables shaded by striped umbrellas, uniformed waiters serving drinks and food, and the muted beat of canned music. A purple neon sign announced that this was Barney's Cocktail Lounge and Restaurant. Only some undisciplined hens pecking about on the roadway were a reminder of the old days.

Emmy sighed. 'It's not fair to begrudge them all this,' she said. 'I mean, the place is transformed and they're all doing well. All the same ...'

'Remember what Barney said,' Henry reminded her. 'According to Margaret, St Matthew's now is just what Tampica used to be like – and see what's happening there.'

The road took them through the principal town of Tampica Harbour, which they remembered as a sleepy little waterside community. Now it throbbed with life – new shops, new apartment buildings, new hotels. It took some time to negotiate the town, because the narrow streets were crammed with tourists in parrot-bright resort clothes and big straw hats. There was also a marked increase of new cars. It was easy to see why Barney's business was flourishing.

As soon as they left town, however, and began to climb the sinuous track over Goat Hill, things became more familiar. True, the road was tarred for a mile or so beyond the Lodge – the Prime Minister's residence – but after that it became the old, boulder-strewn dirt track that Henry and Emmy remembered. The views were the same as ever: limpid blue water creaming over coral reefs and breaking on beaches as curved and golden as fresh croissants; white sails of yachts leaning to the breeze; the scatter of tiny rocky islets punctuating the sapphire and emerald sea. Everything was really just the same.

Making the steep descent down the hairpin bends to Sugar Mill Bay, Henry saw what Barney meant about the protective parapet walls. They were tiny and obviously fragile: and yet, it somehow made a big difference to feel that there was *something* between the moke, with its unreliable brakes, and the thousand-foot plunge on to the rocks below. Nevertheless, it was with the usual sense of relief that Henry took the last snaking bend and came out on to the flat coastal track that led to Sugar Mill House, and Miss Lucy Pontefract-Deacon.

Sugar Mill Bay had changed very little. True, there were a couple of jeeps parked near the beach, and a handful of holiday-makers basking on the sand, but otherwise the little settlement of sugar-almond houses was as Henry remembered it, with barefoot children and sleepy dogs and young goats with impertinent tails going about their business. The big gates of Sugar Mill House stood open, and there in the driveway was Lucy Pontefract-Deacon, her arms held wide in welcome.

Henry pulled the moke to a halt, and jumped out. 'Lucy, my dear – you haven't changed one little bit!'

Lucy beamed. 'That is a lie, of course,' she said. 'After eighty, every year leaves its mark. But bless you for saying it.'

'But it's true, Lucy,' Emmy protested. 'You look wonderful.'

'If Emmy says so, then it must be true,' conceded Miss Pontefract-Deacon. Indeed, the old lady was impressive, with her tall, upright figure, her snow-white hair and her sun-tanned face – lined, but astonishing in its look of youthful innocence. 'Well, then, let me return the compliment. You are half my age, so the years show only half as much. And you've lost weight,' she added to Emmy approvingly.

'A little. Not enough.'

'Don't want to get skinny, my dear. It wouldn't suit you. Now, come in and have a drink and tell me all about this dreadful affair on St Matthew's. That's why you're here, of course.'

Henry began, 'How did you – ' and then checked himself. 'I should know better than to ask how. You know everything that goes on.'

'On Tampica, yes. But a few things that happen on the out-islands manage to escape my notice.' Lucy led the way through her comfortable drawing-room, and out on to a shady terrace. 'Come and sit down. Iced tea or rum punch?' She tinkled a small silver bell, and a black lad with a wide grin appeared from the house. 'Three rum punches, please, Martin. Now, where was I? Oh yes – I don't pretend to keep track of everything over on St Matthew's, but Geoffrey Patterson was here to tea the other day – he's an old friend of mine – and he happened to mention that you were coming over to look into this murder.'

' "Happened to mention" indeed,' said Henry with a grin. 'I suppose he had told you all about the case before he even knew he was being pumped.'

'There's no need to take that attitude with me, young man,' replied Lucy, with spirit. 'You're every bit as bad as I am, and you know it. What about that mild mousey manner and positively apologetic interview technique? I know how you get your information.'

Emmy laughed. 'You're perfectly right, Lucy,' she said. 'You and Henry are two of a kind.'

'Our methods are different, but we make a good team,' Lucy agreed. 'Ah, here are your drinks.' She waited until Martin had gone, and then said, 'Well? What do you want to know?'

'Everything that you know,' Henry said.

Lucy considered. 'That doesn't amount to a great deal. I know Sandy Robbins – he once had a girl here on Tampica. It would surprise me if he was guilty as charged.'

'You mean, you don't think he's capable of murder?' asked Henry.

'I mean no such thing, nor did I say it. Sandy handles a machete as well as any man in these islands, and he has a quick temper. If it was a question of a fight over a girl, say ... or if somebody had done a friend of his a really bad turn ... yes, I can imagine Sandy killing. What I do not believe is that he would get mixed up in some extremist political group, much less murder a total stranger as a result.'

'That's the police theory, I understand,' Henry said.

'Yes. That's why I used the words "guilty as charged". The evidence against him is very strong — no doubt about that. Before you rule Sandy out as the culprit, you'll have to dig pretty deeply into his relationship with Senator Brett Olsen.' Lucy stirred her rum punch with a slender silver spoon.

'You think there may be a relationship?'

'I have no idea. I only know Olsen as the name of a committee, and a man who vacations in the Caribbean. I'm just telling you that if Sandy Robbins killed him, it was personal, not political.'

'What possible personal connection could a Mathusian barman have with a US Senator?' said Emmy.

Lucy smiled. 'Islands are small places,' she said. 'Sandy Robbins has lived all his life on St Matthew's, and this wasn't Olsen's first visit. Sandy has always been a great one for the girls, and I understand from Geoffrey that the Senator's wife wasn't with him — she flew back from Europe when she heard the news. There might be a line of investigation there.'

'What's the Governor's opinion?' Henry asked.

Lucy gave a little impatient sigh. 'Geoffrey simply wants the whole thing cleared up and disposed of as soon as possible. I suppose it's inevitable that he should only think of the political angle — and then, he never did have much imagination. He wants Sandy tried, sentenced and hustled off to prison on St Mark's — out of sight, out of mind. Then he feels sure that Owen Montague can deal with the political trouble-makers, given some police reinforcements from other islands. I told Geoffrey that he was making a serious error of judgement.'

'Did you? Why?'

'Because it's too late for those tactics now. The political ball

23

has started rolling and gained momentum, and Sandy's conviction would simply make things worse. People in these parts are volatile and emotional, and a very ugly situation could develop. No – what's needed now is a slow, painstaking investigation, no assumption of guilt, justice being seen to be done. That'll allow a cooling-off period, and if you do find proof of Sandy's guilt – as I am very much afraid you will – at least there'll be nothing hole-and-corner about it. You will also certainly find that the motive was not political, which is very important. So don't let Geoffrey bully you, Henry. Take your time. Get the facts. Above all, don't provoke the trouble-makers. What if a few more windows are broken? It's better than a full-scale riot.'

'You know John and Margaret Colville?' Henry asked.

'Certainly I do. I first met them while they were holidaying here, and after that they came to visit me each time they were on St Matthew's.' The old lady's eyes twinkled. 'In fact, I flatter myself that I may have had a small part in their decision to buy the Anchorage. They are just the sort of people we need on these islands – but residence permits and so on can be tiresome and lengthy to arrange.'

'Unless you know the right people,' said Emmy.

'Exactly, my dear. It is fortunate that I am now on the telephone – an underwater line from St Mark's. Very convenient. I was able to speak to Geoffrey Patterson and get the whole thing fixed up in no time.'

Henry said, 'So you approve of John and Margaret.'

'Of course I do.'

'You know they are convinced of Sandy's innocence?'

'I could hardly fail to know. Margaret has been on the telephone every day. I can only repeat – I do not believe the boy is guilty as charged, but that's a far cry from blameless innocence.' Lucy paused and sipped her drink. Then she said, 'I am very pleased that you are here. Please keep in touch with me – here is my telephone number. And if I can be of any help ...' She glanced at her watch. 'I don't want to rush you, but if you are going to catch the afternoon boat, I think you should be on your way. I don't like anybody to take the Goat Hill road too fast, parapet or no parapet.'

'I agree with you,' said Henry feelingly. 'Thanks a lot, Lucy. We'll be off. If you should happen to think of anything – '

The Tibbetts were already in the moke, and Henry had his hand on the ignition key, when Lucy said, 'You shouldn't overlook Sebastian Chatsworth. Or Teresa.'

Henry said 'Chatsworth? He's the Secretary of the Golf Club, isn't he?'

'He is. And Teresa is his wife. Sebastian is extremely stupid, but he has a lot of influence on St Matthew's. Teresa is ... not stupid. If you handle her right, she will be very useful to you. If not, she would be a formidable enemy.'

'Thanks for telling me,' said Henry.

'I wonder,' said Lucy, 'whose side she is on? It would be interesting to know.'

'I'll telephone you,' Henry said, and turned the key to start the engine.

Chapter 3

The ferry from Tampica tied up alongside the wooden jetty at Priest Town, St Matthew's, just as the sun was going down and the green and red harbour lights began to glow in the brief tropical twilight. On the quayside, a few sparse and inadequate street lamps made it just possible for Henry and Emmy – the only passengers – to make out the figures of John and Margaret Colville, who were waiting to greet them.

It should have been a happy reunion, but inevitably it was not. Margaret's fine-boned, sensitive face looked strained and tired, and her golden hair greyer than Emmy remembered. John's usual bluff good humour was subdued. Hands were shaken, cheeks briefly kissed, and then luggage was loaded into the ubiquitous mini-moke.

The streets of Priest Town were unnaturally quiet. There seemed to be a lot of policemen about. Small groups of black youths lounged on street corners, smoking, smiling slowly, saying little. Several shop windows appeared to have been recently boarded up. There was no music.

Margaret said, 'It's been quiet today, thank God. But you can feel the atmosphere. If Sandy is found guilty . . .'

John said, 'This isn't the way we would have liked to welcome you to St Matthew's. God, why do people have to play politics all the time? This was – this *is* a happy island. Let's hope we can keep it that way.'

'Has it been – ? That is, do they know I'm here, and why?' Henry asked.

'The Governor is making a speech on the radio this evening,' said John. 'He thought it better to get you here safely first.' He changed gear noisily as the moke left the town and began to climb a cliff-side track. 'Trouble is, we don't know who or what is really behind this political unrest. All I'm sure of personally is that someone has really got it in for St Matthew's. Poor old Olsen and Sandy are just pawns in the game – a splendid excuse for a small revolution. Christ, it makes me mad.'

'Well, don't show it, darling,' said Margaret, 'unless you want to land us all in the soup. Major Chatsworth was in the bar at lunch-time, and he said two of his clients had taken one look at your face and cancelled their reservations on the spot.'

'Bloody fool,' muttered John, peering into the darkness ahead, which was only minimally dispersed by the moke's headlamps. On each side of the narrow, rutted lane, hedges of oleander and frangipani stretched out their dark branches, and pale blossoms glimmered.

The man stepped out from the shadows so suddenly that Emmy gave a tiny cry of surprise and alarm. John braked abruptly, swerved to avoid the pedestrian, then began to accelerate.

'Stop, John!' Margaret's voice was sharp and incisive. John hesitated, then stopped. The man was behind them now, running towards the car.

Margaret stuck her head round the canopy and called, 'Daniel! Want a lift to the Anchorage?'

'Thank you, Margaret. Sure do. It's a long dark walk from the Club.'

'Climb in, then. You'll have to sit on the baggage at the back, I'm afraid. Daniel, meet Henry and Emmy, friends of ours from England. This is Daniel Markham. He looks after the greens at the Club.'

'Pleased to know you.' Daniel Markham extended two skinny black hands and gripped Henry's and Emmy's simultaneously. Then he leapt lightly into the back of the moke, and perched on a pile of suitcases. As the car moved forward, Daniel reached in his pocket for tobacco and paper, and began to roll a cigarette, balancing miraculously on his swaying perch. He said, 'Hear you cancelled the dance tonight.'

'It's because of the Governor's speech,' said Margaret easily. 'Everyone'll stay home to hear it. We wouldn't get enough customers to keep the band in beer.'

'Knowing that bunch, you're sure right.' Daniel sounded amused. 'Hear there's to be a dance at the Bum Boat, all the same.'

John, at the wheel, made a sound which started off as a growl and ended as a cough.

'Well, you can always go there, can't you, if you get bored at the Anchorage?' said Margaret, just a shade too brightly. 'Ah, here we are.'

The moke had topped a small hill, and was coming down into a little settlement beside the sea. Henry and Emmy could just make out a few houses – some dark, some glittering with lights. The largest building was a four-square white structure illuminated by a small floodlight. It stood in a garden lit by coloured lanterns, and the rhythmic pounding of the surf on the shore was enhanced by the crisp *obbligato* of a Chopin étude for pianoforte. Outside the building, mounted on a white post, swung a traditional English pub sign depicting an old-fashioned anchor.

'Must've known I was comin',' Daniel remarked. 'Playin' my favourite record. Sandy always –' He stopped abruptly. 'Sorry. For a moment I forgot. Who've you got behind the bar tonight?'

'Me,' said Margaret. 'Harper's just been standing in for me while we went to Priest Town to meet the boat.'

Daniel jumped down from his pile of suitcases. With no particular emotion, he said, 'Reckon you'll have to get another regular barman. Sandy won't be back in a long, long whiles. Well, thanks for the ride . . .' He strolled off in the direction of the bar.

'You'd better get back on the job, darling,' said John. 'I'll help Henry and Emmy upstairs with their luggage.'

'OK.' Margaret climbed out of the moke, took a step towards the bar, then turned back. 'I don't want to rub it in,' she said, 'but tonight was a case in point. If you–'

John held up his hand. 'All right, all right. I thought it was Daniel, but I couldn't be sure. And Henry and Emmy were with us.'

'You see what I mean?' Margaret appealed to Henry. 'You see what's beginning to happen to us? All these people are our friends. If it gets to the point where John's afraid to stop and give a lift to Daniel, then this island is in bad trouble, and getting worse. If I hadn't made John stop – well, every time something like that happens, the wedge goes in deeper. Them and us. Fear and suspicion. It never used to be like this.'

'We'd never had a racist murder before,' said John sombrely.

'Come on, Emmy. This way. Mind, there's a steepish step . . .'

John picked up a couple of suitcases and led the way up an outside staircase to the upper floor. At the top, he stopped, put down the cases and fumbled in his pocket for a key.

'That's another thing,' he said. 'We never locked this door until a week ago, and Margaret still wants to leave it open. Says it's insulting to the islanders. Well, maybe it is or maybe it isn't, but I've got my guests to think of. You'll find a spare key to the outside door in your room. Be a good chap and lock it behind you when you come down, will you, Henry? After all, one does have responsibilities . . .' John sounded defensive.

Henry said, 'Of course. It's only sensible.'

'Well, here you are. Make yourselves at home. Shower through that door, balcony out here. See you in the bar.'

The room was simple but immaculate, and the balcony looked out over a gentle slope towards the silver sea and the lights of Priest Town across the bay. As she unpacked, Emmy said, 'I'm so glad we came. It's one thing to read about things in the newspapers, but quite another to feel them at first hand. It seems to me this is more than just a case to be solved, Henry. It's the future of this island.'

'Is it?' Henry had lit a cigarette, and was standing at the open balcony door, watching the lights of a cruise ship out at sea. 'It all depends how the case comes out, doesn't it?'

'Well . . .'

'Besides, this murder may be a symptom of political change that nobody can stop.' He paused. 'It sometimes seems as though history has been altered by a single event, but it's almost always untrue. The event is produced by the historical process, rather than the other way round.'

'Now you're getting too deep for me,' said Emmy. 'I just want this island to go on being happy and uncomplicated, like it's always been.' She closed a drawer, snapped an empty suitcase shut and swung it up on top of the wardrobe. 'There. All unpacked. Let's go down and have a drink.'

The bar of the Anchorage Inn was roofed, but otherwise open to the lamplit garden. A handful of people – black and white, men and women – sat on tall bamboo bar stools chatting and sipping drinks. Behind the bar, Margaret was busy concocting a complicated rum punch. She looked up and smiled as the Tibbetts came in.

'Ah, there you are. Come and have a welcome drink on the house — I'm just making you a couple of Anchorage punches.' She added some dangerous-looking pink liquid, and began slicing a fresh lime. 'Every bar on every island has its own special recipe, you know. Fortunately, we inherited this one, along with Sandy.' In went a dash from another bottle, a sprinkle of nutmeg and a straw. 'There. See how you like it.'

'It's delicious.'

'Good. Now, you must be introduced. Henry and Emmy Tibbett, great friends of ours from London. Daniel, you know. Sebastian and Teresa — that is, Major and Mrs Chatsworth from the Golf Club. Tom Bradley from Washington DC — he's been staying with us for a couple of weeks. Harper Robinson and — oh, heavens, it's seven o'clock. We'll miss the Gov.'

Quickly, Margaret switched the loudspeaker from turntable to radio, and Chopin was replaced by a silence broken by anticipatory cracklings. Then an announcer with a marked West Indian accent said, 'This is Radio St Mark's, seven o'clock. Ladies and gentlemen, the Governor of the British Seaward Islands, His Excellency Sir Geoffrey Patterson.'

A pause, the clearing of a throat, and then a plummy upperclass British voice took over.

'Good evening, my friends. I'm sure I don't have to remind any of you that our islands — and in particular I am thinking of St Matthew's — is ... em ... are going through a difficult and painful experience. First, we had the savage and meaningless murder of a distinguished visitor from the United States of America. I refer, of course, to Senator Brett Olsen. Then the arrest of a suspect, which was followed by a regrettable outbreak of sporadic violence, on the part of a very few individuals — violence which nevertheless has had and is having a dislocatory effect on the stability of our Crown Colony.'

Sir Geoffrey paused and cleared his throat again. Teresa Chatsworth muttered, 'For God's sake, get on with it,' and Daniel asked nobody in particular what the man was talking about. A voice called, 'About Sandy, man.'

'Now I am sure,' resumed the voice, 'that these individuals are not politically motivated. They are simply unhappy about what they fear may be a miscarriage of justice.' Daniel nodded seriously. 'So it is to these people that I speak first this evening. I want to reassure them that they need have no fear. I have been in personal touch with Scotland Yard in London, and they have sent us one of their most experienced men – Chief Superintendent Henry Tibbett of the CID – to make a thorough investigation into the case.'

Every head in the bar turned to look at Henry, who grinned broadly.

'The Chief Superintendent will stay on St Matthew's until this case has been finally solved beyond a shadow of doubt. He is, of course, completely unbiased, but I happen to know that he holds with the utmost firmness to the basic cornerstone of British law – that a man is innocent until he is proved guilty. He will not be swayed by mere circumstantial evidence. He will track down the murderer – whosoever that may prove to be – until guilt can be irrefutably demonstrated. I ask you all to co-operate with Chief Superintendent Tibbett in his difficult task, and to make him welcome. I also ask all those who have the welfare of our islands at heart to stop the violence, to have confidence in the judicial process, and to ...'

Whatever Sir Geoffrey's next exhortation was going to be, the listeners in the bar of the Anchorage never found out. At that moment, a well-aimed brick – thrown from the outer darkness of the garden – caught the radio fair and square, sending it crashing down from its shelf above the bar, scattering and splintering glasses and bottles as it went. Margaret screamed, ducking down and shielding her face from the broken glass. Sebastian Chatsworth was on his feet, shouting. John Colville came running from the kitchen. For a moment, all was pandemonium. As the confusion subsided, the voice of the Governor came serenely from the radio – now lying on its side under the bar, but still operational.

'– and peace. Goodnight, my friends. Good night.'

John Colville mopped his brow. 'Good ... *night*,' he said. Then – 'Where's Henry?'

'I'm here.' Henry stepped in from the shadowy garden. 'No hope of catching – whoever it was. Got clean away. What's the damage, Margaret?'

Margaret's head appeared from underneath the bar, like an Aunt Sally at a fun fair. 'Just a whole lot of glasses,' she said, 'plus a bottle of Scotch, two bottles of rum and our last real French *crème de menthe* until the next boat comes in. Still, I suppose it could have been worse. I think that merits drinks all round on the house. Teresa, what can I get you?'

'You can get me a dustpan and brush,' said Teresa Chatsworth, 'and let me clear up that broken glass for you. No, no, you get on with serving the drinks. Just leave the damage to me.'

Watching Mrs Chatsworth take charge, Emmy decided that Lucy Pontefract-Deacon had been right, as usual. Teresa was an attractive woman, small, slim and neat. Her brown hair was cropped short, and her skin – devoid of make-up – was deeply and evenly bronzed. By contrast, her husband was a tall man, vague of face and untidily put together. He had managed to add to the general confusion by knocking over several bar stools at the moment of the attack, and was now toppling others as he endeavoured to set the first upright. Emmy decided in her own mind that he had probably been given the job of Golf Club Secretary on the strength of his English accent, his handle-bar moustache and his wife.

'There you are. Two rum punches.' Margaret pushed the drinks across the bar to Henry and Emmy. Her hands were not as steady as her voice. 'Sorry about that. I suppose it was because ...'

'Because of me, I expect,' said Henry. 'Bless you, Margaret. Your health.'

'I think we should drink to yours,' said Margaret.

'Nonsense.' Teresa Chatsworth swept a final sliver of broken glass into the dustpan, and stood up. 'I'll need a lot of old newspaper to wrap this in, Margaret. Thanks. No, you've no need to worry, Chief Superintendent. The people here are basically decent and perfectly biddable. Aren't they, Sebastian?'

'What? Oh yes, rather. I mean, perfectly.' Major Chatsworth looked at his watch. 'Better be getting back to the Club, old girl.

Dinner and all that. Have to put in an appearance,' he added, addressing Henry apologetically.

'Of course,' Henry said. 'By the way, I'd like to come and see you tomorrow, if I may.'

'Certainly. Certainly. Any time. Temporary member, and so forth. We had hoped that you and your wife might have –'

'We're old friends of John and Margaret's,' Henry explained, 'so we decided to stay here.'

Teresa Chatsworth threw the last bundle of newspaper into the trash can, and turned to look Henry squarely in the eye. 'To stay here,' she said, 'and to conduct a completely unbiased investigation.'

Henry smiled. 'That's right.'

'I hope,' said Teresa, 'that you know what you're doing. Come along, Sebastian.'

John Colville reappeared from the kitchen, untying a large butcher's apron from around his waist.

'Dinner in five minutes,' he announced. 'You off, Sebastian? Have a good evening, then. You're eating with us, are you, Tom?'

The dark-haired young man who had been briefly introduced as Tom Bradley got off his bar stool and put his empty glass on the counter.

'Afraid not, John. Sorry I didn't tell you before. I've got a date.'

'And you're not bringing her here?'

Tom Bradley grinned. 'Not that sort of a date. Be seeing you.' He strolled towards the garden, then stopped and turned. He said, to Henry, 'You know the Bum Boat?'

'Where there's a dance tonight?'

'That's right. Might be interesting to look in.'

'So it might.'

'Maybe see you there later on.' He disappeared into the darkness.

John Colville said, 'The table's laid for us in the snug. I'll get one of the girls to keep an eye on the bar, but I don't get the impression that business is going to be exactly brisk tonight.'

The snug was a small room behind the bar, underneath the Tibbetts' bedroom, and with the same view overlooking the sea. A dinner table had been laid for five, but, as Henry and Emmy

33

came in, a small, black-skinned girl was nimbly whisking away one place-setting.

'Sit you down,' said John. 'We eat *en famille* here – with so few guest rooms – '

'And so few guests,' Margaret put in. 'One day were're going to build a proper dining-room and more bedrooms and – '

'Unless, of course,' John said, 'this bloody murder succeeds in bankrupting us all. I've made a salmi of duck for tonight – hope that suits everybody.'

'Whoever would have thought,' Margaret said, 'that John would turn out to be better at cooking than he ever was at economics? That's what makes this place such fun. And with – ' She stopped.

'With what?' Henry prompted.

'Oh, nothing. I keep forgetting. I was going to say that with Sandy in charge of the bar . . . but that's all changed now.'

'As a matter of fact,' Henry said, 'I'm rather glad that Tom Bradley isn't in to dinner. You can tell us about this wretched business from your point of view. I'd like to have that under my belt before I meet the Governor and the Police Chief tomorrow.'

There was a little silence, broken only by the clattering of plates as John dispensed the food. Then Margaret said, 'It sounds so silly, if you don't know the people. I mean – Sandy could never have hoped to be believed.'

'Never mind about that,' Henry said. 'Just tell me.'

'All right. Well, first of all, the facts. I expect you know them. The Senator went off after lunch last Tuesday – March 20th, that is – to play a round of golf with Mr Huberman, and – '

'Just a moment,' Henry said. 'Let's have a bit of background. I gather Olsen was here on his own, without his wife.'

'Without his wife, but not exactly on his own,' said John.

Quickly, Margaret said, 'You've no right to say that, John. You don't know for sure – '

'Potatoes, Emmy? All I meant, my dear Margaret, was that Olsen and Huberman, who were old friends, had come here together for a golfing holiday, each without his wife.'

'Well, if that's really all you meant . . .' Margaret sounded dubious.

'We are sticking to undeniable facts at this stage, aren't we?' said John. 'OK, darling. Go on.'

'Who is Huberman?' Henry asked.

Margaret said, 'Albert G. Huberman. Attorney. Well-known Washington lobbyist. Since he represents a lot of the big cotton interests, he naturally came into contact with Senator Olsen – and, as John says, they came here to play golf, which is precisely what they were doing on March 20th at ten minutes past three in the afternoon. They were on the fifth tee when it happened.'

'When what happened?'

'Well, if we're really to stick to proven facts, the next thing happened at twenty-five past three, when Huberman came rushing into the Golf Club, shouting murder. He'd run all the way from the fifth tee and he was lucky not to have had a stroke on the way. He gasped out that a black man was attacking Senator Olsen with a machete. Major Chatsworth immediately telephoned the police, and then got out his moke and drove as fast as he could to the fifth tee. They found the Senator. It ... it must have been horrible. He'd not just been murdered – he'd been mutilated – hacked up. The police said it looked as though he had put up a fight, but ...' Margaret raised her hands, and let them fall in a hopeless gesture.

'What exactly was Huberman's story?' Henry asked.

'He said that Olsen had just teed up for his drive when the black man came leaping out of the undergrowth, brandishing his machete and yelling. There's a lot of dense scrub there, between the mango grove and the tee, easy to hide in. Huberman was standing on the far side of the tee – he'd already made his drive. He said Olsen shouted at him to save himself, to run for it – and then began grappling with the man. Huberman isn't exactly an heroic type. He ran. That's about all there is to it – except that he definitely identified the black man as Sandy.'

Henry said, 'It seems to me to be simply Huberman's word against Sandy's. Why shouldn't Huberman have killed Olsen himself, and made up the whole story?'

'Because,' said John Colville dryly, 'Sandy doesn't deny that he was there. He admits hiding in the undergrowth and jumping out with his machete.'

Emmy said, 'Well, then, he surely must be guilty.'

'Now we get to the part that sounds silly,' said Margaret. 'You see, Sandy's story is that the whole thing was a practical joke, thought up by Olsen himself. Olsen was ... he had a bit of a sadistic streak in him, I suppose. I remember from Washington days that he was known for playing rather cruel tricks on people. Huberman had been reading about racial murders on other islands, and apparently he was as jumpy as a cat about the whole thing. Sandy says that Olsen came to him and offered him a hundred dollars if he'd hide at the fifth tee that afternoon, and then come leaping out, breathing fire and brandishing his machete. The idea was that Huberman would lose his head and bolt – which is exactly what he did. Sandy would then depart quietly with his hundred bucks, and Olsen would await the arrival of police and ambulances. At that point, he'd say to Huberman, "Black man? What black man? I didn't see any black man. It must have been your imagination. I wondered why you'd gone haring off like that. I think you'd better see an analyst" ... the idea being, of course, to humiliate Huberman and make him look a fool.'

'And Sandy maintains that that is precisely what happened,' said John, between mouthfuls. 'Have some more sauce, Henry. Everything went according to plan, except for one thing. Somebody actually did kill the Senator.'

Emmy said, 'Somebody just happened to turn up with a machete, at that particular time and place ... whoever would believe that?'

'Whoever would?' Margaret echoed. 'That's just the point. Sandy hasn't a hope in hell of being believed.'

'So the police arrested him,' said Henry, 'and as a result people's cars are being burnt and windows broken – not to mention radio sets.'

'That's about the size of it, old man,' said John. 'So if you can do anything about it, get busy, because it could get serious.'

'I'm proposing to start this evening,' said Henry. 'What sort of place is the Bum Boat Bar?'

'There's nothing the matter with the Bum Boat,' said Margaret, on the defence. 'It just happens that ... well ...'

'It happens to be where the trouble-makers hang out,' said John.

'I believe they're having a dance this evening,' Henry said. 'I think I'll look in.'

'I'll come with you,' said Emmy, at once.

'Better not, perhaps. You must be tired, and – '

'I'm coming,' said Emmy firmly. 'If only as an insurance policy. Besides, you know I love West Indian music.'

Henry did not smile. 'I'm sorry, darling,' he said. 'The answer is "no". Please stay here with John and Margaret.'

Emmy sighed. 'O K. But be careful.'

'I will.' Henry turned to John. 'I don't suppose I'll need to take the moke, will I?'

John looked a little surprised. 'No,' he said, 'it's only just down the road. How did you know?'

'I just had a feeling,' said Henry.

Chapter 4

The Bum Boat Bar was strongly reminiscent of Barney's Bar on Tampica, before its transformation into a Cocktail Lounge and Restaurant. The box-like concrete building was painted bright pink, the chairs and tables were green plastic and the music was deafening. The clientele appeared to be one hundred per cent young and black, and since men outnumbered women by about two to one, the bar was crowded with groups of men.

Heads turned and conversations stopped momentarily as Henry came in. There was a certain amount of laughter, of a kind which Henry did not much like the sound of, but no overt hostility or rudeness. Nor was there the warm friendliness which he had come to associate with the West Indies.

He was making his way to the bar for a drink when he spotted Tom Bradley, who seemed to be the only other white person present. He was sitting at a table in the company of two young black men – one tall, lanky and bearded, the other small and slightly-built, both beautifully dressed in slim-hipped flaring pants and denim shirts decorated with coloured sequins. Tom raised his hand in salute to Henry, said something to his companions, and then got up and came over to the bar, glass in hand.

'So you decided to come along?'

'Yes.'

'May I ask why?'

'On your recommendation,' said Henry. 'In any case, I wanted to look around.'

'While you still have a hope of doing it incognito?'

'Exactly.'

'And what d'you think you'll find here?'

Henry said, 'The person who heaved a brick into the Anchorage bar.'

Tom Bradley grinned. 'That's a fair assumption,' he said. 'Do you want some introductions? What are you drinking, by the way? No, no, this is on me. Two more beers, please, Everett. Now, what can I do for you?'

'Your good health,' said Henry, raising his glass. 'What can you do for me? You can tell me what you're doing here on this island, for a start.'

Tom's grin grew even wider. 'Hadn't you guessed? I'm a reporter. Sorry, an investigative journalist. From Washington DC. I'm one of the foot-slogging minions who gather material for Bill Mawson. You must know his column.'

Henry shook his head. 'We're from the other side of the world,' he said. 'You'll have to explain.'

'It's very refreshing,' remarked Tom, 'to meet somebody who has never heard of Bill Mawson. It sort of restores one's faith in the human race. Well, in a nutshell, he operates in and around Washington and his speciality is uncovering hornets' nests – usually political. Some of the stuff he digs out is pure scandal – but he's done his share in sniffing out several nasty cases of corruption in high places. With the help of people like me, of course.'

'And are you here on the track of scandal and corruption?'

'To be honest – no. I'm a very small cog in the machine, and I'm here on a watching brief, simply because the man who got murdered was Senator Brett Olsen. Bill didn't consider it an important enough assignment for one of his top men, so I landed it and I sure am enjoying it. I'm also supposed to keep a weather eye on the political situation and let the front office know if it looks like blowing up into full-scale riots. Hence, I keep my finger on the throbbing nerve-centre of St Matthew's – which is the Bum Boat Bar.'

'And what's your opinion of the situation?' Henry asked.

'A storm in a teacup,' said Bradley. 'The only mystery is what caused Sandy Robbins to run amok with a machete, and I've a few ideas about that which I won't go into now. The rest is just a few hot-heads looking for an excuse to raise Cain.'

'Revolutions can start that way,' Henry said.

'So they can – but I don't see it happening here. What may

happen, though, is a tricky economic situation, if the tourists get scared away. Sandy was really very thoughtless to kill Olsen on Golf Club property. It's given the members a bad attack of cold feet – and the members are the people who keep this island off the bread line.'

'Who threw the brick?' said Henry.

Tom grinned again. 'Come and meet Brooks and Delaware,' he said.

The two young black men, who had been engaged in serious conversation, stopped talking abruptly as Tom and Henry approached. Tom said easily, 'Brooks ... Delaware ... meet Henry. He's a friend.

Brooks – the tall, bearded man – extended his hand. 'Pleased to know you, man.'

The smaller man looked at Tom and said, 'Is he a brother of the Cause?'

'He's a friend,' Tom repeated.

'You can trust him?'

'He wouldn't be here if I couldn't.'

Delaware seemed to make up his mind. 'O K, man. You're a friend of Tom's, you're a friend of ours, you're a friend of the Cause. Sit down and drink your beer. You from the States?'

'No,' said Henry.

'Cuba?'

'England.'

The two black men exchanged wary glances. Tom Bradley said, 'Not all Englishmen are like Sir Geoffrey Patterson, you know.'

Henry said, 'That was a very well-aimed stone. Yours, I presume – ' he added, to Brooks.

The big man grinned. 'Sure, man. And there's more where that came from.'

'What are you planning next?' Henry asked conversationally.

Quickly, Delaware said, 'We don't discuss that outside of meetings. You'll find out soon enough.'

'Need any help?'

Delaware laughed. 'Sure. A membership card to the Golf Club would come in mighty handy, man. That place is like a fortress, I tell you.'

'People go in there to work, don't they?' said Henry.

'Sure they do. And live there in staff quarters. And any one of them comes just once in here for a beer – wham, he's out. Just like that. And a man who's been fired by the Club don't find no new job easy, not on this island. That's what I call slavery, man. That's what we're fighting. When we're through, there won't be any Golf Club. Nor Chatsworth nor Patterson neither. There'll be the independent republic of St Matthew's, run by and for the people of this island.'

'That sounds like a fine ambition for your home island,' said Henry. 'You were born here, I suppose?'

'No, man. No way. I'm from Tampica, like Brooks here.'

'People born on this island, they're no good,' Brooks explained. ' 'Fraid of the Golf Club. 'Fraid of the Government. 'Fraid of their own shadows. They won't get out and fight for their rights.'

'And yet,' Henry pointed out, 'Sandy Robbins is a native-born Mathusian, isn't he?'

Again a glance was exchanged. Then Delaware said, 'Sandy was framed. A white man's trick.'

'You mean, you don't think he killed Senator Olsen?'

'He wouldn't have had the guts,' said Brooks, in disgust.

'Then who did?' said Henry. 'One of your people, perhaps?'

'Who's this?' The voice was low, feminine, and incisive as an ace service by a tennis champion. All four men looked up. Standing behind Henry's chair was one of the most beautiful girls he had ever seen. She was black as onyx, a good six feet tall and slim as a reed. She wore pink denim pants which flared at the ankle over her two-inch wedge sandals, and a pink cotton shirt whose tails were knotted between her breasts, leaving her midriff bare. Also, in the gloom of the bar, she sported huge dark glasses with rims of glittering rhinestone. Her hair was elaborately plaited close to her head, in the corn-stalk fashion, leaving little lanes of naked, shiny scalp between the neat rows.

Brooks and Delaware seemed to have been struck dumb, but Tom Bradley grinned and said, 'Hi, Diamond. This is a friend of mine.'

The girl called Diamond did not even look at Tom. To the other two, she repeated, 'Who is he?'

Awkwardly, Brooks said, 'Like Tom said . . . a friend . . .'

'Name?'

'Henry.'

'Henry what?'

'Well –'

'I'll tell you, you pair of idiots,' said Diamond. 'His name's Henry Tibbett and he's a pig out of London. What have you told him?'

'Nothing, Diamond,' said Delaware, too quickly. 'Nothing at all. Just drinking a beer, that's all.'

'Talk about Sandy?'

'Well . . . not really . . .'

'Get out,' said Diamond coldly. 'Both of you. And you,' she added, to Tom. 'I'm going to talk to this man alone. Once. After that, nobody talks to him. Understand?'

Like a pair of whipped puppies, Brooks and Delaware shuffled to their feet and made for the bar. Tom stood up and put a hand on Henry's shoulder.

'Don't worry, brother,' he said. 'She doesn't actually eat men, do you, honey?'

Diamond was not amused. 'I said, get out.'

'OK, OK. Cool it, baby. See you at the Anchorage, Henry.' Tom strolled off into the darkness.

Diamond pulled up a chair, turned it with its back to the table and straddled it, her long legs on either side of the seat, her elbows on the back. Henry wished she would take off her glasses, so that he could see her eyes.

She said, 'Now, I'm doing the talking, remember. You come here to solve the Olsen case – Sandy innocent or guilty, right? Now get this. We're a political movement, and no policeman wants to get mixed up in politics – right? We don't care about Sandy any more – innocent, guilty, all the same to us. He's served his purpose by getting arrested. All right, so he's guilty, so that's better for us – but so he's innocent, that's never going to stop us now. We're off the ground and way up out of sight, man.'

Henry said, 'So it was you who framed him?'

'It was not. That's a lie. His arrest was a fortunate coincidence, and that's the truth.' She spoke quite softly and very deliberately.

'The murder was an even more fortunate coincidence, wasn't it?' Henry remarked.

'That's all I'm saying. Now I'm going to show you something.' With a quick movement, Diamond whipped off her sunglasses, and Henry drew in his breath in sharp shock. Her right eye was as lovely as the rest of her face – huge and dark, with long curling lashes and elaborately made-up. Where her left eye should have been, there was nothing but a hideous mass of scar tissue.

Watching Henry's face, Diamond smiled slowly. 'I won't wear a patch over it,' she said. 'I want it to be seen.' She leaned towards him over the back of the chair. 'You know how that happened? It's funny. Very funny. That was done by a golf ball.' Henry said nothing. 'I am sixteen, come from Tampica to work at the Golf Club. Very good money, they say. Very rich men, very good tips. All true. Plenty of rich Americans, leave their wives at home, like to find a nice friendly girl on St Matthew's. But what happens if the girl's not friendly? You tell me, Mr Tibbett.'

'You're not implying that it was done deliberately, are you?'

'You decide, Mr Tibbett. Here am I with a very rich American, and I say "No". "All right, Diamond. No hard feelings. Quite understand. We can be friends, can't we?" "Sure," I say. "Then come round the golf course with me tomorrow, Diamond. I'm playing a round alone. Come with me, just walk and talk." "Okay," I say. Fifth tee. "Diamond, you mind stand just there . . . just a little ahead of me? You watch my left arm, see if it's straight as I drive." "Sure, I'll watch." So I stand where he says and he winds himself up and he hits that ball hard and . . . They get me to the doctor's house – he's out at a party. So they get me on a boat to Doc Duncan on Tampica. Nothing he can do. Might just have saved the eye if he'd got to it right away.' Diamond replaced her glasses and stood up. 'Don't expect me to give up the Cause,' she said.

Henry said, 'Diamond, who was it?' – but she had gone. Henry finished his beer and made his way back to the Anchorage.

At ten o'clock the following morning, Henry reported to the Golf Club for his first official meeting – a conference with the

Governor (who was arriving that morning on his private yacht) and the Police Chief, Inspector Owen Montague. The original idea had been to foregather in the Inspector's office at the Priest Town police station, but Sir Geoffrey opted in favour of the more luxurious setting of the Golf Club. He was, of course, planning to stay there.

John Colville drove Henry over to the Golf Club, between hedges of oleander and hibiscus. Remembering the manicured lawns surrounding Pirate's Cave Hotel on Tampica, Henry was prepared for an abrupt contrast between the Club compound and the island wilderness outside: what he was not prepared for was to find himself entering what looked like a military encampment.

The perimeter of the Golf Club was surrounded by a stout wire fence, eight feet high, and the gate to which John drove was defended by a prettified structure in white concrete with red roof tiles, which was nevertheless a guard house. As the moke approached, a tall young man dressed in a musical-comedy uniform, with a gun holster at his hip, strolled out and barred the way.

'May I see your pass, sir?' The accent was unmistakably American.

John pulled the moke up to a standstill. 'You know me, Hank,' he said. 'And this is Chief Superintendent Tibbett from Scotland Yard. He has an appointment with the Gov. So just kindly move your ass and let us in.'

'OK, John. Sure. Sorry, Superintendent. We have to be careful, you see. The members expect it.' The guard pulled a bunch of keys out of his pocket and began unlocking the heavy metal gate.

'What's the number of the Gov's cottage?' John asked.

'Twenty-three. Round to the right, past the tennis courts. Have a nice day.'

As the moke passed through into the sacred precincts, Henry heard the heavy gate slam shut, and the key turn in the lock. They were inside the fortress.

'And very pretty it is, too, as you can see,' John was saying. 'Seven hundred of the most beautiful acres in the Caribbean. The golf course was designed by Scotland's greatest expert, I need hardly say, and the gardens were landscaped and planted by a specialist from Kew. The outside staff alone runs to thirty people.'

'All the same,' Henry said, 'it strikes me rather like a luxurious maximum security prison. Are all those guns and fences really necessary?'

'I'm afraid they are. Of course, security has been tightened up since Olsen's murder – but even before that, the committee didn't take any chances. This is a private club, after all – and at any one time the number of potential targets here must be enormous.'

'Targets?'

'For robbery, blackmail, kidnapping, political demonstration and even murder. Not to mention plain hounding by newsmen or fans. The people who come here are prepared to pay astronomic prices for security and privacy.'

'Poor things,' said Henry. And then – 'In view of all that, how is Sandy Robbins supposed to have got in? Unless he was invited by Olsen, as he says.'

'By water,' said John. He drew up outside one of the white-painted Spanish-style cottages. 'Here we are. And there's the beach. It's discreetly guarded by a posse of bouncers disguised as sunbathers, of course. But at certain points the golf course runs close to the sea, and – '

'And under British law, all land below the high-water line is public property,' said Henry. 'How about the fifth tee?'

'Separated from the beach by about a hundred yards of mango grove,' said John. 'Perfect cover. Well, this is number twenty-three. I'll be getting back to the Anchorage.'

The door to the cottage stood open, leading into the sitting-room, which had a red-tiled floor scattered with Scandinavian rugs, and was furnished in bamboo and brass. Beyond, on the verandah overlooking the beach, Henry could see three men sitting round a glass-topped table, sipping long drinks and obviously in conference. One he recognized as Major Chatsworth. Of the other two, Henry decided that the tall, thin, distinguished-looking character with the greying goatee beard was probably the Governor, Sir Geoffrey Patterson, while the dark, tubby little man with the black moustache who was continually mopping the sweat from his brow must be Inspector Montague, chief of the island's police force. Henry walked through the sitting-room, paused at the open door to the verandah, and said, 'I'm Henry Tibbett. May I join you, gentlemen?'

The three men looked up abruptly, as if caught off balance. Then Major Chatsworth said, 'Ah, Tibbett. Good morning. Sir Geoffrey, may I present Chief Superintendent Tibbett of Scotland Yard? Chief Superintendent, Sir Geoffrey Patterson – ' and he indicated the small, rotund man who was now sweating more profusely than ever.

'Ah. Yes. Tibbett. To be sure.' Henry recognized the plummy voice from the previous evening's broadcast. 'Glad to see you. Hope you can help us clear up this sorry affair. This is Inspector Montague.'

The third man had risen to his feet, and now resembled a shakily-planted bearded beanpole. He said disdainfully, 'I certainly hope we can dispose of this horrid thing as quickly as possible, Chief ... am I right? ... Chief Superintendent. Goodness me, what a mouthful. I'm afraid you won't find us equipped with all your newfangled scientific dodges. We're not used to sophisticated crimes like murder on St Matthew's, I fear. Very much behind the times, we are.'

Sir Geoffrey cleared his throat, passed a handkerchief over his brow, and said, 'Hrrrmph. Yes. Well, sit you down, Tibbett. Now, this needn't take long. Just fill you in about the general background of the whole business, and we can leave you and Montague to get things settled, eh?'

'I hope so,' said Henry.

Major Chatsworth, who had disappeared into the interior of the cottage, came out again with a tall glass full of pinkish liquid, which he placed at Henry's elbow, spilling some in the process.

Sir Geoffrey said, 'You heard my broadcast last night, I imagine?'

'Some of it, sir.'

'What d'ye mean, some of it?'

Quickly, Chatsworth said, 'We were both listening in the Anchorage bar, Sir Geoffrey. Unfortunately, the broadcast was interrupted – '

'By a well-aimed stone,' Henry said. 'Tell me, Sir Geoffrey, what do you know about a girl called Diamond?'

There was a quick, three-pronged glance. Then the Governor said, 'Nothing, Tibbett. Who is she?'

Montague said, 'She's a trouble-maker from Tampica, Sir Geoffrey. A girl who imagines she has a grudge against white people on this island.'

'She also has one eye missing,' Henry said. 'She lost it on the fifth tee of this golf course, when somebody drove a golf ball into it.'

Sir Geoffrey looked startled. 'Gracious me, what a bizarre story. What do you know of this, Chatsworth?'

Major Chatsworth's normally ruddy complexion had deepened to strawberry. 'Girl's a confounded nuisance,' he said. 'Tried to put the blame on the Club. Her work had been unsatisfactory for some time, and the committee was planning to fire her – pity we didn't get around to it sooner. Matter of fact, the Club behaved very handsomely. Paid her medical expenses and offered a thousand dollars' compensation, which is a fortune to these people. Naturally, she couldn't be kept on, after an episode like that. She took the money, of course, and ever since she's been stirring up trouble. She's the one who's behind all this unrest, Sir Geoffrey.'

The Governor looked puzzled. 'I thought it was a gang of young men.'

'So it is, my dear fellow,' said Montague languidly, 'but who puts them up to it? Ask yourself that.'

'For heaven's sake, Owen,' said Major Chatsworth, 'can't we have her deported, or something?'

'What, and have a real riot on our hands?' Montague lit a small cigar and blew out a plume of smoke. 'Don't be idiotic, Sebastian. What we have to do is to play the whole thing very slowly, very quietly – until this wave of violence dies down. Meanwhile, as long as Diamond is on this island, you're going to have trouble, dear soul. Might as well admit it.'

'Why have I not been told about this woman before?' Sir Geoffrey might be unimposing physically, but now his voice had the unmistakable ring of authority. 'You know that I rely on your reports, Montague – and this is the first I have heard of her. And yet, within twenty-four hours of his arrival, Chief Superintendent Tibbett has been able to pinpoint – '

'Oh, don't go on like that, Geoffrey,' said Montague pettishly. 'Sandy Robbins killed Senator Olsen. There can't be any possible argument about that. The sooner we get him tried and convicted, the better. Diamond and her merry men have been having their little fling, throwing stones and setting cars on fire – but once the trial is over and Sandy is safely behind bars in St Mark's, the steam'll run out of these silly demonstrations, you mark my words.'

'I'd be happier if that girl was back on Tampica, where she belongs,' said Major Chatsworth. The others ignored him.

Sir Geoffrey said, 'As to getting the trial over as quickly as possible, I entirely agree with you, Montague. On the other hand, Tibbett has come all this way precisely so that people here can be convinced that justice is being done. He must at least make a show of conducting an investigation.'

Henry opened his mouth to protest, thought better of it, and shut it again.

The Governor glanced at his watch. 'Well, gentlemen, I don't think I can help you any further. Good luck to you, Tibbett, and – make it as quick as you can, won't you? Nothing to be gained by dilly-dallying. Facts are clear enough. Don't hesitate to call on me if I can help at all. I'll be on the golf course if you need me. Pray use this cottage as your HQ, if you wish. Good day to you.'

When the Governor had left, Henry said, 'Who was the wealthy American who put out Diamond's eye, Major Chatsworth?'

'I really can't tell you, Tibbett.' The Major was decidedly flustered. 'The whole thing happened four years ago – before my time. I was told about the incident and the financial details and so on, but no name was mentioned. The whole episode was . . . kept in low profile, as you might say.'

'I suppose your predecessor would know,' Henry said.

'Of course – but he's dead. That's how the job came to be vacant.'

'Anything suspicious about his death?' Henry asked.

'Not unless you call D Ts and cirrhosis of the liver suspicious,' Chatsworth remarked tersely.

'Ah, well. Never mind.' Henry turned to Montague. 'I'd like to see Sandy Robbins as soon as possible.'

'Easily done. He's in the lock-up in Priest Town and he has very few social engagements.' Montague sniggered.

'Can you fix it for me to see him this morning – say, twelve o'clock?'

'Consider it done.'

To Chatsworth, Henry said, 'Is Mr Huberman still at the Club?'

'Yes, he is. Won't go near the golf course any more, but he'd booked in for three weeks, and ...' The Major's voice trailed away.

Henry said, 'I'm surprised he stayed on, after what happened. And since he came here to play golf – '

Once again, Chatsworth's face had assumed its crushed-strawberry hue. He said, 'I may as well tell you, because you'd find out anyhow. There's a young woman – '

'Huberman's girl-friend?'

'That's right. A remarkably pretty girl, a fashion model, I believe. Miss Candida Stevenson, known as Candy. I understand that she ... em ... expressed a wish to stay on and finish her holiday, and so of course Mr Huberman ... that is ...'

'I understand,' said Henry. 'Now, I have to make a phone call, and then I'd like to see Mr Huberman. Can you contact him and make a date for me around eleven o'clock?'

'Surely. He'll be on the beach. I'll have a word with him.'

'Thanks.' Henry hesitated for a moment. Then he said, 'Is there a telephone I can use?'

'Right here, sir. Just ask the operator for the number you want. Run along now, Owen. Can't you see the Chief Superintendent wants a bit of privacy?'

'Oh, very well.' Owen Montague stood up reluctantly. 'We'll co-operate, won't we, Chief Superintendent? Or may I call you Henry? My name's Owen.'

'Certainly you can call me Henry. I'll see you at the lock-up at twelve.'

Montague giggled a little. 'Not a very romantic assignation,' he said. 'Oh, all right, Sebastian. I'm going.'

When Montague had gone, Major Chatsworth leant towards Henry, and said in a conspiratorial voice, 'I thought you'd like to know, Mr Reynolds has arrived. On the *Island Queen*. He's in number seventeen.'

'Good,' said Henry. 'By the way, you're the only person who knows who Reynolds is, aren't you?'

'Absolutely. Even Teresa and Owen don't know. Nor the Governor.'

'Good. Keep it that way, won't you?'

'Of course. Of course. Oh, and I've arranged for one of our mokes to be at your disposal, Tibbett. Just ask at the bar. You'll be lunching at the Club House, I trust?'

'That's very kind of you.'

'A pleasure, sir. Well, I'll get along to the beach and find Mr Huberman.'

Henry waited until Chatsworth was well away from the cottage, and then lifted the receiver. A minute later he was connected to Sugar Mill Bay, and Lucy Pontefract-Deacon was saying, 'I'm ashamed of myself, Henry. I must be getting old.'

'So it was Senator Olsen?'

'Of course it was. I remember distinctly, now that you mention it. Of course, Olsen was just a name to me – and not a very memorable one at that. And it's so long since Ethel left this island.'

'Ethel?'

'Ethel Drake. The girl who now calls herself Diamond.'

'What do you know about her, Lucy?'

'Bright. Ambitious. Quite ruthless, I should think – especially after she lost her eye.'

'Why did she leave Tampica?'

'To make money. Can't really blame her. It was before independence, and Tampica was something of a dead-end for up-and-coming youngsters. She was one of a big family, and she was determined to get out of the rut. And then, of course, there was Sandy Robbins. You remember I told you he had a girl here?'

'That's very interesting,' said Henry. 'Tell me, Lucy – how are Diamond's family doing now?'

Lucy laughed. 'Famously, most of them. One brother is a qualified motor mechanic, working for Barney. The eldest girl is Reservations Manager at the Barracuda Bay Hotel. One brother stayed on St Matthew's with the Club, but the youngest runs the best seafood restaurant in Tampica Harbour.'

'That's what I meant,' said Henry. 'I'd have thought that Tampica might be a more attractive place than St Matthew's right now. Especially since the Golf Club is out, as far as Diamond is concerned.'

'I see what you mean. You think she had some special reason for staying on?'

'I'm beginning to think,' Henry said, 'that she had two reasons – at least one of which no longer applies.'

Chapter 5

Albert G. Huberman lay flat on his back on a chaise-longue, listening to the rhythmical plashing of the sea and soaking the sunshine into his plump near-naked body. He was not looking forward to his interview with Henry Tibbett, but he had decided that the best thing to do was to get it over with as quickly as possible.

All other things being equal, Huberman would have been back in Washington by now – but things were far from equal. As a lobbyist working for a group of cotton producers, his assignment had been to establish contact with and influence over Senator Brett Olsen, Chairman of the Olsen Committee. Hence his presence on St Matthew's. Now, Brett Olsen was dead, and Huberman's masters had decided to keep in him in cold storage in the Caribbean until they embarked on a new strategy – and that, of course, depended on who was nominated as the new Committee Chairman. Besides, Huberman's role in the attack on Olsen had been unheroic, if not ridiculous. Candy Stevenson provided a useful excuse, but in fact she had very little to do with Huberman's protracted stay on St Matthew's.

'Ah, here we are. Em . . . Mr Huberman . . . ?'

Huberman opened his small brown eyes at the sound of Major Chatsworth's voice. Squinting up into the sun, he could see the tall figure of the Secretary accompanied by a smaller, undistinguished-looking man in beige cotton pants and a pale blue shirt.

'Hi,' said Huberman, and closed his eyes again. He saw no reason why he should make things easier for this damned interfering policeman from England.

'This is Chief Superintendent Tibbett, Mr Huberman. As I told you, he would just like a word with you . . . pure formality . . .'

'Siddown,' said Huberman. He did not open his eyes.

'Well, Tibbett, I'll leave you to your little chat with Mr Huberman. I'll see you later . . .'

Major Chatsworth hurried away, enveloped in a palpable cloud of relief. He had never found Albert Huberman an easy member to get along with, and the present situation was acutely embarrassing. He was glad not to be in Henry Tibbett's shoes.

As a matter of fact, Henry was not wearing shoes. He had left them in the Governor's cottage. He sat down on the sand beside Huberman's beach bed, and said, 'I'm glad to know you, Mr Huberman.'

Huberman grunted. Henry went on, 'I understand you and Senator Olsen were here together for a golfing holiday. Is that right?'

Another grunt.

'And you were playing a twosome on the afternoon of March 20th, when – '

Huberman opened his eyes enough to let a slit of sunshine in. He said, 'For Chrissakes, stop beating about the bush. You want me to tell you what happened on the fifth tee, don't you?'

'Not particularly,' said Henry agreeably. 'I think I know that part. Sandy Robbins jumped out from the mango grove, brandishing a machete and yelling. Senator Olsen shouted to you to run for your life, and you did. When you got back with Major Chatsworth, you found the Senator dead – murdered with a machete. That's right, isn't it?'

Huberman made an indistinct sound indicating assent, and added, 'Then what the hell do you want to know?'

Conversationally, Henry said, 'I'm interested in your job. I believe you are a lobbyist.'

'That's right.'

'We don't have them in England,' Henry explained. 'Just what do you do?'

Huberman heaved a sigh, as of an unwilling fool-sufferer. He said, 'I'm employed by the CPF – the Cotton Producers' Federation. I look after their interests in Washington.'

'By influencing politicians?'

'By talking to them. Putting our point of view. Nothing illegal in that, is there?'

'Apparently not,' said Henry. There was a dryness in his voice that made Huberman open his eyes a further eighth of an inch.

'What do you mean by that?'

'Nothing. The whole conception is – well – a little difficult for an Englishman to understand. Olsen was Chairman of the Olsen Committee, wasn't he?'

'Of course he was. Goddamit, there was no secret about it. I was working on Olsen to get the higher cotton subsidies through the Committee. Ledbetter and I– '

'Who's Ledbetter?'

'Jackson P. Ledbetter. President of the CPF. He was staying here up to the end of last week. We're – we were, I should say – both personal friends of Brett Olsen's, but I'm not going to pretend to you or anybody else that it was just coincidence we were vacationing here, or that we didn't talk cotton from time to time. Olsen and I were just playing a friendly round that day. You make it sound like we were criminals, or something.'

'I'm sorry. I didn't intend to. Mr Ledbetter doesn't play golf, then?'

'Sure he does, but he was off the island that day – went over to St Boniface to do some shopping.'

'And after the murder, Mr Ledbetter went back to the States, but you decided to stay on here.' Henry sounded guileless, but Huberman was not deceived.

'Now, see here. Jackson Ledbetter went back to Washington because he had work to do. I stayed on because I'm on vacation. You're here to investigate a crime, not to pry into innocent people's private lives. Is that clear?'

Before Henry could answer, a small, clear, feminine voice said, 'Hi, Al. Who's your friend?'

Henry looked up, and found himself staring at one of the prettiest girls he had ever seen. She was slender and long-limbed and her body – where it was not covered by a scrap of string bikini – was evenly tanned to a deep honey-colour, so that the tiny sun-bleached hairs on her legs and forearms glistened like silver against her skin. She had evidently just come out of the sea, for she was dripping wet and carried a snorkel mask and rubber fins. She shook the water from her long blonde hair, which clung like seaweed around her shoulders, and picked up an enormous towel from a neighbouring beach bed.

Huberman said, 'Hi, honey. This is Chief Superintendent Tibbett from England. Tibbett – Candy Stevenson. How was the snorkelling?'

'Fantastic.' Candy sat down astride the chaise-longue, and began languidly to towel the water from her golden skin. 'There's a biggish barracuda in Mango Trunk Bay. Six foot or so. We had quite a game.'

'This girl,' Huberman explained to Henry, 'swims like she should be a mermaid. And faces up to those big fish – '

Candy said, 'Barracuda never attack, Al. You know that. They just look a mite fierce.'

'A mite too much for me,' said Huberman. 'More up your street perhaps, Tibbett? Or do you specialize in sharks?'

Henry said, 'I'd better explain, Miss Stevenson – I'm a policeman, and I'm making inquiries into Senator Olsen's death.'

'Go right ahead,' said Candy. 'Don't mind me.' She lay down on the beach bed and closed her eyes.

Henry looked at Albert Huberman, who also appeared to be asleep. He said, 'Shall we go on with the questions, Mr Huberman, or would you rather talk in private?'

'Oh, the hell ... get on with it.' The eyes did not open. Henry noticed that a stubble of beard was beginning to appear on Huberman's multiple chins. It occurred to him to wonder just what the attraction was for Candy Stevenson.

He said, 'You're quite certain that the man with the machete was Sandy Robbins?'

'Of course I'm certain.'

'You'd seen him behind the bar at the Anchorage, I suppose?'

There was a tiny pause, and then Huberman said, 'No.'

'No?'

'Never been there. One-horse little joint, so they tell me.'

'Then where – '

This time, Candy spoke. 'Shall I tell him, or will you?'

55

Henry was finding it somewhat unnerving to carry on a three-sided conversation in which two of the participants never opened their eyes. He felt a strong urge to lie down on the sand and feign sleep himself, but in duty bound he had to keep the ball rolling.

'Who is going to tell what to whom?' he asked, acutely aware of his English accent and careful grammar.

Huberman grunted.

Candy said, 'Sandy is the best underwater swimmer I've ever met. He used to take me out to West Sound Reef after lobsters. Then sometimes we'd come back here for a drink. It made Al very cross – didn't it, sugar?'

Huberman said, 'Now don't misunderstand me, Tibbett. The fact that Sandy was ... is ... black is neither here nor there.'

Candy Stevenson gave a little, half-amused sigh, but said nothing. Huberman went on. 'Neither here nor there. Nobody can call me a racist. No, the thing I objected to ... what made it awkward ... was that Sandy was an employee of a small and inferior establishment on this island. Not the sort of person you expect to meet at the bar of the Golf Club.'

'But members may invite guests to the Club?'

'Certainly – but Candy is here as *my* guest. She's not a member herself. It was ... well, it was a hell of an unsatisfactory situation. I won't go further than that.'

'Did Major Chatsworth ever raise any objections to Robbins coming here?' Henry asked.

'Certainly not. He's much too tactful. Besides, you know what these British are like.' Huberman paused, and then added, 'Funnily enough, if Robbins had been white, I think there might have been some open objections, from other members if not from Chatsworth. But everyone's so darned scared of being accused of colour prejudice these days ... Well, I asked Candy to stop bringing the boy here. Go out skin diving with him by all means, if you want to, I said. Only just keep him away from the Club. Was that too much to ask?'

'Yes,' said Candy shortly. There was an oppressive silence.

Henry said, 'So presumably Senator Olsen had also met Robbins in the bar here.'

'Of course,' said Candy. She sat up, picked up one of her sand-encrusted feet, and began examining the toes intently, picking at them with inch-long, carmine-painted fingernails. She did not look at either of the men.

'Do either of you know,' Henry said, 'of any reason why Robbins should have killed Olsen? Was there ever a quarrel or – '

'No, no. Nothing of that sort,' answered Huberman quickly. 'These people are emotional, you know, and – '

Candy looked up from her toe examination and winked at Henry. She said, 'Come off it, Al. There was a very good reason. Brett was jealous as hell of Sandy.'

'Jealous?' Henry echoed. 'Why?'

'Because of me, of course.' Candy sounded impatient at his slowness.

'But I thought that you and Mr Huberman . . .'

Candy returned her foot to the sand, and squinted up at Henry through her veil of golden hair. 'Hey, when were you born, mister? Or don't they do things that way in England?'

Henry said, 'If you mean what I think you do, the practice is universal. But you might just spell it out for me.'

'Now, Candy – ' Warningly, from Huberman. He did not open his eyes.

'OK. Well, sure I came here with Al, as his . . . guest. But in fact I was intended as a nice little gift – unsolicited of course – from the CPF to Senator Brett Olsen. To sweeten his vacation.'

'Candy – '

'Shut up, Al. So of course Brett got sore when I started to go scuba diving with Sandy. He reckoned I was his personal property, like. After all, he'd paid for me, hadn't he?'

'Had he? I thought you said the CPF – '

'Ah, but – '

Huberman sat up, his eyes wide open. 'Tibbett, you mustn't believe a word of this. Candy's a great little kidder, aren't you, honey? Why, she hardly exchanged a word with Senator Olsen, did you, baby? She went swimming with Sandy Robbins, and . . . everything else she did with me. Still does. Isn't that so, Candy?'

Candy lay back on the chaise-longue. In a tired voice she said, 'I guess so, honey. I was just kidding. You know me.'

On impulse, Henry said, 'Candy, do you know a girl called Diamond?'

There was an apparently endless silence. Huberman was looking at Candy, bewildered. The girl lay as if asleep, but Henry felt that she was tense. At last she said, 'No.'

Another silence. Huberman said, 'Who is this Diamond dame? Why should Candy know her? What are you getting at, Tibbett?'

Henry grinned. 'Oh, nothing. Just trying to find some sort of a pattern, you know. Well, I won't bother you any more.' He scrambled to his feet. 'Thank you both, you've been very helpful. I hope we'll meet again. Now I have to go to the lock-up – to meet Sandy Robbins.'

Candy opened one eye. 'Give him my love,' she said.

'I'll do that,' said Henry. He walked a few steps down the beach, then paused and looked back. Huberman and Candy were lying, one on each beach bed, their eyes closed. Like corpses.

Henry had walked a hundred yards or so up the beach towards the bar, when his eye was caught by a figure at once familiar and incongruous. A tall, athletic young man in a khaki-coloured shirt and rather long Bermuda shorts, impeccably creased, below which paper-white legs proclaimed him a new arrival from a less clement climate. He stood out among the bronzed, near-naked sun worshippers like a bowler-hatted City gentleman at a rock concert. Henry raised a hand in greeting.

'Good morning, Mr Reynolds,' he said. 'Fancy meeting you here, of all places. Did you have a good journey?'

'Oh, good morning, sir. Yes, thank you, very good. I was just looking for you, sir. They told me you were conducting an interview on the beach.'

Henry grinned. 'If you can call it that,' he said. 'What d'you think of this place?'

'Like Dartmoor on the outside, isn't it, sir? What are they all so scared of?'

'Robbery, murder and journalists,' said Henry.

'But once you get in ... well ... I've never seen anything like it.' He paused. 'I hope you and Mrs Tibbett are comfortable, then?'

'Very, thanks. Not in this class, of course, but the atmosphere's cosier. You must come slumming one day.'

Reynolds went slightly pink. 'Thank you, sir. I'd appreciate that.' He cleared his throat. 'Well – how are things going, sir?'

'Interestingly, so far. I'm just off to the nick to talk to Robbins.'

'You want me to come along, sir?'

'No, I don't think so. We don't want to scare the young man. No – you stay here, have a swim and do some sunbathing. Keep your ears open – I'm interested in the sort of gossip that may be running around this place. You might find a spot in the sun up there – near a fat man called Huberman and his girl-friend. You can't miss her – a smashing blonde in a green string bikini. They're the people I've just been talking to.'

'Will do, sir.'

'And ... Reynolds ...'

'Sir?'

'For heaven's sake get into swimming trunks and stop looking like a copper. I can see your boots.'

Reynolds glanced involuntarily down at his bare feet, then grinned sheepishly. 'I see what you mean, sir.'

'And stop calling me "sir". Now, Major Chatsworth has kindly invited me to have lunch here. Wait for me in the bar, will you? I'll be there around one, and we'll lunch together. Remember that you're just a casual acquaintance of mine from London.'

'I'll be there, sir ... that is ... I'll be there.'

Henry made his way to the beach bar, and asked that a car should be sent round to the Governor's cottage in five minutes. Then he retrieved his shoes, and soon was outside the formidable main gate, and bumping along cheerfully over the rutted dirt road towards Priest Town, at the wheel of the inevitable mini-moke.

The police station was a grey stone building on the quayside, next door to the Customs' House. The waterfront was bustling with activity, as fishermen sorted their catch and sailing yachts motored out of harbour, their white sails flapping. The *Island Queen* was still berthed at her pier, taking on passengers and merchandise for the return run to Antigua. It was a busy scene, full of life and colour, and several tourists were recording it on movie cameras. Henry wondered how many of the holiday films would feature the tall, unsmiling black girl in the dark sunglasses who was lounging against the side wall of the Customs' House.

Diamond gave him no sign of recognition, but he knew very well that he was being observed, and also that she had intended him to notice her. He pushed open the shabby green door of the police station and stepped inside, into the cool shadows.

Inspector Montague was all smiles. 'Ah, twelve on the dot. Punctuality is the politeness of kings, or so they tell me. I'll take you along to Robbins right away, Henry. Do you think I should sit in at the interview? It's just as you like, of course, my dear fellow.'

'If you don't mind, I'd rather see him alone. I want to get his confidence, you see.'

'I don't see why *my* presence –' Montague began, then broke off with a nervous smile. 'Of course, of course. I take your point. I was just going along to the Anchorage for lunch, in any case. Shall I see you there?'

'As a matter of fact, no. Major Chatsworth has invited me to eat at the Golf Club.'

'Oh, please yourself, of course. I hope it's on the house, that's all. For your sake, I mean. Well then, Sergeant Ingham can look after you.' He pressed a bell on his desk, and a burly black man in tropical uniform appeared. 'Sergeant, this is Chief Superintendent Tibbett. He wants a private talk with Robbins. See to it, will you?' To Henry, he added, 'I'll be here this afternoon, if you want me. So long for now.'

'This way, if you please, sir.' Sergeant Ingham's gentle voice belied his tough appearance. 'Just ring the bell in the cell when you're through, sir. Then I'll come and let you out.' Apologetically, he added, 'We have to try to keep Sandy . . . Robbins, that is . . . as carefully as we can. Of course, we don't have anything like maximum security. We've never had a murder here before that I can remember.'

'I know,' said Henry. 'That's what makes it so distressing.'

'That's right, man. I mean sir. Distressing is right. Just down this passage, sir. Here we are.'

Sergeant Ingham produced an iron key of medieval dimensions, and turned it in the lock of one of the three small, barred cells at the back of the building. He said, 'Hi, Sandy, man. Got a visitor for you. Chief Superintendent Tibbett from London, like Mrs Colville said. Well, I'll leave you now, sir.'

Sandy Robbins, who had been lying full-length on the narrow bed, reading a paperback detective book, jumped to his feet. Beaming as though his handsome black face would split in two, he held out his hand and said, 'Henry Tibbett. Man, am I glad to see you! So Margaret finally sent you.'

Henry shook hands, smiled back, and said, 'Not Margaret, Sandy. Scotland Yard.'

Robbins brushed aside this technicality. 'Margaret and John,' he said, 'told me that if there was any man in the world could get me out of this mess, it was you.'

'Look,' Henry said, 'I'm not your lawyer. I'm a policeman, investigating the case. If you would like your lawyer present at the interview – '

'Him? He's a no-good nothing, man. You're the fellow I want to see.'

'Have it your own way. Mind if I sit down?'

'Help yourself.' Sandy Robbins moved so as to leave room for Henry to sit beside him on the bed. 'Now, where do we start, Mr Tibbett?'

Henry said, 'Why don't you tell me your side of the story – exactly as it happened.'

'From the beginning?'

'From the beginning.'

'Well, now.' Robbins ran one hand through his frizz of black hair. 'I guess you'd say the beginning was when Olsen came down to the Anchorage Monday evening – '

'The day before he was killed?'

'That's right. We were quiet that night – there was a big dance on at the Bum Boat, see? John and Margaret were in Tampica, visiting Miss Lucy. I was in charge of the Anchorage, and planning to shut up early since we had no custom. And then, in walks Senator Olsen.'

Henry said, 'There was nobody else in the bar? Just the two of you?'

'That's right. He sits down and orders a pina colada, and then he comes out with it.'

'With what?'

'This crazy idea of his. He's telling me about Huberman – you know Huberman?'

'I've met him.'

'Well, Olsen starts talking about Huberman, and how he's been reading about black guys carving up rich white fat cats on other islands, and now he's got so he's scared even to go out on the links, man. And Olsen says, "I've finally talked him into playing a twosome tomorrow afternoon, and he's nervous as a kitten. Boy, wouldn't it be something if he did get attacked?" Then he looks at me, speculative like, and he says, "Hey, Sandy, you got a machete, haven't you?" "Sure I have, Senator." And he says, "You got a sense of humour, Sandy?" and I say, 'You tell me, Senator." Then he says, "OK. You hide yourself in the mango grove beside the fifth tee tomorrow afternoon, and when Huberman and I arrive, you leap out yelling and waving your machete. How about it?" '

'And what did you say?'

Sandy grinned. 'I said, "You crazy, Senator? I got no idea of cutting up this Huberman." "Of course not, Sandy," he says. "Now, listen, this is the action. I act like I'm as scared as he is – but braver, see. I tell him – you run for help, I'll deal with this fellow. And boy, will Huberman run! Then you go off home – and when Huberman comes back with the police and all, I'll just play it cool and say, 'What man with what machete? I didn't see no man."' And he started to laugh, like he was really crazy.'

'And so you agreed?'

'Well . . .' Sandy hesitated.

'Margaret says he offered you money.'

'Sure. Hundred dollar. I showed Montague the bill, but it didn't do any good. Made them think I might have robbed Olsen. Fact is, Mr Tibbett, I was a fool. I admit it. I didn't want any part of that damn silly business – but I needed that hundred.'

'Will you tell me why?' Henry asked.

'Sure, man. You know Candy?'

'Slightly. I've seen her.'

Sandy grinned. 'Then I needn't say any more, I guess. She's something, that girl. Not like what you'd think, just to look at her, I mean. Intelligent, I mean. And she's learning to swim and dive real well, too. Well, after we'd come in from swimming, we'd go to the Golf Club, and . . . well . . .'

'And Candy would pick up the tab,' said Henry.

'That,' said Sandy, 'I wouldn't have minded. She's my friend. No, sir, what got me was that I knew all the time it was Huberman paying. Now, I don't ... didn't earn that much at the Anchorage. Not John and Margaret's fault,' he added hastily. 'They don't have the cash, not yet. Got to build up the business. But I wanted – just once – to be able to take Candy out, and show her a good time, and pay the check myself. I was planning to take her to Tampica, go to Pirate's Cave for dinner, order the wine, dancing after, order the Golf Club launch home. You understand how I felt, Mr Tibbett?'

Henry nodded. 'I understand,' he said. 'But it doesn't help much, does it?'

'Sure doesn't.'

'Now,' said Henry, 'how did you get to the mango grove?'

'How? Swam, of course.'

'Where from?'

'There's a little beach near the Anchorage – Pelican Bay. About a mile from Mango Trunk.'

'That's a long swim,' Henry said.

Sandy laughed. 'Long? You crazy, man? With my flippers and snorkel, five mile is nothing. Ten, even.'

'So you swam around to Mango Trunk, virtually under-water.'

'That's right, man. Nothing above the water but the tip of my snorkel tube. I didn't want to be conspicuous, see?'

'So it's a fair bet nobody saw you,' said Henry. 'Did you see anybody?'

'Difficult to see much beside fishes when you're snorkelling, man.' Sandy sounded amused.

'I meant after you surfaced at Mango Trunk.'

Sandy shook his head. 'Don't often get people on Mango Trunk. It's not one of the best beaches around, and there's no way to it but by water. Unless you come down off the golf course and through the mango grove, of course – but you don't find Club members dropping off at the fifth tee to take a dip.'

'O K,' Henry said. 'Go on from there. You came out of the water and walked up the beach. You had your machete with you.'

'That's right, man. Had it in a special sheath on my belt, for swimming. So I waited, nice and hidden in the trees, and before long Olsen and Huberman show up.'

'They didn't have a caddy?'

'No, sir. Well, Huberman drives his ball, and Olsen's looking into the grove, sort of anxious in case I don't turn up. So when he starts his swing, I reckon the moment has come, and I leap out, yelling and waving my machete.' Sandy grinned broadly. 'Must have looked a proper lemon, like Margaret says.'

'I gather the scheme worked?'

'Sure did, man. Olsen played up to the hilt. "Run, Al! Run for your life! Get help!" He didn't really need to carry on so. That Huberman was off the tee and legging it for the horizon in two seconds flat. And Olsen began to laugh. Man, I've never heard a man laugh so loud. He gives me the hundred, and pats my arm, and makes with his head that I should beat it.'

'What did he actually say?'

'He didn't say nothing. He was laughing too hard, man. So I tuck my hundred in the waterproof bag with the machete, and get back in the water. Next thing I knew was when Montague comes into the bar at the Anchorage that evening, looking all solemn, with Sergeant Ingham along. I'm behind the bar, and I ask them what they fancy to drink. And they tell me they're not interested in a drink and that I'm under arrest for murder. Man, that's the worst moment of my life, I'm telling you.'

Henry said, 'You could hardly blame them, Sandy. Obviously Huberman identified you, and the fact remains that somebody did murder Senator Olsen. Somebody who was an expert with a machete.'

Sandy gave Henry a sideways look. 'What makes you say that?'

'Well . . .'

'Now, see here, Mr Tibbett. I didn't get to look at Olsen's body, but they tell me he was all cut up.'

'That's correct.' Before leaving London, Henry had been shown photographs of the Senator's body and they were not pretty. 'Whoever did it must really have hated Olsen, to do that to him.'

Sandy leant forward and tapped Henry on the arm. 'That's where you're wrong, man. All that shows is that the fellow with the machete was no expert. He didn't know how to handle it.' He paused. 'You know what a machete's really for, don't you?'

'Not precisely. Cutting down vegetation, I suppose.'

'No, man. It's for cutting coconuts. You climb up the tree with your machete and cut down the coconut. Unless you really know what you're doing.'

'Then what do you do?'

'You don't climb, man. You just throw the machete up, and get the nut you're after, and down they both come.'

'That's the way you do it?'

'Sure is, man. But that's not the important part. The important part is once you've got the coconut down. Ever tried to split a coconut?'

'No, I haven't,' Henry admitted.

'Well, man, it's an art. I'm telling you. One stroke with the machete – straight down the middle. Coconut's in two equal halves.'

'Yes, but – '

Sandy went on, unperturbed. 'Now, I'm not saying a machete's never been used to kill a man, because it has. And there's a way of doing it – a right way, like an expert would use. You get it?'

'You mean – the victim's head – ?'

'Right, man. Like a coconut. From behind. One neat stroke. That's how the expert would do it. You believe me?'

For a long moment, the two men looked at each other. At last, Henry said, 'Yes, Sandy. I believe what you say about the expert method. But a possibility occurs to me – '

'What possibility?'

'You're bright,' Henry said. 'Work it out for yourself. By the way, Candy sends her love.'

Gravely, Sandy said, 'That's kind. I appreciate that. Will you give her mine?'

'I'll do my best,' Henry said. Then, 'How much have you seen of Diamond lately?'

Sandy's face hardened. 'What d'you know about that?'

'Just that it's old history. When did it end?'

'Long ago, man. Long ago.'

'Before you met Candy?'

'Oh, sure. Long before that.'

'And you never went along with Diamond as far as politics – '

'Cut it out, man.' Sandy sounded really angry. 'I broke with Diamond long before she ever . . . before she . . .'

'Lost her eye?'

'Before that, man. Who's been telling you – ?'

'Nobody, Sandy,' said Henry. 'Nobody at all.'

Chapter 6

Lunch-time at St Matthew's Golf Club. The dining-room was a long shady terrace overlooking the beach, and it had been laid out with an impressive buffet. Lobsters and Parma ham, sides of roast beef and whole hams stood among herbaceous borders of green salad, rose bushes of pink shrimps on sticks, bosky copses of soft beige mushrooms scattered with parsley, carrots and radishes sculpted into flowers and snowflakes; whole pineapples had been scooped out and filled with fruit, cakes frosted and iced like fairytales, tiny tangerines candied, leaves and all, and platters of cheeses shaded from creamy white Brie to the deep orange of Double Gloucester. Sergeant Reynolds was trying hard not to appear impressed, but Henry saw his eyes widen despite himself.

When both their plates were laden with good things, they carried them to a secluded table. A short conversation with the wine waiter produced two glasses of beer. Under the protective cover of buzzing conversation from other tables, Henry said, 'Well, Mr Reynolds? How did you get on?'

'With Huberman and the girl? No dice, I'm afraid. Chatty as a couple of clams.'

'You were close enough to hear anything they said?'

'I was lying on the beach right next to them. Well, that is . . . as close as I could . . .'

'And they didn't say anything at all?'

'Not a word. He was lying on his back on that beach bed thing. She spread out a towel on the sand and lay on her face.' Reynolds paused. 'Next thing, it was half past twelve and the girl sits up and says, "OK, Al. Lunch-time." He sort of grunts, and sits up, and they go off up the beach together. I haven't seen them since. They've not been in here or the bar.'

Henry said, 'There's something else, isn't there? Something puzzling you.'

'Well – yes, actually. I could have sworn I didn't miss anything, but – '

'But what?'

'Well, Huberman did make one remark, and I can't make head nor tail of it. They were both lying there, not moving, when suddenly Huberman says, "And you can put *that* idea out of your head for a start." But she hadn't said a word – not even moved.'

'Did she react?' said Henry.

'Not really. She just rolled over on her side, so that her back was towards him. And there we were for another ten minutes, until she said it was lunch-time. It did occur to me,' added Reynolds diffidently, 'that perhaps he was taking up an old conversation – I mean, answering something that she had said much earlier on. You see what I mean?'

Henry swallowed a delicious mouthful of lobster, and said, 'I do. Very interesting.'

'How did you make out – ?' Reynolds nipped the word 'sir' off his tongue. 'Did you see Robbins?'

'I did. A very attractive young man.'

'D'you think he's innocent?'

Henry meditated a moment. 'Too soon to say. I've certainly established that he had a couple of good reasons for wanting to do away with Senator Olsen.'

'You mean, he was mixed up with this political business after all?'

'No. No, I don't think so. These were personal reasons, and therefore more plausible, as Lucy said.'

'Lucy?'

'A friend of mine on Tampica,' Henry explained. 'We discussed the case. She knows most of these people. You must meet her.'

'I'd like that,' said Reynolds. 'There's some smashing girls on these islands, if Miss Candy is anything to go by.'

Henry smiled. 'Miss Lucy Pontefract-Deacon is eighty-four,' he said. 'But all the same, I don't think you'll be disappointed. However, for the moment I've a more congenial job for you. You're a nice-looking, unattached young man, and Candy Stevenson is obviously bored with Huberman. Play it very lightly –

don't let her think you're after information. I want to know more about her relationship with Olsen – and with Sandy Robbins. I want to know what Huberman meant by that cryptic remark. I want to know more about Jackson Ledbetter.'

'Jackson Who?'

'Ledbetter. He's an American business man, very high-powered. Chairman of the Cotton Producers' Federation. He was here until a few days ago, but now he's gone back to the States.'

'Just what do you want to know about these people?' Reynolds sounded anxious.

'Whatever Candy Stevenson knows,' said Henry. He grinned at the sergeant. 'Just relax and enjoy yourself. You're not likely to get another assignment like this in your entire career. Now, whatever you do, don't let on that you're a policeman. You're a business man from London. Do you know anything about cotton?'

'No, sir. Sorry, I mean – no.'

'What do you know anything about?'

Surprisingly, Sergeant Reynolds reddened. 'Well, sir ... that is ... stamp collecting. It's my hobby. Would that be any good?'

'That would be splendid.' Henry was enthusiastic. 'You're a dealer in rare stamps, and you're here on holiday but also hoping to pick up a ... what would you be hoping to pick up?'

'A purple Tampica fourpenny oblong, of course.'

'Of course. A what?'

'A purple Tampica fourpenny oblong. One of the rarest stamps there is. The purple Tampica fourpenny was a square stamp, you see – but in 1934 a couple of sheets were mis-perforated as oblongs, by mistake. They're not all accounted for, and collectors think some may still be around on the islands – probably privately owned by people who've no idea what they're worth. That was the first thing I thought of when I heard about this job. I mean, I thought that if I had some time off I could go to Tampica and – '

'Mr Reynolds,' said Henry, 'you never cease to amaze and delight me. Go off and dazzle Candy Stevenson with purple oblongs. If she asks why you were lunching with me, say we are acquaintances from London. Refer to me rather patronizingly as

69

some sort of a bobby. Whatever you do, don't forget you're very rich.'

'About that,' said Reynolds. 'What do I do for money?'

'You put everything on the bill. The people here are much too wealthy to dirty their hands with actual money. You'll have to get used to that.'

'Shouldn't be very hard,' said Reynolds with a grin.

'You'd be surprised,' said Henry.

On his way back to the car park, Henry stopped at the Secretary's office, where Major Chatsworth was engaged in a passionate telephone conversation with Her Majesty's Customs' House on St Mark's. Apparently there were difficulties over a consignment of frozen beef from the United States.

'I suppose you know that the Governor is staying at the Club?' he shouted, playing his trump card. 'Yes, and I've promised him roast ribs of beef for Saturday night, and I can assure you that if ... oh, you will? Well, so I should hope ... yes, yes, I'll send the boat ... and a very good day to you, sir.' He slammed down the telephone and looked up balefully at Henry, mopping his brow with a white linen handkerchief. 'Officious jacks-in-office! Making smugglers out of all of us, that's what they're doing! I could have run that consignment out of Tampica in my own boat and no questions asked. A man tries to play by the rules, and where does it get him – ? Oh, forgive me, Tibbett. Just a little bother with Customs and Excise. Charming fellows really, of course. Now, what can I do for you? You've had lunch, I trust?'

'I've had lunch,' Henry said, 'and I'm on my way back to the Anchorage. It's all right if I keep the moke, is it?'

'My dear chap – it's yours for as long as you're here.'

'Thank you. One other thing. About Sergeant Reynolds.'

'You found him all right, did you?'

'Yes, indeed. And I want to fill you in on his assumed identity. He is Mr Derek Reynolds, a wealthy philatelist from London.'

'A philatelist?'

'It happens to be true,' said Henry. 'Except the wealthy bit. So play it up, will you? Especially to Sir Geoffrey and Montague ... and your wife.'

The Anchorage was deserted, except for John Colville, who

was sitting behind the bar reading the *Financial Times*. He looked up as Henry came in from the blazing sunlight of the garden into the cool shadows under the palm-leaf roof.

'Hi, Henry. Care for a drink? Emmy and Margaret have gone to the beach. I'm minding the shop.'

'I'll have a fresh guava juice, if you've got one.' Henry sat down on a bamboo bar stool. 'I see you're keeping up with your old profession.'

John grinned. 'Hardly,' he said. 'Look at the date. Three weeks old. Just arrived by surface mail. I suppose it has a sort of quaint, historical charm. One guava juice. How are things going?'

'I saw Sandy,' said Henry.

John's face brightened. 'You did? How is he?'

'Remarkably cheerful, in the circumstances. He also seems to have a touching faith in me, which is hardly justified. He also seems to have had a couple of good reasons for disliking Senator Olsen.'

'Nonsense, Henry. What reasons could Sandy possibly have had?'

Henry took a drink from the cool, dark-pink glass. He said, 'Their names are Diamond and Candy.'

John made an impatient gesture, as if brushing away a fly. 'Oh, Sandy and his chicks. He doesn't take them that seriously. He'd never commit murder – '

'I hope you're right,' said Henry. 'Tell me, can Sandy handle a machete?'

'Better than any man on the island.'

'He tells me there's a right and a wrong way to kill people with those things.'

John's smile was worried. 'If he said so, you'd better believe him. But don't expect me to know.'

'They're pretty easy to come by, I suppose,' Henry said. 'I mean, if anybody wanted to buy one – '

'Oh, certainly. All over the islands. Most of the men carry one, for coconuts. I expect Sandy told you.'

'Yes. Yes, he did.'

There was a clatter of feet on the outside staircase leading to the bedrooms. John looked up and said, 'Hello there, Tom. Want your bill?'

'If you please, John. Hi, Henry. Hail and farewell.'

Tom Bradley was almost unrecognizable in a navy blue light-weight suit and a polka-dotted bow tie. He said, 'Don't smirk at me like that, you lucky devil, just because you're staying on here.'

'Sorry,' said Henry. 'You just look a little out of place. I didn't know you were leaving.'

'Nor did I.' Tom made a face. 'Summoned back to Washington by Head Office half an hour ago. Bill's got a whiff of some sort of a story maybe breaking, and he wants me on it. Just my lousy luck.'

Henry said, 'Has it anything to do with – ?'

'Don't ask me, pal. Not the sort of thing one discusses on a public telephone line.'

'It just occurred to me – '

'It occurred to me, too,' said Tom. 'Thanks, John. God, did I drink all that? Oh, well, Mawson's expense account can stand it. Charge it on my American Express, will you? Here . . .' He fished the magic plastic rectangle from his wallet. 'And can you call a cab for me? I want to make the three-thirty boat from Priest Town.'

Quickly, Henry said, 'Don't bother with a taxi. I've got a moke outside. I'll run you to the harbour.'

Tom Bradley gave him a quizzical look. 'OK. Very kind of you.' He scrawled his signature on the bill and picked up his cases.

'So long, John. Say good-bye to Margaret for me. Oh, and . . . don't let my room for a week or so, there's a dear chap. I just might be back.'

In the moke, bouncing over the dirt road towards Priest Town, Tom said, 'All right. It may be something connected with Olsen. Naturally I thought of that when Bill called. But get this straight. It may be a hundred other different things. And what's more, there's no question of revealing my sources to a policeman. I've got my job to do, and you've got yours. You can't ask me to – '

Henry said, 'I haven't asked you anything, Tom.'

Tom grinned. 'No, you haven't, have you? Well, get this. *If* it's to do with Olsen, and *if* it's not going to harm me or Bill or the column, and *if* it's going to help Sandy . . . well . . .'

'Thanks a lot,' said Henry.

'Probably wouldn't be anything specific, you understand? Just a tip-off . . . a direction to look in . . .'

'Huberman?'

'I told you, I don't know.'

'Ledbetter?'

'That's quite enough of that. Turn right here, and the second left will bring us to the harbour. And get a move on, or I'll miss that boat.'

Henry stopped the moke near the dockside, where a battered little steamboat called *Pride of St Mark's* was puffing out ineffectual bursts of black smoke from her grimy funnel. Tom jumped out of the car, grabbed his cases and ran up the gangplank, just a matter of seconds before it was hauled inboard. The *Pride of St Mark's* gave an asthmatic hoot, ropes were cast off, and the steamer moved with a certain slow dignity towards the harbour mouth. Henry reversed the moke, and drove back into the narrow streets of Priest Town.

If he had not had so much to think about apart from actually driving the car, Henry might have seen his attacker. As it was, the jagged brick smashed through the windscreen with no warning, shattering the glass and sending the moke into a skid on the slippery cobblestones, as Henry fought with the wheel to regain control. He brought the little car to a screaming stop half-on and half-off the narrow pavement. The street, which a moment before had boasted a sprinkling of pedestrians and cyclists, was suddenly deserted.

The brick had come from the right, slightly ahead of the moke – in fact, from the direction of a narrow alley running between two tall grey buildings. Henry leapt out of the car and raced for the alley's entrance. He got there just in time to see a lanky figure on a bicycle disappearing round the corner at the far end, before he collided violently with Diamond, who had stepped out of a doorway and was standing fair and square in the centre of the alley. She was wearing her dark glasses and a sardonic smile, and she halted Henry's progress with one strong black hand.

'Looking for somebody, Chief Superintendent?'

Henry regained his balance and glared at her. 'Not any more.'

Diamond's smile deepened a little. 'That was just to show you,' she said. 'We're watching you. We know what you do and who you talk to.'

'There's no secret about what I do. For God's sake, Diamond, Olsen's dead. Aren't you satisfied with that?'

'A year ago, I might have been. Not any more.' Diamond looked down on Henry, using her height as a weapon. 'You'd better take the moke back to Chatsworth, and get one with a windscreen. A strong windscreen. It might be a bullet next time.'

Henry grinned wryly, and shook his head. 'Which is it to be, Diamond? Personal or political?'

'Bit of both, man. Bit of both.'

'Can't you feel any pity for – ?'

'Who felt pity for me? Tell me that.'

'Plenty of people,' Henry said. 'But it's a perishable commodity, you know. It won't last much longer.'

'Unless you do something foolish. Like arresting me. Or Brooks. Or Delaware.'

'My dear young lady,' Henry said reasonably, 'if you or Brooks or Delaware break the law, and I catch you at it, I'll arrest you just as I would . . . Major Chatsworth.'

'Or Owen Montague? Or Sir Geoffrey Patterson?' Diamond spat the names out.

'Nobody is above the law,' said Henry.

Diamond did not reply. She laughed, shortly and without amusement. Then she turned on her heel and walked off down the thin alleyway, casting a larger-than-life shadow which flicked up the grey walls behind her. Henry did not attempt to follow her. He went back to the abandoned moke, and, as she had advised, drove it back to the Club.

Major Chatsworth was predictably irritated. 'Surely you could have called the police and had the girl arrested, Tibbett?'

'What for?'

'Well – disturbing the peace . . . breaking your windscreen . . .'

'Diamond didn't throw that brick, Major Chatsworth. And I warn you – if you have her arrested before the Robbins case comes to trial, you're going to have bad trouble on this island.'

'That's blackmail.'

'Call it what you like, it's a fact. Robbins must either be cleared or convicted before anything worse happens.'

'Well, isn't that what you're here for, Tibbett?'

'Yes,' said Henry. 'Yes, of course it is. I'm sorry about the moke.'

'Good God, the moke doesn't matter. Pick up another one on your way out. What matters is to get this island back to normal.'

'It's possible,' Henry said, 'that nothing will ever be what you call "normal" again.'

'What do you mean by that?'

'Just that it's easier to start things than to finish them. As Miss Diamond may find out.'

'I don't pretend to understand you, Tibbett.'

'I'm not surprised. I don't really understand myself. I'll be at the Anchorage if you want me. By the way, there's no need to make a big thing of this stone-throwing incident. I'd be obliged if you didn't mention it to anybody.'

As soon as Henry had left his office, Major Chatsworth picked up the telephone. 'Get me the Governor. Yes, if he's on the beach, have him paged. It's urgent.'

Seven o'clock. The Colvilles and the Tibbetts were enjoying a cool drink in the Anchorage bar, with Emmy recounting the delights of snorkelling in Cedar Valley Bay. As the sun dipped towards the western horizon in a blaze of red, yellow, purple and gold, John Colville suddenly said, 'Listen. Isn't that – ?'

'It's the Club launch,' said Margaret. 'I'd know her motor anywhere. Yes, there she goes.'

Around the headland, travelling fast, came a sleek white boat cutting through the rippled water and leaving an arrow of creamy wake.

John looked puzzled. 'Heading for St Boniface, no doubt about that,' he said. 'Picking up some new guests? But there are no planes due.'

'Perhaps somebody's leaving,' Margaret suggested.

'Why leave now?' remarked her husband. 'The only plane any-body could catch before morning is the cut-rate night excursion flight to Washington, and that's not the way Golf Club members travel.'

They watched the boat in silence as it ripped across the bay and finally disappeared from view. 'I wonder – ' John began, but

75

was cut short by the shrilling of the telephone. He heaved himself out of his comfortable chair and went to answer it.

'Anchorage Inn. Yes ... who wants him, please? ... I see ... just a moment.' He put his hand over the mouthpiece. 'For you, Henry. Mr Reynolds from the Golf Club.'

Henry stood up. 'He's due here for dinner in half an hour,' he said. 'I wonder what he wants.' He took the phone from John. 'Yes? Tibbett here.'

'Oh ... sir ... Mr Tibbett.' Reynolds sounded both furtive and uneasy. 'It's ... that is, something has come up. It's a little awkward.'

'What is, Mr Reynolds?'

'Well ...' Reynolds lowered his voice. 'It's not very easy to talk. I'm not alone, you see.'

'Well, then, come down here at once and – '

'That's just it. I ... I really can't. The young lady ... well, she insists I go to Major Chatsworth right away, and now that Mr Huberman has gone ...'

'Gone?'

'Just a few minutes ago. He suddenly decided to leave. Got himself a booking on the night plane to Washington and called the launch to take him to St Boniface right away. And Miss Stevenson ... ah, that's better.'

'What's better?'

'She's gone off to the bar to get a drink. So I can talk more freely. She wouldn't go with him, you see. There was quite a row. Well, I'd been making up to her, like you said, and when Mr Huberman told her she'd have to leave with him, as she wasn't a member but only his guest, she turned right round and said that her new friend Mr Reynolds the well-known stamp collector would sponsor her at the Club. I didn't know what to say – I really didn't. Anyhow, Mr Huberman has gone and Candy is still here, and she wants me to fix it with Major Chatsworth right away, and ... is there something wrong, Mr Tibbett?'

'No,' said Henry. 'I'm sorry. It just struck me as rather funny. Though the reason Huberman is making tracks for Washington may not be a laughing matter. Anyhow, don't worry. I think it's an admirable arrangement. Just tell the young lady that everything is in order, and I'll speak to Major Chatsworth. Go ahead and enjoy yourself.'

'I could tell her I had an appointment for dinner – '

'You'll do nothing of the sort. Find out anything useful she can tell you, and let me know tomorrow.'

'Sometimes,' said Sergeant Reynolds, on a note of slight desperation, 'I think it would be nice to be back in Victoria Street.' Then, more loudly, 'Yes, my dear. Just coming. Well, let me know if you get on the track of a purple oblong, won't you, old man? Thanks. See you tomorrow.' The line went dead.

Chapter 7

The reception clerk at the Golf Club informed Henry that Major Chatsworth was out, but could be contacted at the Anchorage Inn: and sure enough, hardly had Henry recradled the telephone than the Secretary's bright red jeep turned into the parking lot. The Major was alone, and looked worried.

'Evening, Margaret ... John ... how are you, Tibbett ... Mrs Tibbett ... ? Make me a Bloody Mary, will you, John?' He sat down heavily on a bar stool.

'Good evening, Sebastian,' said Margaret. 'Henry was just trying to call you. I understand Mr Huberman has left us.'

'Good God,' said Major Chatsworth, in a flat voice. 'I knew this island had an efficient grapevine, but that takes the cake. I only heard myself about ten minutes ago. How on earth – ? Oh, I suppose you saw the launch. And if Tibbett was on the blower to the Club ... thanks, John. I needed that.' He took a gulp of his drink. 'You heard what happened to Tibbett this afternoon?' he added.

The other three turned to look inquiringly at Henry, who said, 'I hadn't mentioned it, actually.'

Emmy said, 'What happened, Henry?'

'Oh, some idiot in Priest Town heaved a brick at my car. It was nothing.'

'Well, Sir Geoffrey Patterson doesn't consider it nothing,' said Chatsworth. 'He's extremely upset.'

Henry said, 'Major Chatsworth, I did particularly ask you not to – '

'It was my clear duty to inform the Governor. I wasn't chatting about it in bars.'

'Well, you are now,' said Henry. A couple of black men, one of whom Henry recognized as Daniel Markham, had come in and seated themselves at the far end of the bar. John went off to serve them.

Sotto voce, Major Chatsworth said, 'Naming no names, but Sir Geoffrey has been in touch with Montague. A certain person will not be at liberty very much longer.'

'In that case,' said Henry angrily, 'I shall have to – '

He got no further. A second jeep had pulled up with a squeal of brakes, and Teresa Chatsworth jumped out of it and hurried into the bar. It was obvious that she was very angry, and although she spoke little above a whisper, it sounded like a shout.

'Sebastian! You must come back to the Club at once. That girl is still there!'

'Girl? What girl?'

'The Stevenson girl, idiot. Huberman has gone back to Washington, but she's still at the Club.'

Chatsworth hesitated a moment, as this information sank in. Then he said, 'But she's not a member.'

'Precisely.'

'She was Huberman's guest. She had to leave when he did.'

'Well, she didn't. According to a garbled story from Reception, she has found herself another ... protector.' Teresa spat out the word. 'Now, once and for all, Sebastian – '

The Major held up a hand in mild protest. 'All right, all right, my dear. I know – '

'I was against letting her in in the first place,' Teresa went on. 'If it had been anybody but Mr Huberman and Senator Olsen ... anyhow, I gave in, against my better judgement. And now this happens. Please understand, Sebastian, that I am running a golf club, not a brothel.'

'To be absolutely accurate, Teresa dear, you're not running anything. I am.'

'Oh, don't be childish, Sebastian. Come back this moment and get rid of her. As soon as the launch gets back from St Boniface, she's going to board it. I don't care where she goes. She's not spending another night at the Club.'

The Major did not seem unduly intimidated. He said, 'For heaven's sake, Tess, simmer down and have a drink. John! A rum punch for my old lady, if you please. She's somewhat over-excited.'

'Sebastian, I – '

'Who's she found to sponsor her, I wonder?' Chatsworth went on. 'Pretty quick work. Of course, some members are on the qui vive for – '

Henry said, 'I think I can throw some light on that, Major. In fact, it's what I was trying to telephone you about. Miss Stevenson is now the guest of Mr Derek Reynolds, the wealthy English philatelist.'

Teresa Chatsworth turned on Henry, furious. 'You lunched with him today,' she said accusingly.

'That's right. He's an old acquaintance from London.'

'Then you're behind this. You put him up to it.'

'I certainly did not, Mrs Chatsworth. At lunch-time, nobody had any idea that Mr Huberman would be leaving. But I won't deny that when Reynolds telephoned me just now to tell me what had happened, I didn't discourage him.'

'Well, you should have. It's disgusting.'

Henry said, 'The point, Mrs Chatsworth, is that I think the Stevenson girl may be useful in my investigation – and once she leaves here, she'll disappear into the United States like an eel into the mud. Not like many of your members, who are public figures and therefore always traceable, even if not available for comment.'

'The reputation of the Golf Club,' said Teresa icily, 'is more important than your investigation. It's perfectly obvious that Sandy Robbins killed Senator Olsen, and all we have to do now is tie it up in blue ribbons for the public. I can't see how Candy Stevenson can help with that.'

Henry smiled, in a way calculated to infuriate Mrs Chatsworth. He said, 'I'm afraid our priorities are different. My object is not to convict Robbins, but to find out what actually happened. Candy Stevenson was a close friend of both Olsen and Robbins, and so her testimony is important. With Huberman out of the way, I think she'll talk more freely.'

Teresa shot him a nasty look, and took a pull at her drink. She said, 'If Sebastian won't ask her to leave, I will.'

'Don't be silly, Tess,' said Major Chatsworth. He shot an uneasy glance at Henry. 'You can't do that. Club rules. Members are allowed to bring one guest, and Mr Reynolds is a member.'

'A temporary member,' said Teresa with a sniff. 'Anyhow, I never said I was going to order her to leave. I shall ask her to do so – quite politely. And I shall make sure that everyone in the Club knows it, and for what reasons. It may be quite embarrassing, both for her and for Mr Reynolds, if she stays.' She finished her drink, and stood up. 'Well, I'd better get back. We have some members arriving in the morning, and there's a lot to be done.'

She marched out of the bar, and Major Chatsworth turned to the others, with a small, hopeless gesture. 'Nothing I can say will stop her,' he remarked gloomily. 'She'll do nothing but harm, mark my words.'

'I'm sorry, Major,' said Henry, 'if I've put you in a difficult position by wanting Candy to stay on – '

'That's not the point, Tibbett. If Tess is as good as her word, and everybody knows that Candy's been asked to leave, and why . . . well . . .'

Emmy said, 'You mean, there are other members – ?'

Sebastian cleared his throat. 'Don't misunderstand me, Mrs Tibbett. I just meant that a lot of members' wives don't play golf, and some of them – '

'I understand you perfectly, Major Chatsworth,' said Emmy.

'I fancy you do, Mrs Tibbett. The last thing we want is the wrong sort of publicity, especially after the murder. Oh, well, no use sitting here crying over spilt milk. Better go after her and see what I can do . . . chalk up the drinks on my bill, will you, John?'

When Chatsworth had gone, John said, 'I can't think what's got into Teresa.'

'Can't you?' Margaret sounded amused.

'No, I can't. As Sebastian almost said, everybody knows a certain amount of extra-marital high jinks go on at the Golf Club – hell, it's one of the things that members pay for. Discretion.'

'Exactly,' said Margaret.

'So I don't – '

'Candy Stevenson,' said Margaret, 'was expected to leave when Mr Huberman did – but instead she's staying on. There must be at least one other member who feels that life would be easier if she were out of the way.' She turned to Henry, raised an eyebrow and smiled. 'Right, Chief Superintendent?'

'Right, Margaret.'

'But if that's so,' John protested, 'Sebastian would know – '

'I doubt it,' Henry said. 'If I were a member, and wanted to make arrangements of a . . . a certain delicacy . . . I don't think I'd approach the Major. I'd go to Mrs Chatsworth. Right, Margaret?'

'Right, Henry.'

At ten o'clock the following morning, Saturday, Tom Bradley telephoned Henry Tibbett at the Anchorage Inn, speaking from Washington.

'Hi, Henry. Got to make this short and sweet. I've got some information for you, and I hope you'll have some for me.'

'What do you want to know?'

'Where's Albert Huberman?' Tom asked.

'Not here,' said Henry. 'He left in a hurry last night. Ordered the launch around seven o'clock and caught the night flight out of St Boniface to Washington.'

Tom Bradley swore softly. 'That's what the Golf Club told me,' he said, 'but I hoped they might just be covering up. You're sure of your facts?'

'I have it from both Major and Mrs Chatsworth,' Henry said, 'and I saw the launch leaving myself. The girl Candy Stevenson is still at the Club. She might be able to help you.'

'Nope. I tried that. She left this morning, early.'

'So Teresa did get rid of her. Pretty smart work.'

Bradley was not listening. 'As far as anybody can make out, Huberman isn't in Washington. He must be hiding out somewhere, damn his eyes.'

'Why should he be hiding?'

'That's the news I have for you. The story hasn't broken yet, but it'll be all over the papers in the Bill Mawson column on Monday morning. Big kick-back scandal involving the Olsen Committee.'

'That's the cotton subsidies affair?'

'Right. Seems the Justice Department was about to move in on Olsen when he was killed. Now Bill's got a leak from a Justice aide, and it seems that the probe won't die with Olsen. Huberman's in a hot spot, and he's conveniently disappeared.'

'Kick-backs from the cotton people?' Henry said. 'Does that involve Ledbetter?'

'It might. Anybody's guess. As President of the CPF, he's bound to come under suspicion.'

'He hasn't disappeared, too?'

'Ledbetter? Far from it. He's in New York. One of our guys managed to see him yesterday afternoon. He's issuing a statement, timed to coincide with Bill's column, deeply regretting any implication etc. etc. The usual stuff. So far, nobody has traced any money further back than Huberman. Dammit, where is that bastard?'

'Not here,' said Henry.

'Well, I'll tell you something. He wasn't on that plane last night. I met it at Dulles myself, and there's no way I could have missed him.'

'Couldn't the airline have arranged to smuggle him off by some different exit?'

'Sure they could. But they swear they didn't, and why should they do such a thing? They also maintain that he was on the flight. His name's on the manifest and his baggage was claimed. Well, I guess he could have fixed that. He's hiding out somewhere and I'm going to find him.'

Henry said, 'Did the Golf Club say where his girl-friend had gone?'

'Nope. Just that she left early this morning. Candy wouldn't know anything, anyhow. Strictly a sex symbol. She'll have gotten herself a fresh millionaire by now. Well, I gotta go. If you get any word on Huberman, be a pal and call me – Margaret has my number. And watch out for Monday's *Post*. Bill Mawson's column. See you.'

At half past ten, Daniel Markham drove up in a Golf Club jeep and came into the bar of the Anchorage. He waved aside John's suggestion of a drink.

'Can't stop, I'm afraid, John. On my way to Priest Town – we're expecting a load of fertilizer on the Tortola boat. Just dropped in to deliver this – for you, I think, sir – ' and he handed Henry an envelope discreetly emblazoned with the insignia of the

Club, and addressed to Mr Henry Tibbett in a hand which Henry recognized at once as that of Sergeant Derek Reynolds. 'Gentleman asked me to deliver it personally. Well – so long, all. See you later.'

Daniel was vaulting into the jeep again before Henry had time to open the envelope. The letter, on Club notepaper, was written in a hurried scrawl. It read as follows:

Dear Mr Tibbett,

Sorry I couldn't keep our appointment, but I'm off on a swift boat trip, on the trail of one of those rare stamps I told you about. Don't worry, I won't go over the side – you know I can't swim!

Miss Stevenson has decided to leave, too – she went golfing early this morning, but her opponent pulled a stroke on her, which made her very fed up, I'm afraid. I rowed her out to the launch and punted around till it left.

I hope I won't be away too long – I've left all my things at the Club, including my shoes. I'll get in touch with you as soon as I get back. Until then, there's no point trying to contact me – I don't know where I'll be.

Yours,
Derek Reynolds

Emmy strolled into the bar, shaking the sea water out of her wet hair. 'Mail from home?' she asked.

'No. From our friend Mr Reynolds.'

Emmy took the letter, read it, and said, 'What an odd communication. Did you have an appointment with him?'

'No, I didn't.'

'Then what does he – ?'

Henry glanced around him. The bar was empty, except for John Colville, who was rearranging bottles and glasses in anticipation of the noontide rush of business. He said, 'I feel like a swim. Coming?'

'I've only just got back from the beach!'

'Then you'll need a dry swimsuit. Come on upstairs.'

Emmy was well-trained. 'OK. See you later, John.' She led the way up the outside staircase to the bedroom. Once inside, she said, 'Now, what's all this – as your constables are supposed to say?'

'This letter from Reynolds.'

'Sounds slightly crazy to me. Has he taken a real shine to the Candy girl, and done a bunk with her?'

'Of course not. The letter sounds odd to you, because Reynolds wrote it in police jargon. Not a bad effort, considering he must have been in one hell of a hurry. I'll translate it.'

Henry studied the letter for a moment, and then went on, 'He's off on some ploy that isn't strictly legal or authorized. That's what "swift" means.'

'On a boat,' said Emmy.

'Not necessarily. He needed the boat to be able to assure me that he wasn't over the side.'

'What does that mean, for heaven's sake?'

Henry grinned. 'Attending to his own affairs, usually sexual. In fact, that there's nothing personal in his going after Candy Stevenson, who is obviously the "rare stamp" in question. Somebody has played a dirty trick on her – "pulled a stroke" – and Reynolds believes she's innocent.'

'How on earth do you know that?'

'Because he says he rowed her out to the launch. "Rowing in" is slang for implicating somebody in a crime, so "rowing out" is the opposite. To "punt around" is to patrol – which I suppose means that he's searched the Golf Club and is now convinced that she's been abducted. So he's gone after her.'

'Without his shoes?'

Henry said, 'That's a private joke. I accused him yesterday of mentally wearing a copper's boots, even on the beach. This must mean that he's disappearing into the undergrowth, especially as it's followed by a clear warning not to go after him. Don't call us, we'll call you.' Henry sat down heavily on the bed. 'I hope to God he knows what he's doing. If it were anybody but Reynolds – '

'Derek Reynolds is OK.' Emmy spoke decisively. Several times she had worked very unofficially with Reynolds, and she held him in great esteem.

'I never said he wasn't. I just hope he's not being a bloody fool. Well, the next thing is to contact Mrs Chatsworth, and find out what she said to Candy Stevenson, and where *she* thinks she is.'

'Miss Stevenson has left, Superintendent.' Teresa's voice was clipped and very upper-class English. 'I have no idea where she has gone. She went on the first launch to St Boniface, at eight-thirty. Yes, I spoke to her last night. No, I don't think I was rude in any way. I just pointed out that Mr Reynolds was only a temporary member, and therefore didn't enjoy the same privileges as – '

'Is that true, Mrs Chatsworth?'

'In the circumstances, yes. We have a certain latitude in the case of temporary members.'

'Did she seem upset when you spoke to her?'

'She did not.' Down the telephone line, Henry could imagine Teresa's mouth set in a thin line of disapproval. 'She was extremely flippant. I did not press her. I made my point, and left it at that. I was gratified but not really surprised when the reception clerk told me she had departed on the eighty-thirty.'

'I suppose you know,' said Henry, 'that Mr Reynolds has also gone.'

'Has – what?'

'Gone. Presumably with Miss Stevenson.'

'How on earth do you know that, Mr Tibbett?'

'Because I had an appointment with him this morning, and he sent a note via Daniel.'

For a moment, there was silence. Then Teresa Chatsworth said, 'So that's why she went. Well, Mr Reynolds has not checked out, and so he will be charged for the room until he returns.' She replaced the receiver with a noisy click.

At eleven o'clock, Sergeant Ingham and two of his constables, on orders from Inspector Montague, broke into the Bum Boat Bar and arrested Diamond on charges of creating a public disturbance. They handcuffed her and marched her out into the police wagon and drove her to the police station in Priest Town, where she was booked under her legal name of Ethel Drake and locked into a cell adjoining that of Sandy Robbins.

At twelve o'clock, the rioting began in earnest.

It started in the area around the Bum Boat, led by Brooks and

Delaware, who had been buying drinks freely for all comers. It spread through the streets of Priest Town like a brush fire. The Golf Club shut and barricaded its formidable iron gates, incidentally imprisoning both Sir Geoffrey Patterson and Inspector Montague.

Small bands of three or four black youths quickly merged themselves into more menacing groups, their numbers building up into the fifties and sixties. Most of them had very little idea of what it was all about, but the momentum was irresistible. When they had satisfied their first frustrations by breaking windows and overturning cars, they converged as if by common consent on to the police station.

The news was brought to the Anchorage by a badly-shaken Daniel, who had narrowly escaped while driving his load of fertilizer back from the Priest Town dock. John Colville immediately closed the bar, lowering the protective iron grilles around it with much difficulty, for they had not been used in years.

Despite vigorous protests from Emmy and the Colvilles, Henry insisted on getting into his moke and heading for Priest Town. He abandoned the vehicle well outside the town, and made his way on foot towards the quayside, breasting the hysterical tide of tourists and Golf Club members who were struggling out of the danger zone. He arrived at the waterfront in time to see the police station merrily ablaze, surrounded by revolutionaries of both sexes throwing blazing petrol cans into the building.

By the time the flames were finally brought under control, Sergeant Ingham was in the local hospital, one constable was dead and three more injured – and there was no sign whatsoever of either Sandy Robbins or Diamond Drake.

Their mission accomplished, the arsonists melted quietly away. There were no arrests, because the police force of St Matthew's had been effectively put out of action, and by the time reinforcements arrived from St Mark's, there was nobody to arrest.

At seven o'clock in the evening, when some sort of order had been restored, and Sir Geoffrey was preparing to broadcast another of his soothing messages to the population, a maid at the Golf Club went into the cottage previously occupied by Mr

Albert Huberman. Two minutes later, she arrived screaming in Major Chatsworth's office. It was with some difficulty that Sebastian extracted from her the information that the cottage was not empty. It contained the body of Mr Albert Huberman, who had been brutally hacked to pieces by a machete, and was very dead indeed.

Chapter 8

It was Sunday morning, in Sebastian Chatsworth's office at the Golf Club, and Henry Tibbett was very angry.

'I made it absolutely clear that this would happen if Diamond was arrested. The stone thrown at my car couldn't matter less. Now you have two murders and two escaped prisoners on your plate, and frankly you're welcome to them. Maybe it's no coincidence that this is April Fools' Day.'

'You made nothing of the sort clear, Tibbett.' Sir Geoffrey took an indignant puff at his cigar and strutted across the room, punctuating his words with emphatic gestures. 'Nobody could have foreseen that Robbins and Drake would escape from prison. Still less did anybody – let alone you – imagine that a man would be murdered ... a man, mind you, who was supposed to have been back in the United States for at least twenty-four hours. The whole thing is disgraceful and I demand an explanation.'

'You'd better ask Inspector Montague about the prison breaks,' said Henry. 'And about the murdered policeman. That's his department.'

Owen Montague, who had been lounging against the window-sill, stood up abruptly and stamped out his cigarette on the marble-tiled floor. He had gone very pale. 'I don't think that's fair, Tibbett,' he said. 'My men behaved splendidly. There was simply nothing they could do. They were outnumbered and the place was on fire. And I may say that I was against arresting the Drake girl from the beginning. It was Sir Geoffrey and Sebastian who – '

'I did no more than my duty,' said Sebastian Chatsworth. 'I informed the Governor of a breach of the peace.'

'Now you're all insinuating that the whole thing was my fault, is that it?' demanded Sir Geoffrey.

'Oh, for heaven's sake,' Henry said. 'I'm sorry. I lost my

temper, and I apologize. Let's not quarrel among ourselves. What's happened has happened, and the best thing we can do now is get on with our respective jobs.'

The Governor cleared his throat. 'Just what I was about to say, Tibbett. Co-operation is the key. Montague and I are due at my cottage in ten minutes for a meeting with Commissioner Alcott from St Mark's, to talk about riot control. As you know, the Executive Council has already imposed an eight o'clock curfew, on my advice. The tracking down of the escaped prisoners would seem to me to call for a joint effort by Montague and Tibbett.'

'Of course I'll help all I can, sir,' Henry said, 'but I do have my terms of reference. I'm here to investigate the murder of Senator Olsen.'

'And of Albert Huberman, Tibbett.'

'Strictly speaking, sir – '

'Please let me finish. It's perfectly obvious what happened yesterday. Robbins escaped from gaol, and took advantage of the general confusion to come here to the Golf Club – once again by water, of course – and finish off what he had started. The double murder of Olsen and Huberman. In fact, for all we know, Huberman may have been the intended victim all along, but the first time he escaped, and Olsen had to be silenced. You only have to consider . . . Robbins's escape, the same murder weapon, the same horrible mutilation . . . it all fits. Agreed?'

'I'm afraid not, Sir Geoffrey,' Henry said, 'but no matter . . . I agree that the two crimes are related – but there are a lot of unanswered questions.'

'Well, put your questions and find your answers, Tibbett, and good luck to you,' said Patterson. 'Come along, Montague. Commissioner Alcott will be waiting.'

Henry said, 'Just one question before you go, Inspector. Can you tell me exactly how your officer was killed at the police station?'

'How? With a machete, of course. You knew that.'

'But the actual wound?'

Montague looked sick. He said, 'It was most unpleasant – but certainly efficient. Just one stroke to the head – '

'Like splitting a coconut?'

'If you must put it like that – yes.'

'Thanks,' said Henry. 'Well, I won't keep you any longer, gentlemen.'

Alone with Sebastian Chatsworth Henry said, 'Now please tell me about Mr Huberman.'

'About him? What about him? He left here about seven o'clock the night before last – '

'Why?'

'How should I know why? He decided to go back to the States, and ordered the launch. Our members are busy and important people, Mr Tibbett. They frequently have to make quick changes of plan – and we pride ourselves on serving them efficiently. We certainly don't ask questions.'

'All right. But the man is dead. Did he get a phone call or a telegram – ?'

Chatsworth looked uncomfortable. 'I understand from Reception that he received a call from New York around six o'clock. Naturally, the operator asked who wished to speak to him – we protect our members from unwanted callers . . .'

'And who was it?

'The caller was a woman – a secretary, I suppose. She told our operator that Mr Jackson Ledbetter was on the line for Mr Huberman. Naturally, Mr Huberman accepted the call – and immediately afterwards asked the desk to book him a seat on the night flight to Washington, and to order the launch to take him to St Boniface without more ado. It all seems very logical. After all, Mr Ledbetter was Mr Huberman's employer, in a manner of speaking. The CPF clearly wanted Mr Huberman back in the States – '

'Did anyone listen in to that telephone call?' Henry asked.

Chatsworth looked deeply shocked. 'How can you suggest such a thing, Mr Tibbett? Don't you realize that our reputation with our members rests on a foundation of absolute discretion and trust? Why, if Mr Huberman had not been killed, I would never have dreamed of divulging the mere fact that Mr Ledbetter had called him – even to you.'

'All right. So we have to presume that Ledbetter did speak to Huberman, and did ask him to return to Washington at once. The next question is – why didn't he?'

'My dear Tibbett, I have no idea. Our boatman took Mr

Huberman to St Boniface and put him ashore soon after eight o'clock. After that, there's nothing but conjecture. Presumably he changed his mind.'

'Then why didn't he get the Club launch to bring him back? In fact – how did he get back, Major Chatsworth?'

Chatsworth smiled, and settled more comfortably in his cane chair. 'No mystery to that. He must have persuaded a local boat-man to bring him over. Our launch service stops at ten o'clock, you see, unless special arrangements have been made in advance. Hire boats aren't allowed to land at our jetty during the day, and most of them don't work at night – but you can generally find a skipper prepared to make an extra buck.'

Henry said, 'Something puzzles me, Major Chatsworth. You take fantastic precautions to prevent the Club from being broken into from the land – and yet it seems relatively easy to get in from the sea. You mean that Huberman could have been landed back here, at your jetty, in the middle of the night – by a boatman from St Boniface – and nobody would have known?'

Chatsworth looked shocked. 'I mean nothing of the sort. Let me explain. It's perfectly true that our security is far stricter on the landward side – simply because that's the way interlopers try to get in. You see, only small boats skippered by people who know the local conditions can get past the reef and into the bay, even in daylight. At night, there's only a handful of local people and a couple of the St Boniface boatmen who would dare try it.'

'There's no buoyed channel?'

'Goodness me, no. These people know every rock and every piece of coral. There are guiding lights on our jetty – but they'd be little use to a helmsman who didn't know the waters.'

'And your jetty is manned twenty-four hours a day?'

'Of course. In the daytime, the Customs and Immigration Officer is there, as well as our Harbour Master. At night, one of our men is always on duty. If a member should arrive on the night flight – a very unusual occurrence – he makes out the documents and has them ready for the Immigration people in the morning.' Major Chatsworth looked a little embarrassed. 'I suppose it may strike you as somewhat informal, but this is the Caribbean. And, of course, our members are above suspicion.'

'Supposing somebody tried to land who wasn't a member?'

Chatsworth laughed shortly. 'He wouldn't succeed. The only way it could be done was as Robbins did it – underwater swimming to a remote bay like Mango Trunk, and overland across the links. And that's never happened before.'

'Right.' Henry stood up. 'Let's go and talk to the man who was on duty at the jetty on Friday night.'

The Golf Club jetty was spick and span and decked out in teak and white-painted wrought-iron to look like an idealized Victorian yacht club. Two Club launches were moored alongside, busily loading up with members and their luggage – for the riots and the death of Albert Huberman had turned the exodus into a rout. The only thing keeping visitors on the island was the lack of seats in aircraft returning to the United States, and Teresa Chatsworth reported that the snapping sound of frantically pulled strings was audible as far away as Miami. It was even rumoured that some members had accepted economy-class seats, while others were roughing it in ordinary luxury hotels on St Boniface, waiting for first-class seats. Henry noticed that the jetty was being patrolled, as unobtrusively as possible, by several brawny armed guards. The Club was in a state of siege.

Major Chatsworth led the way to a cute little white-painted pavilion at the head of the pier. It bore two black-painted notices which read, respectively, 'St Matthew's Golf Club. Harbour Master', and 'H.M. Customs and Immigration'. The red, white and blue of the Union Jack fluttered merrily above the pagoda-like conical roof.

Inside, two officials with important-looking black and gold epaulettes attached to their spotless white shirts were stamping passports and collecting documents from the departing travellers, while at another desk a small, cheerful black man in Golf Club uniform was making entries in a large log book. He jumped to his feet as Henry and Chatsworth came in.

' 'Morning, Major Chatsworth. Busy time we're having. Both launches just about loaded and ready to be off. Reckon we'll have to run an extra trip.'

'You don't have to rub it in, Franklin,' remarked Sebastian gloomily. 'You're making sure to get addresses where everybody

93

can be reached, aren't you? And warning them they may be asked for a statement?'

'Sure, Major Chatsworth.'

To Henry, Chatsworth said, 'It's Montague's opinion that we can't stop these people from leaving, and in any case none of them really knew Huberman. His cronies were Olsen, who's dead, Ledbetter, who's in New York, and the girl Candy Stevenson, who's heaven knows where. You agree?'

'Reluctantly,' said Henry. 'I understand the cottages on either side of Huberman's were empty when he was killed –'

'That's right. One couple were scared off by the trouble here and cut short their stay, and the other people had cancelled.' Chatsworth sighed deeply, then changed gear and said briskly, 'Well, now, Franklin, you can tell us who was on duty here on Friday night.'

Franklin consulted a wall chart. 'Let's see. Friday March 30th. That was Addison Drake, sir.'

'Right. Get me the Assistant Secretary's office on the blower, there's a good chap.'

Henry noticed that Franklin gave the Major a curious sidelong look, but all he said was, 'OK, sir.' He dialled a number, said, 'Major Chatsworth for you' – and held out the telephone to Sebastian.

'Hello? Oh, it's you, Tess. Well, you can help me. Just get hold of Addison and ask him to come down to – what? He's what?' Sebastian Chatsworth had gone very red. 'When did this happen? Why wasn't I informed?' Faintly, from the telephone receiver, Henry could hear Teresa's voice talking rapidly and decisively. At last Sebastian said, in a chastened tone, 'Yes, of course I realize . . . well, we shall just have to . . . Tampica, you said . . . yes, dear . . . no, of course you couldn't . . . no, I wasn't implying . . . yes, I'll see you for lunch . . .' He rang off and mopped his brow.

'I gather he's gone,' said Henry.

Franklin grinned. 'Sure. Addison went off Saturday, back to Tampica. Had it in mind for some time.'

'These people – !' The Major raised his eyes to heaven, but saw only the Union Jack. 'We'll get after him, of course – but it may be difficult, now that Tampica is independent. To think that nobody raised a finger to stop him – '

'On Saturday,' Henry pointed out, 'nobody knew that Mr Huberman had come back to the Club, much less that he had been or was going to be murdered. His body wasn't found until the evening.'

'Well, it should have been,' said Chatsworth peevishly. 'Even if the Club wasn't full, there was no excuse for leaving that cottage uncleaned until ... oh, well, what's the use? These people are utterly feckless, they come and go as it suits them. In any case, it's of no great importance. The Harbour Master's log for Friday night will show us exactly when Mr Huberman returned. Let's see the log, Franklin.'

'Sure, sir.' Franklin beamed again, with a slight suggestion of a wink towards Henry. He held out the book. 'You'll find it all in there, sir.'

Chatsworth was turning the pages. 'Let's see, this is today, Sunday. Here we have Saturday, and here ...' He broke off and then said, 'I don't understand.'

'What's the matter?' Henry asked.

'There's nothing. Look for yourself. Nothing!'

He thrust the book at Henry. The page marked Friday March 30th ended with two terse entries. '7.10 p.m. Launch Island Eagle dep. for St Boniface. Skipper Sylvester Markham. Passenger Mr A. Huberman. 9.29 p.m. Launch Island Eagle returned. No passengers.'

Sebastian Chatsworth was slowly becoming very angry. 'It's a conspiracy! Addison Drake must have been in on it, and probably the Stevenson hussy as well, never mind how many people! How did Robbins get into the Club to murder Huberman? I'll tell you, sir! In all probability the guard unlocked the gate and begged him to step inside!' He turned fiercely on Franklin, who backed away, looking not unnaturally apprehensive. 'I'll get to the bottom of this! I'll find out who's sabotaging this Club! Heads will roll – you mark my words!'

Several departing members exchanged nervous glances and crept out of the office. The sight of them seemed to jolt Chatsworth to his senses. With an effort, he said, 'Well, as you remarked earlier, Tibbett – no use losing one's temper. Now at least we know where we stand.'

'Do we?'

'I for one certainly do, and I shall explain the matter to the Governor. We must get hold of Addison. And come to that – where the blazes is Mr Reynolds?'

'That's just one of the many things we don't know,' said Henry. 'Now, may I borrow your office? There are some people I'd like to talk to.'

The maid who had found Huberman's body was a pert slip of a girl who looked no more than sixteen. She seemed to have recovered from the shock of her gruesome discovery, and was now enjoying her new-found importance. She told Henry that her name was Marietta Markham.

'You're from this island?'

Marietta beamed. 'Yes, sir. I'se born here.'

'You're related to the other Markhams, then – Daniel and Sylvester?'

It was an unfortunate question. Marietta immediately launched into a highly intricate account of the family's contorted tree. Henry remembered too late that island marriages are often flexible affairs, and that illegitimate or 'out' children take their father's name and are cared for by his family. He stopped the flow by bringing the conversation back to Marietta's discovery of Huberman.

She was only too eager to talk about that. 'That old blood – that was every*where*,' she said with relish, rolling her eyes. 'That man was done *for*, sir. Worse than I ever see in the movies in Priest Town.'

Henry said, 'Why didn't you go in to clean up the room earlier, Marietta? After all, Mr Huberman left on Friday evening – '

Marietta looked pained. 'Wasn't my job, sir. Saturday, that's my day off. I'se off Friday afternoon to Saturday afternoon. I didn't go in there to clean – that was for the mornin' maid. I went in to turn down the bed and put fresh towels. And there he was, lyin' there in all that blood . . .'

'Did you see what killed him – the weapon, I mean?'

Marietta gave him a sideways look. 'I seen a machete,' she said. 'On the floor beside him.'

Henry had seen it, too, when a distraught Sebastian Chatsworth had called him to report the murder. It was almost new, of a kind that could be bought anywhere, and it had been wiped clean of prints. He said, 'So you did see the murder weapon.'

'Well . . .' Marietta drew the word out to impossible lengths, and grinned. 'I guess so. Yes, sir, I guess so.'

'You mean, you don't think he was killed with that machete?'

'Well, sir. Mr Montague say he was, and Major Chatsworth, and they're clever men. They know.'

'But you know better?'

Marietta giggled. Then she said, 'I say this to you, sir. If Mr Huberman was killed with that machete, it wasn't no man from this island did it. You wouldn't understand.'

'I think I do,' said Henry. 'Anybody experienced with a machete would kill with a clean cut to the head, like a coconut.'

Marietta looked surprised, and nodded. Henry added, 'But supposing somebody who did handle a machete killed Mr Huberman, and deliberately tried to make it look like an amateur job?'

Marietta considered this, her little-bird head tilted to one side.

'That would be a very smart man. I don't think men on this island smart like that.'

'What about women?'

Marietta giggled again, shook her head, said nothing. Henry changed the subject. 'You cleaned Mr Huberman's cottage every day while he was here, did you?'

'Every day but Saturdays, like I said.'

'Did you happen to notice his luggage?'

Suddenly, Marietta was scared. 'I never touch guests' luggage. Never, never. I never take anything. I never open suitcase . . .'

'Of course you don't, Marietta. Nobody said you did.'

'You sure?' She was still doubtful.

'Of course I'm sure. I only asked if you noticed what the luggage looked like.'

Reassured, Marietta said, 'Sure, I did. Very beautiful. All real leather. Black, very expensive.'

'With initials on it?'

'Sure. In gold. A.G.H. on every bit. Beautiful.'

'All right, Marietta. That's all. Thanks a lot.'

'Thank *you*, sir.'

Marietta stood up, grinned at Henry again, and walked to the door. As she did so, she began to hum softly – a calypso which Henry recognized but could not place. It was not until the door had closed behind her that the song clicked into place in Henry's head. It was an old Harry Belafonte number, and the refrain went, *'An' I say the woman of today ... smarter than the man in every way ...'*

Sylvester Markham could not contribute much. He had ferried Mr Huberman and his black, gold-embossed luggage to St Boniface on Friday evening, leaving at 7.10 p.m. and docking soon after eight. He had then come straight back to St Matthew's and checked in with the Harbour Master, Addison Drake. Yes, he had helped Mr Huberman ashore with his luggage – in fact, he had carried it into the United States Customs and Immigration area for him.

'That would be a Customs post on the harbour-side.'

'No, man. Right in the airport.'

'You mean, your launches actually dock in the airport?'

'Right. We have a special wharf alongside the terminal building, right by Customs and Immigration. The town quay is different. That's down by St Boniface Harbour.'

Henry was looking thoughtful. 'Let me get this straight. You personally ushered Mr Huberman and his luggage into the United States Customs and Immigration area?'

'That's right. Saw him checking it through.'

'Then how did he get out again?'

'No problem, man. Mr Huberman sees his baggage through Customs, checks his ticket in for the flight, then comes out again and goes to dinner. His plane don't leave till three in the morning.'

Henry said, 'So Mr Huberman's luggage must have been on the plane, even if he wasn't.'

'That's right.'

'So if, after ten o'clock when the Club launches stop running, he'd changed his mind and decided to come back to St Matthew's, he'd have had to abandon his luggage, go to the town quay and hire a boat?'

'Right, man. And that wouldn't be so easy, not at night.'

When Sylvester had gone, Henry picked up the telephone and

put a call through to Tom Bradley in Washington. The journalist did not sound amused.

'If you're calling me to tell me what happened to Huberman – thanks a lot. Didn't I tell you he wasn't on that plane? He sneaked back to St Matthew's to hide out, just like I said – and you were too goddam dumb to find him until he was good and dead. Dear God – there he was, right under your nose – '

'I'm sorry,' said Henry. 'It never occurred to me that he could use the Club as a hideout. I mean, he had to eat. Somebody would have known – '

'Sure as hell somebody knew.'

'Teresa Chatsworth?'

'Of course. She knew all right, or I'll eat my brown derby. Why wasn't he found until Saturday evening?'

'Because nobody went in to clean the room ... yes, yes, I know, I'm working on that angle. Meanwhile, what about Bill Mawson's column?'

Bradley made a small disgusted sound. 'You might say it's been overtaken by events. If friend Albert had committed suicide, we'd have been in business – but who's going to run a smear column on a guy who's just been cut up with a machete? With sob-shots of his widow and kids on page one? How low can the press sink?'

'You tell me,' said Henry amiably. 'Now will you do something for me?'

'If you make it quick. I'm about to start packing.'

'Packing? Where are you off to?'

'You are about,' said Tom, 'to have the pleasure of my company once more. There have been riots in your neighbourhood, or perhaps you haven't noticed. Not to mention a couple of murders. Nothing to compare with a CPF kick-back scandal, but good for a paragraph. Having failed to locate Huberman, I'm being sent off to the sticks in disgrace. In Bill's own words – "You started the story, Bradley, and I can't think of a more fitting punishment than to make you finish it." ' Tom laughed, somewhat sourly.

Henry said, 'Don't despair. This could be a big story.'

'Har, har.'

'Now, before you take off for St Boniface, can you root around

99

at Dulles Airport and find out anything you can about the person who claimed Huberman's luggage?'

'Hell, Tibbett, I told you before . . .'

'Look,' said Henry. 'Huberman's luggage was on that plane. He wasn't. But somebody claimed it.'

'And how in hell am I expected to – ?'

'I know it's a long shot, but the luggage was very distinctive. Extremely expensive, black leather, each piece embossed in gold with the initials A.G.H. Somebody just might have noticed it.'

Bradley sighed. 'OK. I'm booked on the five o'clock flight. I'll get out there ahead of time and do what I can.'

'You know there's a curfew here? All in by eight p.m. without a special pass.'

'Don't worry. I'm fixed up with a press pass, and I've organized a boat to bring me over from St Boniface.'

'How will you get to the Anchorage?'

'Relax, my friend. John Colville has a pass, and he's going to meet me at the dock. Unless you feel like doing the job yourself.'

'It'll be a pleasure. What time should I be there?'

'Let's say nine-thirty . . . be seeing you.'

Next, Henry asked the Club switchboard to connect him to the Governor's cottage.

'Patterson speaking. Yes, Tibbett? Anything to report?'

'Not really, sir. I wondered how you were getting on. Is the pathologist's report in yet?'

'I think I can say we are making progress, Tibbett. Commissioner Alcott is getting in touch with Tampica with a request to send Addison Drake back for questioning. Meanwhile Montague is going to organize a posse of policemen to search the rain forest for Robbins and Diamond. All other Seaward Islands have been alerted, in case the fugitives escaped by sea. Warrants are out for the arrest of the men Brooks and Delaware, who have also disappeared. That seems to be all we can do for the moment.'

'And the pathologist's report?'

'Oh yes. It's here. Haven't really had time to study it – all Greek to me, in any case.' Sir Geoffrey laughed with the braying self-deprecation of the British upper classes. 'It'll make more sense to you than to me. I'll let you have it when you come up to lunch.'

Henry said, 'Perhaps you can have it sent down to Major Chatsworth's office, Sir Geoffrey? I'm going back to the Anchorage for lunch.'

'You are?' Sir Geoffrey did not sound pleased. 'Oh, very well. But be back here at three. I've arranged a meeting with Montague and Commissioner Alcott to plan our strategy for the search party.'

'I'll be there, sir.'

Henry had a couple more jobs to do at the Golf Club. He located the girl who should have cleaned Huberman's cottage on Saturday morning. She volunteered that her name was Leontine, and that Mrs Chatsworth had told her not to bother about unoccupied cottages, as no new arrivals were expected and there was other work to do. She had cleaned two occupied cottages, and spent the rest of the morning taking an inventory of bed linen with the housekeeper. Then Henry put through a call to Miss Lucy Pontefract-Deacon.

Back at the Anchorage Inn, Henry lay on his bed and read the autopsy report on Albert Huberman, while Emmy took a shower to rinse the salt water off her rapidly-bronzing skin. The report was predictable. Translated into lay terms, Albert Huberman had died of multiple wounds inflicted by a sharp instrument such as a machete. The body was well-nourished despite the fact that the deceased had not eaten a substantial meal for some twelve hours before his death. The wounds could not possibly have been self-inflicted. The time of death was difficult to pinpoint, owing to the delay in finding the body. All the doctor was prepared to say was that Huberman had died between twelve and twenty-four hours before the autopsy, which was held at midnight on Saturday night in the Hospital on St Mark's.

Emmy emerged from the shower, towelling vigorously. She said, 'John and Margaret are really broken up, Henry. The curfew means no bar trade after eight o'clock – and just about the end of tourism on this island. By God, I hope you find Sandy Robbins and let him have it.'

'You've decided he's guilty, have you?'

'Well, I'm not blind or an imbecile. Even Margaret admits now that . . . well, she tries to stick up for him . . . but once he got out of gaol, why didn't he come back here? Why did he have to – ?'

'We don't know what he did or where he is,' Henry pointed out.

Emmy suddenly stopped towelling and stood quite still. She said, 'No, we don't. And we don't know where Sergeant Reynolds is either, do we?'

Chapter 9

If Derek Reynolds had not been a highly-trained and alert policeman, it is probable that he would have felt nothing but relief at the departure of Candy Stevenson from St Matthew's Golf Club. A note pushed under the door of his cottage at seven o'clock on Saturday morning informed him, in a childishly rounded hand, that 'the old bitch' had been 'so bloody rude' that she, Candy, had decided to pack up and leave on the first launch to St Boniface. 'Darling Derek' had been a 'cutie angel pie', and she hoped they would meet again some day.

The note was delivered as silently as possible, and most people would not have been woken by the tiny, dry sound of the paper under the door. Reynolds, however, was up and out of bed in an instant – just in time to see a black masculine backview slipping away into the shelter of a hedge of pink oleanders. This fact was not in itself particularly sinister, but it was enough to send Derek Reynolds struggling sleepily into his pants and shirt, and out into the early-morning quiet of the gardens.

Although the whole compound seemed to be asleep, Derek Reynolds took care to remain unobtrusive as he made his way towards the jetty: and, as he approached it, he was glad he had taken this elementary precaution, because – unlike the rest of the Club – the jetty was not deserted.

The Harbour Master's office was empty, and the Club launches and small Boston Whalers rode quietly at the quayside, jostling each other gently on the sparkling water. In another twenty minutes or so, the first of the staff would arrive to check, refuel, scrub and swab down the boats for a new day. Meanwhile, two black men – one of whom Reynolds recognized as Addison – were loading the last of a pile of luggage on to the *Island Eagle*. Derek Reynolds ran down the jetty, waving his arms.

'Candy! Miss Stevenson!'

He found himself confronted by the bulk and muscle of Addison, who smiled and said, 'Hi, Mr Reynolds. Looking for something?'

'For Miss Stevenson. She left a note – '

'She ain't here, man. Best go back look in her cottage. We're just loading her luggage. She's off at half past eight.'

'If I could just go on board – '

'Sorry, sir.' Addison had been joined by the second black man, who was every bit as formidable as his companion. 'Are you travelling to St Boniface on this launch?'

'Yes,' said Reynolds.

'Then I'll have to see your pass from the reception desk, sir.'

'I haven't got a pass. I've only just decided – '

'Well, sir, I'm afraid I can't let you on board without a pass. But we don't sail till eight-thirty. Plenty of time to go up to the desk and get your pass and – '

'Plenty of time to go back to Miss Candy's cottage,' added Addison, helpfully.

The two of them presented a solid front, and Derek Reynolds had the sense to realize that he could not penetrate it single-handed. At the same time, he was reasonably certain that he could glimpse, in the dark recesses of the boat's cabin, a slim golden-skinned leg protruding from beneath a blanket. As he watched, the leg gave an indignant kick, which only served to shroud it under a falling fold of grey wool.

Reynolds chafed miserably under his assumed civilian status. He could not demand to go on board. He said, 'I think Miss Stevenson is on that boat.'

The two black men looked at each other and smiled. Addison said, 'There's nobody on that boat, man. Just the luggage. It don't sail till eight-thirty. And *nobody* gets on that boat without a pass from reception. You want Miss Stevenson, you'll find her in her cottage. You want a pass for the launch, you get it from the desk ... sir.'

Derek Reynolds knew enough to accept the setback gracefully. 'OK,' he said. 'When can I get a pass from the desk?'

'Eight o'clock, sir.'

'Thanks a lot. Be seeing you.'

Predictably, Candy Stevenson's cottage was empty. Even more

predictably, at twenty-five minutes past seven, the reception desk was locked and shuttered. Reynolds arrived back at the jetty to see to his dismay that the *Island Eagle* was moving away from the quayside, heading for the narrow channel through the reef and to the open sea. Several boatmen were already setting about their day's work, and the on-coming Harbour Master was opening the door to his office. Seeing Reynolds' dismayed face, he smiled and said, 'Don't worry, sir. She'll be back for the eighty-thirty trip. Just out for a trial run – skipper wants to check on one of the fuel lines.'

The *Island Eagle* had by now negotiated the gap in the reef, and turned to starboard, opening up her powerful engines. She roared away round the point and out of sight. Ten minutes later she was back. The skipper moored the boat, jumped ashore and made for the Harbour Master's office – giving Reynolds an unfriendly look as he passed. There was no sign of Addison. Reynolds made for the launch. Candy Stevenson's baggage was neatly stacked in the forward part of the cabin, and, as Reynolds watched, porters began carrying more luggage down the jetty and loading it on to the boat. Otherwise, the cabin was quite empty.

The Harbour Master's office was by now humming with activity. The Customs and Excise men had arrived, and departing members were crowding the little hexagonal pavilion, fluttering boat passes and US Customs declarations and exit cards.

Reynolds fought his way to the Harbour Master's desk. Without looking up, the latter said, 'Boat pass, please, sir.'

'I haven't got a pass. I – '

'This launch is full, sir. If you haven't a pass, you'll have to wait for the next one. Sorry, sir.'

'I'm not catching a boat. I – '

'In that case,' said a loud female voice with a Western twang, 'kindly make room for people who are.' A large lady wearing a brilliantly-striped shirt and pants, a cartwheel hat and enormous sunglasses placed her elbow firmly in Derek Reynolds' stomach and ousted him from his place at the desk.

As the mass of humanity thinned out, Reynolds managed to re-attract the Harbour Master's attention. 'Miss Stevenson,' he said. 'Candy Stevenson. Is she supposed to be on that boat?'

The Harbour Master ran his eye down a list on his desk. 'Yes,' he said. 'She was one of the first on board. Here's her pass.'

'Well, she's not on board.'

'For heaven's sake, come along, Francine, or we'll miss the boat. Excuse me.' This time it was a tall, thin man with an East Coast accent and an imperious air who elbowed Reynolds aside.

The Harbour Master became all affability. 'Ah, Senator. Sorry you're leaving us. Hope you enjoyed your stay. Come again soon ... yes, yes, it'll all blow over. You know St Matthew's – our people will soon put a stop to all this nonsense ...'

From the doorway, a voice called, 'All aboard for St Boniface! We're leaving now, ladies and gentlemen! All aboard!'

Sergeant Derek Reynolds had never felt more frustrated or more ineffectual. Accustomed to being backed up by all the majesty of the law, he felt naked in the unfamiliar role of an ordinary member of the public, forced to wheedle rather than demand. If only he had been able to reveal his identity to this stupid little man ... he pulled himself up sharply. This was just the attitude that the Chief disliked so much.

The office was now empty except for the various officials, busy completing forms. Reynolds perched on the edge of the desk, at which the Harbour Master was making his final notations. He reminded himself that his new role had some compensations: he was, after all, a member of one of the most exclusive clubs in the world. He might be pretty small beer compared with Senators and movie stars, but so long as he was the only member present, he was surely entitled to a little respect from the staff.

He smiled, and said, 'Sorry I bothered you when you were so busy.'

The Harbour Master smiled back, with rather less enthusiasm. 'That's all right, sir. Sorry I couldn't give you more time.'

'Now that things are quieter, could I see the passenger list of the *Island Eagle*? I'm not sure which of my friends sailed on her.'

There was a moment of hesitation, and then the Harbour Master said, 'Right, sir. Here it is. I can't let you take it out of the office, but there's no reason why you shouldn't look at it.' He pushed a piece of paper across the desk. 'You'll see the names are checked off when the passengers hand in their boat passes.'

'Anybody missing?'

'No, sir. Our boats out to St Boniface are all full, I'm sorry to say. Had to turn several members away this morning.'

Reynolds studied the manifest. Miss C. Stevenson was checked off, and her boat pass was among the sheaf attached to the passenger list. Another interesting entry was a note at the bottom of the list, stating that Addison Drake, staff member now resigned, was aboard this launch for repatriation to Tampica via St Boniface.

'Thank you.' Derek Reynolds returned the paper to the Harbour Master. 'Well, it seems my friends did leave, after all.' He paused. 'I'd like to take a motor boat out today, if there's one available.'

'Surely, sir. Where would you like to go?'

'I'm not sure. One of the bays on the north shore – east from here. What do you suggest?'

'Well, sir, there's Apple Tree Bay – that's the closest and always very popular. Excellent snorkelling. Then comes Jellyfish Bay – but I doubt if you'd like that.'

'Why not?'

'Because of the jellyfish, like I said. It's a beautiful beach, but the swimming's no good, sir. After that, it's a longer ride – '

'How long?'

'Oh, fifteen to twenty minutes in a Boston Whaler, out to Village Point Bay, sir.'

'No, that's too far. I'll take Jellyfish Bay. By the way, can the big launches put ashore there?'

The Harbour Master looked surprised. 'They certainly could – there's no reef. But they never do. When would you like the boat to be ready, sir?'

Reynolds glanced at his watch. 'Five minutes. I've something to do first.'

'And when shall we come back to pick you up, sir?'

'Don't bother. I'll walk back.'

'Walk?'

'I presume it's possible.'

'Well – yes. But it's rough going, sir. You have to climb up through the forest behind the beach to get to the road. It'll take you a good hour.'

'That's OK. I need the exercise.'

Reynolds sprinted back to his cottage, and quickly filled a beach bag with a curious assortment of items – long trousers, a sweater, socks and stout shoes, a knife, a whistle, a powerful torch, a compass, binoculars, a flask of water and the rudimentary map of the island provided by the management. Then he scribbled a note on Club writing paper, pausing every so often to find the right phrase. He read over what he had written and sighed. Not very good, but it would have to do. Pray heaven the old man understands.

Daniel Markham was a dedicated gardener. Although officially head greensman in charge of the golf course, he kept a strict eye on the Club's exotic gardens, and he had had several unpleasant encounters with the head gardener, with whom he did not always see eye to eye. As a consequence he had formed the habit of visiting the gardens early in the morning, before the arrival of the regular staff, to make sure that all was well.

So it happened that, while bending over to inspect the trunk of a *lignum vitae*, he was accosted in the rear by a member, unknown to him, who urgently thrust an envelope into his hand, and begged him to deliver it as soon as possible to Mr Henry Tibbett at the Anchorage Inn.

Daniel said he would be only too pleased. He remembered Mr Tibbett well, and his wife too – why, he had ridden with them in John Colville's moke up from Priest Town the day they arrived. He was disposed to settle down to a leisurely session of island gossip, but the member appeared to be in a curious hurry for anyone on a Caribbean island before nine o'clock in the morning. Muttering that he would see Daniel later, the member rushed off in the direction of the jetty, with his beach bag bumping heavily against his shoulder. Daniel shook his head, having long since ceased trying to make sense of the ways of members. He trousered the letter and returned to his arboreal inspection.

The boat was waiting at the quayside, its motor ticking over gently. A smiling boatman helped Reynolds aboard; if he was surprised by the heavy beach bag, he did not say so. He simply slung it into the boat, cast off, and set course for Jellyfish Bay.

The Harbour Master had been quite right. The beach was a crescent of pink-white coral sand, ringed by a grove of palm trees, and protected by a steeply-rising wooded hill to landward. The place was completely deserted, and Reynolds, peering over the gunwale of the boat at the floating forest of jellyfish in the clear water, was not surprised.

The boatman drove the flat-bottomed craft skilfully up to the beach, and kept it steady while Reynolds jumped ashore with his bag. He said, 'You know about the jellyfish, sir? Don't try to swim.'

'Yes, thanks. I know.'

'Well, have a good morning. What time shall I fetch you?'

'No time. I'm walking back.'

Like Daniel, the boatman had ceased to be surprised at the vagaries of members. He just grinned, waved his hand, and manoeuvred the little boat in a tight circle before it roared off round the point and back to the Golf Club.

Reynolds slung his beach bag on to the ground and began a careful inspection of the sand and surrounding scrub. The tide was coming in, washing over the traces of any previous occupancy – but there, on the firm sand just below the high-water line, was the deeply indented print of a large, naked foot. Reynolds just had time to see it before the next wave erased it like chalk from a blackboard. Higher up, in the soft dry sand, footprints were indistinguishable but, following the line from the boat's landing place, through the footprint and up the beach, Reynolds began a painstaking examination of the prickly bushes and sea-grape trees which led up to the forest.

There was no path, but it seemed to him that twigs had been broken and leaves bruised as somebody had passed this way – possibly somebody carrying a heavy burden, causing a deep footprint and a clumsy passage through the shrubs.

Then, suddenly, he saw what he had not dared hope to find. A thread of grey wool caught on the sharp spine of an aloe. He did not hesitate. If the trail were ever to be successfully followed, it must be now. He had caught the vanishing footprint by a matter of seconds. The fragile grey thread would blow away at any moment in the steady north-easterly trade wind. He knew he was alone and unarmed and at the grave disadvantage of being totally lacking in local knowledge – but there was nothing for it. If he could follow, unseen, pinpoint a position and return with help –

well, it would be the best he could do. Besides, Candy Stevenson was an exceptionally pretty girl.

Reynolds went back to the beach, picked up his bag and swung it over his shoulder. Then he began making his way through the sea-grapes and cotton bushes, under the carob trees and the white cedars, up towards the dark rain forest where the wild white orchids grow.

Chapter 10

Sunday lunch at the Anchorage was by no means its usual convivial self. The Tibbetts and Colvilles were the only people eating, and the bar was almost empty. Outside, the hyacinth sea curling over coral in the sunshine seemed a cruel mockery: a dark shadow was lying over St Matthew's island. All the departing boats were full, and all the returning boats were empty, and the people had stopped smiling.

John had prepared an adequate but uninspired buffet of cold meat and salad. He apologized for it with a shrug and a wry smile. 'I just can't understand it,' he said, for the fifth time. 'Someone like Sandy ... someone I'd have trusted with my life ...'

Margaret said glumly, 'Let's face it, John. We've been living in a fool's paradise, like everyone who first comes to an island. There *is* a difference between races, and there's always going to be them and us, whether we like it or not.'

'No!' Emmy had not meant to sound so vehement, but the word came out of its own accord. 'You know you don't really mean that, Margaret. Or if you do, there's no hope for anybody, anywhere.'

'Oh, I don't know what I mean any more,' said Margaret. 'If Sandy didn't kill Senator Olsen, why did he run away when the prison burnt down? And if he didn't kill Mr Huberman, then who did?'

Henry said, 'Don't rush to judgement, Margaret. Supposing Sandy didn't disappear voluntarily? He was one against a mob when they stormed the gaol.'

'All right, but they couldn't have forced him to kill Huberman, could they?'

'Nobody knows who killed Huberman,' Henry pointed out.

'Everybody knows.' John Colville stood up. 'Pass up your

plates, will you? We seem to have run out of help. Margaret's right. We've got to face up to it. Sandy isn't really important – that is, he's important to us as a person, of course – but the bigger issue is these islands. Not only St Matthew's – the whole British Seawards group. The Executive Council on St Mark's has been working with the British Government on a whole new plan to redevelop the islands – tourism on the one hand, and a revival of the Sea Island Cotton trade on the other. I know all about it – they called me in as a consultant, because I'm an economist. It was a marvellous plan, and would have brought a real future to these islands . . . and now . . . By God, I wish they'd deported all these bloody Tampicans and other out-islanders before it got to this point.' He pulled himself up short. 'Sorry, Emmy. Henry. I'm afraid both Margaret and I get a bit emotional on the subject of the BSI. There's cheese, fresh fruit and coffee.'

At two o'clock, Henry looked at his watch and said, 'Well, I'm off to the Golf Club for yet another meeting. Why don't you come with me, Emmy?'

'Me? You surely don't want me at your meeting.'

'No – but you should see the place. It's spectacular.'

'Go on, Emmy,' said Margaret. 'Have a last dance on the volcano. They'll probably blow it up tomorrow.'

'Nothing like looking on the bright side,' said Emmy. 'OK. I'll go and get a dry swimsuit.'

In the mini-moke, as Henry drove along the twisting dirt track between the Anchorage and the Golf Club, Emmy said, 'You see what I mean – about Margaret and John?'

'Don't worry about them for the moment,' said Henry. 'You've got work to do.'

'Work?'

'Why do you think I brought you along?'

Emmy sighed. 'I might have known. All right, what is it?'

'Candy Stevenson and Derek Reynolds both left the Club early on Saturday morning. Candy apparently went on the eight-thirty launch to St Boniface. After that, we can't trace her. Maybe she's still there, maybe she boarded an aircraft under another name, maybe the airlines don't keep accurate manifests. Anyhow, Montague's people haven't been able to trace her further than St Boniface – and Reynolds's note made it perfectly clear that he suspected some sort of villainy and that he was going after it. Now – what I want to know is when and how he left the Club. Where he was aiming for - what transport he used – what time – anything you can find out. OK?'

'Y-e-s,' Emmy agreed doubtfully. 'But where shall I start?'

'At the Harbour Master's office,' Henry suggested. 'Be a member wanting to take a boat trip . . . be a friend of Mr Reynolds, the philatelist from London. Play it by ear – it's all you can do.'

The guard on the gate was even larger and grimmer than usual, and it took a call to Major Chatsworth before Emmy was admitted, as a non-member without documentation. Finally, however, the big gates swung open and the moke rolled through.

'There's the jetty over there, and the comic-opera pavilion is the office,' said Henry. 'I'll see you in the bar some time after four. Good luck, darling.'

Commissioner Alcott and Inspector Montague were waiting for Henry in the Governor's cottage, which seemed to have become a sort of unofficial GHQ. The Governor himself was not there, but the party was completed by Sergeant Ingham, on crutches and festooned with bandages, but in good heart. A detailed map of the island of St Matthew's was laid out on the table, and an earnest discussion was in progress – a discussion cut short by Henry's arrival.

The Commissioner was a tall, skinny white man, with an untidy shock of pure-white hair and a small white moustache. He wore khaki shorts and a white open-necked shirt with epaulettes of rank on the shoulders, and Henry could see that he was as lean and spare and muscled as a racing greyhound. He spoke with the accent of his native Lancashire, and he laughed a lot.

When introductions had been completed, Alcott said, 'Well, now, Tibbett, before we get down to this hunting expedition, let's fill you in with what's been 'appening. Noothing mooch. No trace of Miss Stevenson – I think you knew that. But there's another "no trace" that's interesting – Addison Drake. Duty 'Arbour Master, Friday night. Seems 'e 'anded in 'is notice Friday afternoon, said he'd work 'is night shift and be off to Tampica in the morning. Well, that's what you expect in these parts. People like to move around. No 'arm in that, is there?'

Before Henry could agree, he went on. 'Well, 'e didn't turn oop in Tampica. Mind you, that doesn't mean mooch – I wouldn't say they've a record of every Tampican as comes in from St Boniface on the ferry boat – '

Henry said, 'Commissioner, might I interrupt you to make a phone call to Tampica? I think it may clear this matter up.'

Alcott looked surprised, but he said, 'Go ahead, chum. Help yourself.'

A few moments later, Henry was saying, 'Lucy? Any news for me? You have? Well? . . . Oh, I see. Yes, we rather thought that . . . I don't know, Lucy. Well, he is her brother, after all . . . no, of course not, Lucy. The police are not . . . yes, I promise you . . . good-bye, my dear.'

Commissioner Alcott was regarding Henry with a cocked eyebrow. He said, 'You've bin in these parts before, 'aven't you?'

'Well, actually – '

Montague broke in precisely. 'I explained, Commissioner, that the Chief Superintendent was sent over because of his experience in – '

Sergeant Ingham was grinning from ear to ear. 'What does Miz Lucy say?'

'Who is this Lucy?' Montague demanded. 'What has she to do with the case?'

Henry said, 'She's an elderly English spinster who lives on Tampica. She has the reputation of knowing everything that happens on that island, and she deserves it. I called her earlier today and asked her if Addison had come home. It was she who pointed out to me that he is Diamond's brother, Addison Drake.'

Alcott turned to Owen Montague. 'Did you know that, Inspector?'

'My dear chap, don't take on so. Drake's an extremely common name on these islands, and family relationships boggle the imagination. There are four Drakes on the staff of the Club, not including Addison. I have a Constable Drake on my force, and there's a Drake girl working at the Anchorage. Really, you can't expect me to keep up with island families.'

'Well,' Henry said, 'it may or may not be significant, but Lucy does keep up with Tampican families, and she assures me that Diamond and Addison are brother and sister, and very close.

Diamond's the older, and Addison didn't come over to St Matthew's until after Diamond's accident. She is also quite positive that he has not come home. I think you can add him to our list of missing persons.'

'Making,' said Commissioner Alcott, 'five in all. Diamond and Addison Drake, Sandy Robbins, Brooks and Delaware. And if all I've been told is accurate, Montague, that's a nasty, dangerous little lot to be hiding out in the hills. Probably armed and certainly vicious.'

'Don't rub it in, dear soul,' said Owen Montague. He was very pale. 'For a start, they'll be almost impossible to find. They know the island like the backs of their hands, and there's about a hundred square miles of rain forest up there on the mountain. Unless they're foolish enough to light a fire, we couldn't spot them even from a helicopter – which in any case we haven't got. And supposing we do find them – ' he paused.

'We'll find them,' said Alcott.

'All right, go ahead and find them,' snapped Montague. 'Bring them down to Priest Town in handcuffs and see what happens.' He appealed to Henry. 'You said there'd be trouble if we arrested Diamond in the first place. If we round them up now – '

'The situation is quite different,' said Alcott. 'We've got the men now. Twenty constables from St Mark's. With guns.'

'And whose side do you think most of *them* will be on?' Montague demanded. 'Really, Commissioner, you are naif.'

'I beg your pardon, Inspector. I'm wot?'

Henry said quickly, 'It's a bad situation, Commissioner, and I think Inspector Montague is right to be alarmed. I'm sure you agree we have to move very delicately.'

'We 'ave to apprehend that dangerous lot.'

'Of course. But the first thing to do is locate them. And then ... how are they living, up in the forest? Either they'll have to send somebody down for food, or supplies are being brought up from the valley. I think that's our best lead.'

'True,' said Alcott. He scratched his head with a bony hand. 'You think we should 'old our 'orses and joost watch, like?'

'Of course, you must do whatever you think is best,' Henry said, 'but in your place I think I'd take a small band of men I could really trust and begin with the idea of locating the camp, not capturing it. I presume your men have walkie-talkies to keep in contact with each other and headquarters.'

'That's an excellent notion, Tibbett. When will you start?'

'I'm afraid I can't go myself,' Henry said. 'I have to meet somebody this evening – someone arriving from Washington.'

'Well, obviously I can't go,' said Alcott. 'You're the local man, Montague.'

'All right, all right. I'll go.' Montague sounded peeved. 'Sergeant, I'd be obliged if you would detail the men you think suitable. Four. Chaps who know the interior of the island. Tell them to meet me at the police garage at' – he glanced at his watch – 'at four.'

'Very good, sir.' Sergeant Ingham stood up, adjusted his crutches, and hobbled out of the room.

Montague said, 'We'll only have about three hours of daylight – it would be the luck of the devil if we found anything today. Has anybody considered that they might have got away by boat to another island?'

Alcott gave him a sideways look. 'My men have checked on every motor boat on this island.'

'What about a sailing boat?'

'The Governor,' said Alcott, ' 'ad the sense to get on to me on Saturday, right after the gaol break. Oonlike soom. Any'ow, we 'ad a Piper out in no time, flying low, observing any sailboats leaving this island. All checked up on. You take it from me, that little lot's still on St Matthew's, and planning mischief.' He paused. 'Where d'you plan to start, then?'

Montague was gazing at the map of the island. He said, 'The whole of this central area is dense rain forest. That's where they'll be. But they must have got away from Priest Town in some sort of vehicle, and there's a jeep reported missing. My guess is that they drove up the mountain road as far as they dared, then drove into the undergrowth to hide the car, and went on on foot. The best we can hope for today is to find that car. It won't be much, but it'll give us a lead. Tomorrow, we can begin the search in earnest.'

'If things work out,' Henry said, 'I'd like to come with you before this search is over.'

'Can't think of anything I'd like more, dear boy. Well, I must be off.' He strode out of the cottage, banging the door behind him.

'Curious bloke, that,' Alcott remarked. 'Bit of a fairy, I always thought. Yet 'e's got guts, in a funny way.'

'That's not unusual, you know,' said Henry.

'No. No, you're right, Tibbett. Doesn't do to generalize.' He produced an ancient pipe from his pocket and began to stuff it with tobacco. 'I joost 'ope they didn't get away by boat.'

'I thought you said –'

'Certainly I said it. 'Ad to, didn't I? But it could 'ave been done, all the same. Ah, well. Now, what news 'ave you got for me, Chief Superintendent?'

'Just about none, so far. Did your men have any luck on St Boniface?'

'About the boat? No, and I didn't think they would. Oh, the US authorities co-operated all right, but those lads know they're American and we're British. Not likely that any of them would admit 'aving ferried Huberman back here, is it? Any road, it's not important 'oo brought him. Point is, 'e got back here, went to his cottage, and next day was murdered, and there's no prizes out for 'oo did it. Wot beats me is – wot do they expect to get out of it? Diamond Drake and Sandy Robbins and that lot? Either they stay on the run, or they don't. Either we find them or we don't. Doesn't seem to me they stand to gain, one way or t'other.'

Henry said, 'That's the aspect that's been interesting me, Commissioner. I was sent out here to investigate one particular killing, but now it's becoming less and less important, on its own. The pattern is something much bigger.'

'Well, you tell me wot it is, Tibbett, because I'm damned if I know.' Commissioner Alcott sucked on his pipe, then took it out of his mouth and banged it on the ashtray. ' 'Oo're you meeting this evening, if it's not a tactless question?'

'Not at all. A journalist from Washington.'

Alcott's white eyebrows went up. 'Indeed? Interesting. Keep me filled in, won't you, Tibbett? And if you need any men, I've a few good 'uns. And rather more not so good, but we'll skip that. Well, I'm off. Need a lift?'

'No, thanks, sir. I've got transport, and I'm picking up my wife in the bar at four.'

'And you make sure it's your wife, young fellow,' chuckled Alcott. 'There's been more than loose change picked up in this bar, I can tell you. Keep in tooch.'

Emmy was waiting for Henry, perched on a high stool beside the open-air bar, with its sweeping seascape view. She was excited.

'I think I did rather well, darling. I mean, I found quite a lot of people who saw Mr Reynolds on Saturday morning, and I've been able to put it all together to make sense.'

'OK. Shoot.'

'Well, he was up and about early, for a start. That nice Daniel Markham – you remember – he saw him at about half past seven, at Candy Stevenson's cottage. Says he opened the door – it wasn't locked – went inside for a moment, then came running out again and hurried through the grounds and up to the reception desk. Of course, it was closed at that hour, so Derek ran back towards the jetty. Daniel didn't see him again until about a quarter to nine, when he – Daniel, that is – was inspecting some trees near Derek's cottage. He says he came out, obviously in a hurry, carrying a heavy beach bag. He saw Daniel, gave him the note to be delivered to you, and shot off towards the jetty again.'

'Sounds as if he was chasing a boat,' Henry said.

'Wait a minute. I'm coming to that. The Harbour Master says Derek was hanging around the jetty even before he took over at eight o'clock – that is, when Addison was still on duty. He then proceeded to make a nuisance of himself, asking to see the passenger list for the eight-thirty launch to St Boniface. The Harbour Master explained that it was very awkward, with so many out-going passengers to be processed. He had to keep Derek waiting until the boat had gone. Then he let him see the passenger list. Derek read it and said something about his friends having left. Then he ordered one of the Club's little motor boats to take him to Jellyfish Bay.'

'Jellyfish Bay? Where on earth is that?'

'I don't know,' Emmy said. 'We can find out. Anyhow, this is the really interesting part. He said he wanted the boat in five minutes and went off. Five minutes later, he turned up with a beach bag and boarded the boat – *but* ...'

'But what, for heaven's sake?'

'*But* . . . both the Harbour Master and the boatman asked what time he wanted to be picked up again, and he said he didn't.'

'He didn't?'

'Said he'd walk back to the Club. They warned him that it would be a long, hot walk, but he said that didn't bother him. When he didn't turn up for lunch, the Harbour Master as a matter of routine sent a boat to Jellyfish Bay, but there was no sign of him. And there hasn't been ever since!' Emmy ended on a note of triumph. 'Does that entitle me to a drink?'

'Certainly. It also entitles Derek Reynolds to the Idiot of the Year Medal, with bar. Why didn't he get in touch with me by phone?'

'Maybe,' said Emmy, 'he didn't have time.'

'Or thought he didn't. O K – what's it to be?'

'A fruit punch, please. I'm thirsty.'

Henry called the barman and ordered two fruit punches. When the tall pink drinks arrived, Henry signed the chit and said, 'We were thinking of going to Jellyfish Bay tomorrow. Is it a good place to spend a day?'

The barman smiled widely. 'Depends how much you like jellyfish.'

'You mean . . . ?'

'No good for swimming. Get yourself stung to Kingdom Come. The beach is fine, if you don't plan to go in the water.'

'Where is it?'

'Why, just around after Apple Tree Bay – that's the nearest to the Club.'

'I thought Mango Trunk was the nearest.'

'That's in the other direction. Westward, man. Out of the bay, turn east round the headland, and there's Apple Tree. And next one is Jellyfish. After that, there's nowhere a boat can land for quite a way.'

Emmy said, 'It doesn't sound very nice, darling. Let's go somewhere else.'

'Sure, lady,' said the barman. 'The whole island is empty now. You go anywhere you like – not meet anybody. Not anybody.'

'I'm afraid you're right,' Henry said.

'About what?' said a cool English voice in his right ear. He turned to see Teresa Chatsworth, crisp as ever in black pants and a white shirt. She climbed on to a bar stool, ordered an iced tea and – without waiting for an answer to her question – said, 'What a day. I suppose the High Command at Dunkirk must have felt much the same. An efficient defeat is almost as good as a victory, and our evacuation has gone without a hitch.'

'As bad as that, is it?' Emmy said.

'Worse. The Club is getting it both ways.'

'How do you mean?' Henry asked.

'Well, we might just have survived the riots and the curfew – this place is a sort of enchanted enclave, and most of our members hardly know the rest of the island exists. We might even have recovered from Olsen's murder, if Sandy Robbins had been quickly tried and convicted. Even the combination of the two wouldn't have been quite impossible – but Huberman's murder on the premises and Robbins's escape . . .' Teresa shrugged her thin shoulders.

Henry said, 'It's a small point, Mrs Chatsworth, but I wondered why Mr Huberman's cottage wasn't cleaned on Saturday morning. It would have helped a lot to know whether Huberman was alive or dead – '

Teresa gave Henry a small, icy smile. 'As you undoubtedly know, Mr Tibbett, it was on my orders. The Club was almost empty, and the housekeeper badly needed to take her linen inventory. We fit these things in when we can spare the staff, and it was an obvious opportunity.'

'Oh, well. Just our bad luck.' Henry took a sip of his drink, and went on, 'You know a great deal about the members, don't you, Mrs Chatsworth?'

'What is that supposed to mean?'

'Just what I said. It makes you very valuable to the Club.'

'For God's sake, Tibbett, if you're fishing for information, come right out and ask for it.'

'All right, I will. What do you know about kick-back scandals involving Senator Olsen and Albert Huberman and the Cotton Producers' Federation?'

Teresa let out a long breath, as if in relief. She said, 'What on earth makes you interested in that?'

'Answering a question with a question is a very old device,' Henry said. 'It nearly always means that someone is stalling.'

'I think,' said Teresa Chatsworth, 'that you should wait until Jackson Ledbetter releases his statement tomorrow. Washington is full of cheap columnists like Bill Mawson, who will print deliberate lies just to provoke a reaction. Good God, people come to St Matthew's to get away from that sort of muck-raking. Does that answer you?'

'Yes,' said Henry. 'You've answered me very adequately. Well, Emmy, we should be on our way. We don't want to get into trouble with the curfew regulations.'

'Oh, that,' said Teresa impatiently. 'Geoffrey Patterson has made his tiny gesture, but he can't keep it up. Don't worry, Tibbett. The curfew won't last. Life must go on.'

'Yes,' said Henry. He finished his drink. 'It must, mustn't it? Be seeing you, Mrs Chatsworth.'

Henry and Emmy paused only once on the way out of the Golf Club, and that was at the reception desk. They were in luck – the girl had been on duty on Friday evening, and in answer to Henry's question she replied at once, 'Yes. Yes, that's right. Straight after. Yes, sir.'

Chapter 11

Priest Town under curfew was a silent, unfriendly place. The narrow roadways and alleys were deserted except for an occasional patrolling policeman. Bars and cafés were dark and empty. The headlights of Henry's mini-moke threw angular shadows across the wary streets, and every shuttered window seemed to be listening. Twice, Henry was stopped by polite policemen. He produced his papers, explained that he was meeting a boat from St Boniface, and was allowed to proceed.

The town quay was under strict surveillance, with armed constables waiting to greet every arriving boat. Since no boats were arriving, this was proving a boring occupation, and Henry provided a welcome diversion. He was invited to join the posse in the Customs and Immigration Office for a cup of coffee, and everybody seemed cheered by his assurance that there would be at least one boat arriving before the *Island Queen* docked in the morning.

As Henry sipped his coffee quietly in a corner, conversation returned to the burning topic of the day – the whereabouts of Diamond and Sandy. This took easy precedence over the death of Albert Huberman, which seemed neither here nor there to the islanders. It lay, so to speak, outside their territory. As to the fugitives, opinion seemed to be about equally divided between those who reckoned they had made their getaway by boat, and those who were convinced that they had gone to ground in the rain forest – where, given supplies, they could remain undetected almost indefinitely.

The discussion was interrupted by the throbbing of a powerful outboard motor in the quiet harbour. Coffee was abandoned, peaked caps were pulled on, and the constables went out on to the quayside. Henry followed them, in time to see the red and green navigation lights of a boat coming across the water from the harbour entrance. A few moments later she was alongside the wharf, and Tom Bradley was jumping ashore. The black boatman from St Boniface unloaded the baggage with practised ease, cracked a joke with the police officers, signed a document of some sort, and then put the wheel over, opened up his motor, and roared off again out of the harbour, leaving a wave of silver on the smooth dark water.

Formalities were quickly concluded. Tom's passport was stamped, his baggage inspected with some care, his press card examined and his curfew pass issued. Then the guardians of the law settled down to another cup of coffee and Tom and Henry loaded up the moke and climbed in.

As they drove through the dark, empty streets, Henry said, 'Well? Any luck?'

'About Huberman's luggage, you mean?'

'That's just what I mean.'

'Well, I didn't draw a complete blank. I got talking to the Redcaps at Dulles, and one of them is pretty sure he remembers the baggage. He noticed it partly because it was very fancy, as you said, and partly because it went round the belt several times without being claimed.'

'That's interesting.'

'That's what he thought, because the man who – '

There was a sudden, shocking sound of breaking glass, somewhere ahead and to the right. Henry braked the moke sharply, and switched off the lights. He said, 'I'm going to investigate. Coming?'

'You bet.'

'Well, take care. These people aren't joking.'

'Neither am I,' remarked Tom Bradley under his breath, as he clambered out of the car and followed Henry to the street corner.

They found themselves looking down a narrow street lined with small shops, mostly of the souvenir-boutique variety. On a normal evening, it would have been alive with light and noise and the bustle of commerce, but under the curfew it was dark and shuttered – with one exception. About half-way down the street on the left was Priest Town's newest pride – the supermarket. Recently opened, it would have looked very small beer beside its American or even English cousins – but there were shelves stacked with groceries, a freezer, a fruit and vegetable section and a check-out desk. St Matthew's had never seen anything like it before, and it was the talk of the town.

This establishment had decided, despite the curfew, to keep on its lights, which threw a broad band of radiance across the street; but, as Henry and Tom rounded the corner, the lights suddenly went out, leaving the darkness deeper than before. However, in the split second before blackness fell, Henry had just time to see the big, gaping hole in the store's plate-glass window.

'They're in there,' he breathed in Tom's ear. 'Come on!'

The two men began to run down the street towards the store, their footsteps unnaturally loud in the black silence. Suddenly a single shot rang out, ripping the night. Instinctively, they both stopped. Then Henry shouted, 'Come on, man! What are you waiting for?' – and pelted down the street towards the super-market.

Outside the shop, the pavement glistened with broken glass under the light of Henry's torch. He shone the beam through the jagged hole in the plate-glass window and shouted, 'Police! We've got you covered! Come out with your hands up!'

Absolute silence. Henry stepped forward and began to play his flashlight along the shelves and down the aisles of the market. Without turning his head, he said to Tom, who was behind him, 'Step in carefully, or you'll cut yourself to ribbons. Follow me.'

Gingerly, Henry stepped through the shattered window and into the interior of the store. Holding his torch well to one side of his body, so that anybody firing at it would at worst hit his hand, he began to edge towards the main door. Still the silence was complete and oppressive. At last his fingers found what they were looking for. He pressed the switch, and the building was once more flooded with light.

A careful search of the aisles showed that it was empty – at least of people. However, the looters had left ample evidence of their activities. Shelves were half-emptied of cans, bursting bags of sugar lay on the floor, fruit and vegetables rolled in the aisles as if dropped in the panic to escape: and, at the back of the shop, the door to the dark storeroom stood open.

'That's the way they went,' said Henry.

'What about the shot?'

'We'll find out in a moment.' Henry walked into the storeroom and switched on the light. The back door, leading out into the alley behind the market, swung gently open in the soft night breeze. Henry went over and examined it. 'That's what I thought. They shot the lock out – very neatly, too. They'll be well away by now.'

Tom said, 'At least they didn't have time to get away with much. I suppose we'd better go and tell the police – but they'll have slipped back into Priest Town houses like eels into the – '

'Wait a minute,' said Henry. 'I've an idea. Did you notice that they didn't touch the freezer? Only canned things and fruit. Come on, back to the moke!'

Henry had the engine started and the little car on the move almost before Tom had clambered in. He quickly reversed in the roadway, and set off in the direction from which he had come.

'Hey, what's the idea, Henry?' Tom was clinging to his suitcase to keep it from leaping out of the swaying, bumping vehicle.

Henry said, 'You know this island better than I do. Where's the nearest beach to Priest Town that you could sneak a boat into – well away from the main quay and lighted streets?'

Tom considered. Then he said, 'Frenchman's Bay.'

'Where's that?'

'About half a mile west of Priest Town, across country. More by road.'

'How do we get there?'

'We can't drive all the way. The last part is strictly footwork.'

'OK, we'll get as close as we can. You direct me.'

Tom peered into the darkness ahead. 'I think ... yes, left here!'

Henry turned the wheel violently, and the moke swung round a tight corner. Tom cursed and clung even more grimly to his suitcase with one hand and the iron strut of the moke with the other. Another minute or so, and the houses of Priest Town had thinned out. The road changed from tarred to dirt surface, and the car leapt and bumped over the rutted surface. Past a few more straggling houses, a few goats complaining lazily at being disturbed – and the road, such as it was, ended in a small circular clearing.

'The path goes down from here,' Tom said. 'Look, there's

Frenchman's Bay down there and – by God, you were right. There is a boat.'

They were standing on a rocky bluff separated from the beach below by several hundred yards of thickly overgrown scrub. Above, the velvet sky was studded with outsize stars. In the faint light of a crescent moon, white-creaming waves crawled against the protective reef circling the bay, while gentle waters lapped at the sandy shore. In the centre of the lagoon, riding at anchor, was a small motor boat. It was empty.

Henry said, 'Take the torch and lead the way. You know the path.'

It was rough going – not so much a path as a trail, littered with a selection of obstacles like smooth, steep grey rocks and con-voluted tree roots. Nocturnal crabs scuttled across the sandy track and into the undergrowth, their small hard claws chittering on the dry leaves. A bird rose suddenly from the bushes, with a shocking clatter of sound. A supple green snake uncoiled itself in the beam of Tom's torch and slithered silently away over a rock. At last, they broke from the cover of the trees into the grove of palms that edged the beach, and finally on to the silver sand.

The beach was deserted, but where the retreating tide had left a smooth arc of damp sand, there were two sets of footprints lead-ing down into the sea. Henry caught a sound of water, but not of waves. He whispered, 'Put the torch out. Get back under the trees.'

As they watched, eyes riveted on the little anchored boat, a long black arm came up out of the water to grasp the gunwale. This was quickly followed by a second arm, clutching a bundle of some sort, which was thrown over the side and into the boat. Then a tall, lithe black figure emerged from the sea and hoisted itself into the boat. A moment later, another, paler arm rose from the water, holding its burden aloft like Excalibur. The dark figure in the boat seized the bundle and stowed it, and then leant down to help as the second figure climbed aboard.

In an instant the anchor was up, the motor was on, and the boat sped out of the bay, expertly guided through the narrow channel in the reef. It carried no lights, and at that distance, in the chancy moonlight, it was impossible to be sure of the identities of the occupants. One thing, however, was clear to

Henry. One of them was black and the other white, and they were either girls or young boys.

'Well, I'll be damned,' said Tom. 'Those weren't ordinary looters.'

'They certainly weren't,' Henry said. 'Back to the car as fast as we can. I've got to get to a telephone.'

'Then we may as well go straight to the Anchorage. We're on the way there.'

John, Margaret and Emmy were sitting glumly in the empty bar, and were obviously delighted to welcome Tom, plying him with questions and drinks.

'No time for that now,' said Henry. 'I need a telephone, and fast.'

'A telephone?' said Emmy. 'Why on earth – ?'

Ignoring her, Henry said, 'John, can you connect me with the Golf Club? I want to speak to Major Chatsworth and nobody else. Particularly not Mrs Chatsworth.'

John raised his eyebrows slightly, but only said, 'OK. Whatever you say.' He climbed off his bar stool and went into the small office at the back. A few moments later he reappeared saying, 'He's on the line. Lucky you told me about Teresa, because she did her best to take the call. I don't think you're very popular in certain quarters.'

Henry grinned. 'I can bear it,' he said. 'Thanks, John.' He went into the office and picked up the telephone. 'Major Chatsworth? Tibbett here. This is urgent. Will you check right away and see if one of your Boston Whalers is missing?'

'Our Boston Whalers? Don't be absurd, Tibbett. How could one of our boats be missing?'

'Please hurry, Major. This is important.'

'Oh, very well. I'll send – '

'Don't send anybody. Go yourself and check. And don't say a word to anybody. Anybody at all. I'll hold on.'

Grumbling, Sebastian Chatsworth laid down the telephone in the Golf Club bar. Teresa said, 'What does that man Tibbett want, Sebastian? I do think the Yard might have sent us somebody a little less boorish – '

'Oh, some nonsense about a boat ... back in a minute ...'

Ten minutes later, Sebastian Chatsworth was saying, 'Tibbett?

Chatsworth. Of course there's no boat missing. I checked with the duty Harbour Master – we inspected the trot together. All present and correct.'

'Oh.' Henry sounded puzzled. 'Then I'll come over myself, if I may. Would you tell the guard to expect us – Emmy and me?'

Outwardly, at least, the Golf Club was the only place on the island unaffected by the curfew or anything else. Soft lights illuminated the paths which wound across velvety lawns, and lit up the exotic tropical vegetation – shiny gourds hanging like lacquered green grapefruit from the calabash trees, sweet yellow sugar-apples and orange mangoes. In the distance, the beat of the steel band throbbed on the open-air dance floor – but nobody was dancing. The beach-side bar was as luxurious as ever, but the bar-tender yawned as he polished already spotless glasses, and the waiters lounged against the wall, gossiping. Teresa and Sebastian Chatsworth were the only people sitting at the bar.

Henry said, 'Having a quiet evening, I see.'

Chatsworth gave a laugh that sounded like a bark. 'We've got exactly six guests, not counting the Governor, who's in St Mark's until tomorrow morning. I tell you, Tibbett, this island has had it. We'll never recover from this.'

'Don't be silly, Sebastian.' Teresa Chatsworth was looking elegant if haggard in a pants suit made of creamy slubbed silk. 'The Golf Club is quite wealthy enough to weather a bad patch like this – the members know very well there's nothing in the world to take its place. Besides, a lot of them have a considerable financial stake in it. They'll be back.'

'But what about the rest of the island?' Emmy asked.

Teresa gave her an unfriendly look. 'I'm afraid I am not very much concerned with the rest of the island, Mrs Tibbett.'

'So long as the fence holds,' said Henry.

There was an uneasy pause, then Sebastian Chatsworth rubbed his hands together and said, 'Well, now, Mrs Tibbett . . . Tibbett . . . come and have a drink and tell me about this missing boat which isn't missing.'

'Thanks,' said Henry. 'I'll have a beer. Now, you're sure all your boats are there?'

'Of course I'm sure.'

'Who else on the island owns a Boston Whaler?'

'Nobody, as far as I know,' said Chatsworth. 'We have our fleet of five and that's it.'

'And all five are tied up at their moorings?'

'Certainly. Well, all four. One is in dry dock at the moment.'

Henry was immediately alert. 'Dry dock? What does that mean?'

'In for regular maintenance. We have a small slip and a repair shed on the far side of the bay.'

'And did you check on that boat?' Henry asked.

'Well . . . no, of course not. It's a long walk by land, and – '

'Then,' said Henry, 'I think we should check it now. May we take a boat?'

Sebastian was clearly rattled. 'Now, really, Tibbett – it's eleven o'clock at night and I can't believe it's necessary.'

'I'll take you, Mr Tibbett.' Teresa Chatsworth stood up, and looked at Henry with a curious half-smile. 'I can see that you are determined to go, and I handle a boat very much better than Sebastian does.' She turned to her husband. 'Entertain Emmy while we're away, won't you, darling? It shouldn't take us more than ten minutes or so to satisfy the Chief Superintendent's curiosity.'

Emmy looked at Henry with a question behind her eyes. Things were not going according to the timetable. However, he gave her a reassuring grin, and said, 'That's extremely kind of you, Mrs Chatsworth. Sorry to drag you out so late at night.'

'It's a pleasure,' said Teresa.

It was at once obvious that Teresa Chatsworth was an expert when it came to small boats. Having checked out with the Harbour Master, who seemed half-asleep and unsurprised, she led the way down the jetty, and within seconds had a Boston Whaler cast off, its engine purring gently and its navigation lights throwing ripples of red, white and green on to the crinkled water. Henry's offer to help was rebuffed by a curt, 'Just sit still and keep quiet' – and in another minute the little boat was speeding towards the channel through the reef, which Teresa clearly knew by heart.

The noise of the engine made conversation virtually impossible, so Henry sat still and kept quiet. Once outside the reef, Teresa put the wheel hard a-starboard and headed for a point well inside the jutting headland. As they approached the shore, she reduced speed and pointed.

'There's the slip. See? Over there.'

'I didn't realize it was outside the reef,' Henry said.

'Of course. We couldn't have the Club beach cluttered up with greasy mechanics and repair sheds. You can't see this maintenance area from the Club at all.' The little boat was nosing towards the shore, and in the moonlight Henry could make out the dark shape of a building on the water's edge. He could also see that there was a small white boat, identical to the one he was in, riding at anchor just offshore.

Teresa turned to him, triumphant. 'You see? There she is. Are you satisfied now?'

Henry said, 'Why isn't she on the slip?'

'Why? Obviously because the mechanic finished with her this afternoon and launched her again.'

'Then why didn't he bring her back to the jetty?'

Teresa gave a little impatient laugh. 'Why? Why? Why? I don't know, I suppose it was knocking-off time. Anyhow, you will admit that she's there? You saw the other three on the trot as we came out, and with this one, that makes five. Right?'

Teresa was putting the wheel over to turn away from the land again, when Henry said, 'Just a moment. I'm sorry, Mrs Chatsworth, but I'd like a closer look at that boat.'

'A closer look?'

'Yes. Could we go up alongside her for a moment, before we go back?'

'I suppose so.' Teresa had the air of one humouring an idiot. 'It's the Club boat all right, if that's what worrying you.'

'I'm sorry,' said Henry again. 'If you don't mind . . .'

'Oh, very well.'

Teresa manoeuvred the motor boat adroitly, until it lay alongside its anchored sister-ship. Henry stood up and peered intently over the gunwale of the other boat. He put out his hand – and at that moment Teresa shouted, 'Sit down, you fool!' as the little boat tilted alarmingly, rocked back and finally righted herself as Teresa opened up the engine and sped away.

She said, 'I can see you've never done any boating. Don't you know you can capsize a little craft like this, throwing your weight all over the place?'

'I'm sorry,' said Henry, yet again.

'Oh, forget it. We're used to incompetent land-lubbers. Well, I hope you've seen all you want to.'

'Yes,' said Henry. 'Yes, thank you. I have.'

Half an hour later, a committee of five was deep in conference at the bar of the Anchorage Inn – John and Margaret Colville, Henry and Emmy Tibbett, and Tom Bradley.

John was saying, 'Well, why the hell didn't we get Montague out of bed and go after them straight away, for God's sake?'

Henry said, 'I wish we could, but we can't – for several reasons. The main one being Derek Reynolds.'

'Who in the name of glory is Derek Reynolds?' Tom demanded.

'He's my sergeant from Scotland Yard. He was staying incognito at the Golf Club, posing as a wealthy English stamp collector. On my instructions, he took up with Candy Stevenson after Huberman supposedly left – with the idea of getting information out of her. Now both of them have disappeared, and it's virtually certain that they're both being held by Diamond and her group, somewhere up in the hills above Jellyfish Bay. I intend to get Reynolds out of this in one piece, and the way to do it isn't to let Montague and a crowd of flatfeet from St Mark's go storming up there at dead of night.'

'You're sure about the boat?' Margaret asked.

'As sure as I can be. The boat we saw was a Boston Whaler – right, Tom?' Bradley nodded. 'And Chatsworth confirmed there aren't any others on the island. The repair shed is outside the reef and invisible from the Club. Anybody young and athletic could make their way overland to the maintenance area and steal that boat. Then take it across to Frenchman's Bay and anchor there while they raided Priest Town.'

'For provisions?' said Emmy.

'Exactly. There must be quite an encampment up there, and they need food. Then they made their getaway, landed the bags of provisions at Jellyfish Bay – where others of the troop must have been waiting – and took the boat back around the headland.

They didn't have time to put her back on the slip. But I can tell you one thing – before Teresa Chatsworth staged that near-capsize, I had time to feel the engine, and it was still hot. And there was water in the boat.'

John Colville said, 'You say Teresa staged the near-capsize?'

'Of course she did,' Henry said. 'I pretended to know nothing about boats, but in fact Emmy and I have done quite a lot of sailing. It's perfectly true that you can easily capsize a rowing dinghy of that size by shifting your weight about – but those Whalers are a different design altogether. They sit flat on the water, and it would take a lot more than I was doing to make one as much as rock on that calm water.'

Margaret said, 'So you think Teresa knew – ?'

Henry rubbed a hand on the back of his neck. 'I don't know,' he said. 'I don't know where she fits in.' He turned to Emmy, 'Did Sebastian – ?'

Emmy shook her head. 'No,' she said. 'Just stood me another drink, and rambled on about the disaster to the island.'

'What did you think he might do?' Tom Bradley wanted to know.

Henry said, 'The supposition was that Sebastian would take me out in the boat, while Emmy stayed with Teresa. I had a hunch she might make a phone call while Sebastian was out of the way. However, it didn't work out like that.' He grinned at Emmy. 'Sorry I dragged you up to the Golf Club for nothing, darling.'

'Forget it. Now – who do you think the two looters were?'

Henry frowned. 'Diamond and Candy, Sandy and Candy. Those are the likely guesses – the expert swimmers. I don't know about the others.'

'You're sure one of them was white and blonde?'

'Positive.'

'But if Candy is being held prisoner – ' Emmy began.

'Who knows what's happened to her between Saturday morning and now?' Henry paused, then gave a half-smile and said, 'You know, this is all very sensational, and yet my nose ... I mean, I have a very strong feeling that all this is a sideshow.'

'A sideshow?' Margaret echoed.

'Yes. A diversion. Probably connected in some way with the main entertainment, but essentially unimportant.'

'Henry, how can you say that?' Emmy was outraged. 'With poor Derek probably in danger of his life – and Mr Huberman and the policeman murdered – ?'

'It'll all fit in, in the end, you'll see,' said Henry sombrely. And then, to Tom, 'What were you saying when we were interrupted?'

Tom looked surprised. 'Me? Nothing, old man. Haven't opened my mouth.'

'I mean,' Henry said, 'when we were interrupted by a stone being thrown through a plate-glass window in Priest Town. You were telling me about Huberman's luggage.'

'Good lord, so I was. I'd completely forgotten, with all that happened. Well, nothing very sensational. This Redcap thought he remembered it, and that it was claimed by a tall thin man with a beard. He says he loaded it up and wheeled it to the taxi area, where the bearded wonder told the cabbie to drive him to Washington National Airport.'

'I thought he was there already,' Emmy said.

A chorus of voices rose to explain that Dulles International Airport, some miles outside the city, handled long-distance flights, while the close-in National Airport concentrated mostly on shorter domestic flights.

Henry said to Tom, 'You told me you met that flight. You didn't notice the bearded man yourself?'

'Can't say I did. I was looking for Huberman, hoping to get an interview. When you're after a short, tubby, clean-shaven character, the tall bearded ones are of minimal interest. Anyhow, he may just have been a common thief.'

'You think so?' Henry was surprised. 'How's that?'

'Well, I told you – or I think I did – that what made the Redcap remember the incident was that this expensive luggage had been round the conveyor belt a few times, and nobody claimed it. And all the while, he says, this tall character was standing there, as though he was waiting for his own baggage. Then, the third time round, he suddenly stepped forward and claimed it. Well, it was obviously valuable and probably stuffed with goodies, and that domestic claim area is open to the public. The Redcaps are supposed to check the baggage claim slips, but for a twenty-dollar tip . . .'

'What about this particular porter? Did he take a tip and look the other way?'

Tom grinned. 'You think he'd tell me? Of course not. He swore the man had the baggage claim slips for that luggage. But then, he would, wouldn't he?'

Chapter 12

Derek Reynolds climbed steadily upwards from the beach at Jellyfish Bay, his beach bag slung over his shoulder. Starting from the initial direction indicated by the two footprints on the sand, he was encouraged to find traces that he could follow: broken twigs, clumps of grass bent or trampled, a fresh oleander blossom which had not fallen from natural withering. There was only one route that a man carrying a cumbersome burden could take to travel up the hill, and Reynolds followed it.

In doing so, he knew he was taking a calculated risk, but he thought it was worth it. A few more hours, and the precious clues that were leading him might be lost. He could not imagine why Addison should have decided to abduct Candy Stevenson, and in fact he did not give the matter any thought whatsoever. The important thing was to locate the victim and tell Chief Superintendent Tibbett about it. Then proper forces could be brought in through proper channels to settle the affair. Sergeant Reynolds was not an adventurer. He was an academic police investigator, who worked by the book. He found it quite easy to rationalize his present escapade, and it never occurred to him that the subtle chemistry of the Caribbean might have had anything to do with it.

The higher he got, the more complicated the trail became. Several times, he found himself faced with two apparently feasible paths, so that he had to follow one to its ultimate and impassable conclusion before retracing his steps to follow the other. By now, the trees met densely overhead, filtering out all but the most obstinate slivers of sunshine, although it was almost noon. The quiet darkness of the forest was a different world from the brilliant sunshine of the beaches, the Golf Club, the tourists. Here, in the secret centre of the island, the tiny white orchids put out their small stars of beauty. Here nothing was flamboyant, all was shaded and full of meaning.

Derek Reynolds climbed steadily upwards. Twice, he found himself emerging from the forest on to an open hillside and into full sunshine. He was astonished to find how high he had climbed, and to look down on to the sapphire sea and the tiny white sailing ships, like toys in a child's bathtub, ploughing into the north-east trade winds. He paused, looked, and then went back into the dark, humid forest.

By now, Derek Reynolds was becoming uncomfortably aware of the fact that it was one o'clock and that he had not breakfasted and had no food with him. He had already refreshed himself once from his small flask of water, and wished that it were larger. He admitted to himself that he had not realized how spacious and confusing the wooded highlands of the island actually were, and that finding his way back might be even more arduous than the ascent.

He was in this dubious frame of mind when he suddenly emerged from dense undergrowth to find himself on a recognizable trail. He had read in the welcoming literature provided by the Golf Club that several trails through the rain forest were kept clear and marked, but from his observation of the members he felt sure that these paths were little used, and he was surprised to find that this one did indeed live up to its description. Freshly-painted red arrows on rocks and tree trunks pointed the upward route, and a wobbly wooden notice nailed to a white cedar marked the way to 'Panoramic Tower'. One of the nails securing this notice board had fallen out, leaving the guiding arrow pointing towards the ground, but clearly the intention was to urge the hiker onwards and upwards.

Reynolds made his decision. He would follow the trail up to the Panoramic Tower, whatever that might be. If he still had no clue as to the whereabouts of the fugitives, he would temper adventure with caution, follow the well-marked path back to civilization and contact the Chief Superintendent – who would probably have some sharp remarks to make about CID sergeants who went off on wild-goose chases after pretty girls instead of following authorized police procedure. Feeling easier in his mind, he set off up the steep trail.

Fifteen minutes later, he turned a corner between spidery tree roots to find himself confronted by something huge and weird, standing like a gigantic visitant from outer space in the darkness of the forest. After a moment of instinctive shock, he realized that this was the tower – a perfectly prosaic structure of trellised wood, with its four feet solidly embedded in blocks of concrete and ladders leading up to the observation platform. What made it uncanny was its sudden appearance in the untouched twilight of the dense forest, and the fact that it disappeared upwards into the thick, overhanging foliage, so that its top was invisible and might have led, like Jacob's ladder, to the skies. Reynolds laid down his heavy bag, extracted his compass and binoculars, and began climbing the ladder.

Once, on a winter holiday in Switzerland, Derek Reynolds had had the experience of boarding a bus in a fog-filled valley town, and being driven upwards on sinuous mountain roads until – with no warning – the bus burst out of the fog and into the brilliant sunshine and snow of the high country. He was reminded of that moment when he pushed up through the shadowy coolness of leaves and branches and suddenly found his head and shoulders out in the burning sunlight and looking down on the forest. Just above him, the observation platform skirted the tops of the trees, and all around the sea and sky and islands were laid out like a map. He scrambled on to the platform and looked around him.

Far, far below, the blue and purple sea crawled and crested. The islands of St Mark's and Tampica looked like pieces of a jigsaw puzzle thrown carelessly on to an azure carpet, while immediately below the houses and streets of Priest Town were toy-like and unreal. Matchbox-size boats moved along the buoyed channel to and from the harbour: miniature cars ... Reynolds took another look. Funny. There didn't seem to be any cars moving in Priest Town on this Saturday afternoon, but from the harbour-side a thick plume of black smoke rose towards him, until he imagined he could catch its acrid smell in the limpid air. So there'd been a fire. Well, hardly surprising, in this hot dry climate. Derek Reynolds refocused his binoculars and began to scan the nearer landscape.

All around was a dense canopy of closely-woven tree-tops,

betraying no secrets. Brief glimpses of open glades showed the lighter green of grass, the red and purple of tropical blossoms, but no sign of life or movement. The glint of sun on water drew his attention to a point where a small, leaping waterfall briefly caught the light of day, and at once he began to watch the area more closely. Anybody setting up a camp would need water, and streams were few and far between.

The movement, when he saw it, was so slight that had he not been consciously trying to concentrate on the path of the stream, he would almost certainly have missed it. As it was, it came and went so fast that it was hard to pinpoint – but he was as sure as he had ever been of anything that a figure dressed in some pale colour flitted momentarily into a tiny open glade between dark trees, and then disappeared abruptly backwards, as though pulled from behind back into the gloom of the forest. The spot was about a quarter of a mile from the tower, downhill and to the north-east by north. Reynolds uttered a short prayer and began scrambling down the ladder.

At the bottom, he paused and took stock. However well these local people knew the forest, he reckoned that they would rely on some point or line of reference, and the obvious one seemed to be the well-marked but little-used trail to the Panoramic Tower. In fact, the tower itself would be a useful look-out post. Addison, even encumbered by Candy, would have made good time by a familiar route to the marked trail: followed it upwards to a point not too far from the tower, and then turned off to the right in order to arrive at the spot which Reynolds now marked on his sketch-map of the island. On this map, the trail was marked as a wavily uncertain line between the road from the Golf Club to Priest Town, and a small circle marked 'Pan. Tr.' For navigational purposes, the map was just about useless, but it provided a sense of direction and the comforting assurance that the trail did, indeed, descend to the road.

After about twenty minutes of exploration, Reynolds decided that he had found the exit from the trail. Four or five promising ways through the woods had ended in a blank, but this one – although less inviting from the main path – developed into something like a regular route once away from the marked trail. If he was right, then he should be getting close to the encampment.

The all-important thing now was silence and concealment. Reynolds stepped quietly off the track and into the shelter of a dense hedge of oleander. He put his bag on the ground, crouched beside it, and tried to remember the elementary rules of wood-craft from a miscellany of Boy Scout and police training. He held his breath.

The forest, of course, was not silent. The stream which Reynolds had noticed from the observation platform was close at hand, gurgling and splashing over its steep, rocky bed. A mocking-bird in the trees above kept up an incessant and not very expert imitation of the call of the laughing gull. In the carpet of dry fallen leaves under the trees, lizards darted with crackling suddenness, while overhead the engine of a small plane droned rhythmically as it winged its way from St Mark's to Tampica.

What was completely absent, however, was the sound of the human voice, and so it was with the sensation of a firecracker going off in his ear that Derek Reynolds suddenly heard Candy Stevenson say, 'You'll never get away with it.' She seemed to be speaking from about ten feet away, on the far side of the oleander hedge.

A masculine voice, presumably Addison's, answered, 'That's none of your business, nor mine neither.'

'I mean – it's ridiculous. I suppose they think I left on the morning boat.'

'You left on the morning boat, lady.' Addison laughed.

'Yes, but what'll happen when I don't arrive at the other end?'

'You plannin' a big family reunion? You got people waitin' at the airport? Don't make me laugh. You'se just a travellin' whore.'

'Well . . .' Candy was flustered but not defeated. 'What about my luggage? Somebody's going to – '

'Your luggage, sweetheart,' said Addison, 'is at the bottom of the Caribbean Sea, and it'll take a better diver than you to get it up.'

Candy said, in a sort of exasperation, 'I don't see the *point* of all this. You can't keep me up here for ever in these God-for-saken woods, and when I get away and tell the police – '

'Get away? Tell the police? Them's big words, lady. Don't ask me. That's all. Don't ask me. You and I'se here, and here we stay till further orders. And further orders'll come along, don't you worry.'

'Well, we may as well have something to eat, at least.'

'Sounds OK to me.'

'Untie me, then, and I'll open some tins.'

'And have you try running out on me again? No, lady. I'll get the cans.'

Reynolds could hear twigs snapping and leaves rustling as Addison moved about. He edged forward among the oleanders. Suddenly Addison said, 'What was that?'

'What was what?'

'Something moved. In the bushes.'

'A lizard. Or a bird. Good God, you don't think anyone's come after us up here, do you? As you pointed out, I left the Golf Club of my own free will on the eight-thirty boat – didn't I, Addison?'

'Sure did.' Addison laughed, sounding more relaxed. 'You go for corned beef or ham?'

Reynolds wriggled forward again, to the limits of the hedge: and there, between the slender, spiky leaves and sweet pink blossoms, he saw the encampment.

The undergrowth had been cleared in the form of a rough circle, about fifteen feet in diameter. Above, the thick foliage of the trees shut out the sky, so that the camp would be quite invisible from the air. On the far side of it, the stream meandered downhill, providing a good water supply. Equipment was minimal, but efficient. There were two small tents, set on ground sheets, which would provide cramped but adequate shelter for up to six people in a tropical downpour. As Reynolds watched, Addison came crawling out from one of the tents, carrying a couple of tins. The tent-flaps were neatly rolled back, and Derek could see that inside were rolled-up blankets and watertight chests. The one which Addison had opened had contained provisions. The others might contain anything which required to be protected from damp.

Candy Stevenson was sitting on a ground sheet beside the stream. She wore a loose-fitting cotton caftan, her ankles were hobbled together and her hands were behind her back, presumably also secured in some way. The white caftan and the fact that she wore no make-up seemed to indicate that she had been abducted from her cottage before she was up and dressed in the morning. It occurred to Derek Reynolds that she did not look especially frightened – just dishevelled and extremely cross. He could also see that the rope on her ankles was loosely and not very efficiently tied, and he hoped that the same was true for her hands. Addison had evidently taken the risk of untying her to save himself the labour of carrying her. As Derek had seen from the observation platform, she had made an attempt to escape, and so he had trussed her roughly up again. The most important thing, from Derek's point of view, was that the pair were on their own. Given the advantage of surprise, he was certainly a match for Addison Drake.

'Ham for me,' said Candy.

'One ham, coming up, madam.' Addison was aping a Golf Club waiter. He threw the tin at Candy. It hit her on the leg. She winced, but said only, 'Some use that is, without a can opener.'

'OK, OK, there's one here somewhere.'

Addison turned and crawled back into the small tent. Derek Reynolds knew an opportunity when he saw one. He came out of the bushes like a cork from a champagne bottle, and the next moment the tent was down and Addison Drake was enmeshed in it, struggling and screaming profanities.

It was a one-sided battle – almost too easy. Derek Reynolds had everything on his side, and he used it. Within a couple of minutes, Addison was lying on the ground, neatly trussed like a piece of prime poultry, and Derek was cutting free the ropes which held Candy's wrists and ankles, and Candy was saying, 'Oh, Derek . . .' with stars in her eyes, obviously having the time of her life.

As soon as she was free, Candy flung her arms round Derek's neck and began kissing him with a great deal of enthusiasm, punctuating this activity with a breathless series of questions – 'How did you know? How did you find us? Where are we anyway?' – questions to which Reynolds had no chance to reply, since his mouth was otherwise occupied. He heard the movement in the trees behind him, but had not succeeded in disentangling himself before an incisive female voice said, 'Cut it out and put your hands up, both of you. We're armed.'

Candy gave a startled squeak and clung even more closely to Reynolds. The latter detached her gently and turned to find himself looking at the business end of a Smith and Wesson, held steadily by a tall, striking black girl wearing dark glasses. Immediately behind her stood three young black men. The tall bearded one and the small slim one were on either side of the athletic, crinkly-haired youth whose hands were behind his back.

'Sandy!' shrieked Candy, and made as if to dart towards him.

Derek Reynolds grabbed her, as the black girl snapped, 'Stand still or you'll get hurt. Now, put your hands on your heads, both of you.'

Slowly, Derek and Candy obeyed.

'That's better.' Diamond transferred her attention to the recumbent Addison. 'What are these people and what are they doing here?'

Addison said, 'The girl's Candy Stevenson. Was staying at the Club. Orders from the top to get rid of her.'

'So you're Candy Stevenson. Well, well.' Diamond sounded amused. 'I am Diamond. Sandy Robbins, you know ... very well, so I'm told. The other two are Brooks and Delaware. Who's your boy-friend?'

In a curiously formal voice, Candy said, 'This is Mr Derek Reynolds from London. He collects stamps.'

'Among other things,' said Diamond dryly. 'What in hell is he doing here?'

'He saw me being kidnapped from the Club this morning. He followed me up here – '

'I might have known little brother Addie would bitch things up,' said Diamond, with a sort of exasperated affection. 'So now we've got three of them. One would have been plenty. OK, Brooks ... Delaware ... Tie them up and let Addie go. Then get the tent up again and let's have some food, for God's sake.' Keeping the gun trained on Reynolds, she sat down on the grass, stretching her long, blue-jeaned legs.

'But, Sandy,' Candy began, 'you were in prison – '

'Shut up, or we'll put a gag on you,' said Diamond. She sounded more relaxed. 'Well, it's quite a haul for a small guerrilla group. One wanted murderer, one white whore and one stamp collector. I hope headquarters will be pleased.' She transferred her attention to Reynolds. 'You don't say much for yourself.'

'What is there to say?'

'How did you find the camp?'

'I decided by a process of deduction that she and Addison went ashore at Jellyfish Bay. So I started there, and searched all day, and finally – '

'Why?'

'I don't understand you.'

'Why did you follow her?' Diamond was impatient. 'Why didn't you simply go to the police?' She laughed. 'Not that it would have done you much good. The police station should go on burning for another few hours at least.' She turned abruptly to Delaware, who was pinioning Candy's arms behind her back. 'You know you killed that pig with the keys, Del?'

'Who cares?' muttered Delaware. 'Anyhow, it was Brooks done it.'

'That's not true!' protested the lanky giant. 'You had the machete – '

'You both had machetes,' snapped Diamond. 'Anyhow, it doesn't matter. Hurry up, for God's sake. I'm starving. Get the can opener moving, Addie. Have you and the girl had anything to eat?'

'No, Diamond.' Addison sounded like a whipped puppy. 'We were just going to open some cans when – '

'All right. Spare me the details. I suppose the prisoners will have to be fed – they're more useful alive than dead. Ah, that's better.' Brooks had put the finishing touches to Reynolds's leg and arm bonds, and Diamond put her gun down and stretched luxuriously on the grass. 'Better check on supplies, Addie. Six is more than we bargained for, if we're here for any length of time.'

'How long we here for, Diamond?' asked Addison tentatively.

'How should I know? Until further orders.'

'How'll we get them?'

Diamond shrugged. 'The usual way.'

Addison said nervously, 'Suppose Montague and his cops find us?'

'They won't,' said Diamond easily. 'And if they do – we're in a strong bargaining position. We hold hostages. Now, food, for heaven's sake.'

Addison opened tins of ham and corned beef, cut the meat into chunks and fed the prisoners by hand. After eating, each was given a mug of water from the stream, also administered by Addison, who seemed to have taken over as camp orderly. When the meal was over, Brooks and Delaware retired to the tents and were soon stretched out and snoring loudly. Both men were obviously exhausted. Addison was given the gun and told to stand guard, and Diamond came over to the side of the clearing where the three prisoners were sitting, propped uncomfortably against tree trunks.

'It's time we had a talk,' she said. She looked down disdainfully from her six-foot height and addressed herself to Sandy Robbins. 'You first. You realize you're now wanted for double murder?'

Sandy's mouth dropped open in surprise. 'Me? You gone crazy, Diamond? I been in gaol till Brooks and Delaware come get me out –'

'And you murdered a policeman while escaping. You are the obvious suspect, and Brooks, Delaware and I will all swear we saw you do it.'

'I didn't escape! You know that! I was kidnapped –'

Diamond smiled slowly. 'Try telling that to Montague and the Governor and the pig from London. You escaped in the confusion of the fire, killing a cop in the process. You came and joined us. You've always believed in the Cause at heart, haven't you, Sandy dear?' Diamond was purring, like a tiger. 'I'm just pointing out that your only hope is with us. After independence, the Revolutionary Government will consider dropping charges against you – if you co-operate.'

'You don't seriously think you're going to get independence –'

'Don't underestimate us, Sandy,' said Diamond softly. 'We are more powerful than you think. We have outside help that you know nothing about. And the tide is turning. The island is with us. You saw that today.'

Sandy shrugged. 'You crazy, girl,' he said. 'Your men go buying drinks all round in the Bum Boat, get those kids half-stoned so they –'

'I'm not interested in your opinions. I'm telling you your position. Now.' Diamond turned to Candy. 'You're a useless bitch, and I don't know why headquarters loaded you on to us, but I suppose you've got some value as a pawn. You're a travelling tart, and nobody's going to miss you. If you become useless to us, you will be killed. For the moment, we'll keep you alive, but we have no interest in whether you live or die – only in your usefulness. Understand?'

Candy began to cry noisily. 'You can't kill me! I've done nothing . . .'

Softly Sandy said, 'Don't cry, darling. We'll get out of this.'

'Very touching.' Diamond turned her attention to Derek Reynolds. 'As for you, Mr Stamp Collector, you are a nuisance. On the other hand, you are certainly more valuable as a hostage than the little white tramp. You're a member of the Golf Club?'

'Yes.'

'Rich?'

Reynolds hesitated. Candy, who had stopped snivelling, shouted, 'Of course he's rich!'

Diamond said, 'Right. You will be kept alive on the same conditions as the girl. That is, so long as you're useful.' She turned on her heel and strode off towards the tents, where she started unpacking the waterproof boxes.

Watching her as best he could, Reynolds could see that only one box contained food. The others were a small arsenal – guns, ammunition, hand grenades, devices that looked as if they might be bombs. He cursed himself for a blundering fool. If only he had gone back down the hill and found the Chief Superintendent . . . As it was, all that Tibbett had to go on was a cryptic letter couched in police jargon. Reynolds tested the ropes on his wrists and ankles, but Delaware had done a good professional job, and Addison was prowling the perimeter of the camp, keeping a sharp watch. For the moment, there was nothing to be done.

Candy Stevenson had managed to wriggle close to Sandy Robbins, and was now lying with her head on his lap, sniffling slightly, while he whispered what were presumably comforting things into her ear. It occurred to Reynolds, with a slight shock of surprise, that there was real affection between these two young people, something a million miles away from Candy's extravagant heart-on-sleeve emotion towards himself or Albert Huberman. Well, they didn't appear to have much of a future at the moment, but . . . and then another thought struck him. This was Sanderson Robbins, suspect in the Olsen murder case, whose guilt was supposed to be so self-evident that he, Reynolds, and Chief Superintendent Tibbett had been brought from Scotland Yard merely to put the rubber stamp of impartiality on to the verdict: and yet now, at this moment, Sergeant Derek Reynolds was absolutely and utterly convinced of Sandy's innocence.

By Diamond's own admission, he was being framed for the killing of a policeman: certainly he had also been framed in the Olsen case. How? That was a small academic point, to be worked out later. On that dark, humid hillside in the Caribbean, all of Derek Reynolds's carefully-learned police lore exploded and dissolved to dust like a fragile puffball. At last he understood what the Chief Superintendent meant when he talked about his 'nose'. More than anything, Derek Reynolds wished that he could contact Henry Tibbett and explain to him why Sandy Robbins, although damned by circumstantial evidence, was most certainly innocent.

Evening came with swift darkness and a slight chill. No lamps were lit, nor was there a fire. Food and water were again distributed, guards posted and changed at intervals, and captors and captives got what sleep they could, while the lizards skittered in the dry leaves. Early in the morning, Diamond left the camp, and Reynolds – feigning sleep – heard her say something to Addison about the tower. Half an hour later she was back, apparently with a negative report. Whatever sign or signal she had been expecting had not materialized.

As the sun rose and began its futile attempt to filter beams through the tropical denseness of the forest roof, the encampment stirred into life. Candy demanded to be allowed to wash, and had a basin of water thrown in her face by Diamond in reply. Food – rather less of it – was distributed. Diamond was growing edgy. Twice during the morning she left the camp, and twice returned steel-faced and disappointed. At lunch-time, the final tin was opened and a minuscule ration of corned beef distributed. Diamond, Brooks and Delaware went into conference, and Derek suspected that they were regretting not having killed the prisoners before the food supply ran out. Sandy Robbins and Candy Stevenson were curiously serene, even happy. They sat close together, touching each other, saying little. Derek envied them.

It was seven o'clock by Reynolds's watch when Diamond made

her way across the encampment to the prisoners. She said bluntly, 'We must get more food.'

Sandy looked up at her. 'How?'

'There is a way. We will raid the supermarket in Priest Town.'

'Oh, very funny.' Candy seemed no longer intimidated. 'And how do we get there? Fly?'

Diamond gave her a brief and unamused look. She said, 'It's possible for two people who are in good physical condition and can swim underwater. Unfortunately, that rules out Addison, Brooks and Delaware. Also, I imagine, our stamp collector. That leaves the three of us. I understand,' she added, to Candy, 'that you learnt more from Sandy than merely –'

'Yes, I learned to swim, but I won't do it for you. I'd rather starve.'

Diamond smiled. 'Then Sandy will starve, and also Mr Stamp Collector.'

With a pathetic attempt at cunning, Candy said, 'Why not send Sandy and me? We're the best. We'll bring you back all the food you want.'

Diamond laughed. 'Grow up, little bitch,' she said. 'I have decided. You and I will go. It may be useful in the future that you have co-operated with us in breaking the law. And you will do exactly as I say, otherwise your two friends will die. Understand?'

Candy moved closer to Sandy, and nodded silently.

'Right. Here is the plan. Addison will go down with us to Jellyfish Bay, leaving Brooks and Delaware on guard here with the other prisoners. You and I will make our way overland to the Club maintenance area, where there's a Boston Whaler in working order. We take it to Frenchman's Bay, anchor and swim ashore underwater, making landfall near Priest Town. You know the coast?'

Candy nodded.

'There's a curfew. That means there'll be pigs about, but nobody else. Speed's the thing. Break a window, in and out with all we can get. We'll take plastic bags. Back into the water, back to the boat. I'll drop you and the loot at Jellyfish, and you and Addison will bring it up here. Then I'll return the boat and join you. You understand?'

'I understand, Diamond.'

'And remember,' Diamond added, 'that I shall have a gun. And I won't hesitate to use it.'

'I'll remember, Diamond.'

'And no ideas about escaping when we get to Priest Town. If you do, we shall disappear from this island, leaving Mr Stamp Collector dead and Sandy wanted for double murder. Understand?'

'Yes, Diamond.'

'Very well.' Diamond turned and called her brother. 'Addie, come and untie her feet, I'll deal with her hands myself, when we get to the boat. Now, you all know what you have to do?'

There was a murmur of assent. Diamond took her pistol from her belt and gestured sharply to Candy. 'OK. Get up and get going.'

It was after ten o'clock when a wet, shivering and exhausted Candy arrived back at the camp, escorted by Addison, and carrying a heavy plastic bag full of tinned food. The hungry campers had the can opener in action immediately, and were replete after a good meal when Diamond appeared.

She walked straight over to Sandy, moving unerringly in the almost total darkness. She said, 'Sandy?'

'Yes, Diamond.'

'I learnt some interesting news, in Priest Town.'

'You did?'

'Yes, man, I did. Remember I was talking about double murder?'

'I do.'

'Well, the ante is up. Make that triple murder.'

'What are you – ?'

'Albert Huberman never left the island. He was murdered on Saturday at the Golf Club. After you escaped from prison. In exactly the same way that Olsen was killed. Sleep well, Sandy Robbins.'

Chapter 13

In the small hours of Monday morning, Henry and Tom Bradley were still sitting in the snug of the Anchorage drinking beer, and talking. John and Margaret had gone off to bed before midnight, and Emmy shortly after them.

Tom was saying, 'I don't know what more I can tell you, Henry. I can't reveal my sources – or rather Bill's – and even if I did, it wouldn't get you any further.'

'Let's recap, then,' Henry said. 'Here we have the Senate Committee headed by Olsen, making vital decisions for the American cotton industry. And here we have Huberman – that strange creature of US politics, a lobbyist. His job is to get the Olsen Committee to take decisions favourable to his employer, which is the Cotton Producers' Federation, with Jackson Ledbetter as its President. Right?'

'Right.'

'You and your boss, Bill Mawson, recently unearthed the fact – or at least the suspicion – '

'Fact,' said Tom laconically.

'OK. The fact that Huberman was using more than persuasion on Olsen. He was giving him considerable sums of money for his own use.'

'That's over-simplifying it,' Tom said. 'Since Watergate, politicians have become very, very careful. There's no more of the hundred-dollar bills in the plain manila envelope. This money was laundered – whiter than white.'

'How did it work?'

'Well, for a start, it was Huberman's own money.'

'Was he a millionaire or something?'

'He was a successful attorney, but not that successful. It was paid to him by the CPF for his services as a lobbyist. If it seemed somewhat generous, the Federation simply replied that Huberman was very valuable to them, which he was. In any case, everything was completely above board. Huberman declared every cent, and paid his due taxes on it – after hefty but perfectly legal deductions for business expenses. Huberman was audited by the Internal Revenue Service only last year, and came through without a stain on his character. The money was his.'

'H'm,' said Henry.

'You can say that again – but it was all strictly legal.'

'So what did Mr Huberman do next?'

'Mr Huberman,' said Bradley, 'invested his money in an extremely thriving concern, outside the United States. The St Matthew's Golf Club.'

Henry sat up straight. 'You never told me that.'

'You never asked.'

'How could he do that? I mean, it's not a public company, is it?'

'Oh no. That's the beauty of it. It's a private company, incorporated in the British Seaward Islands, and only members may own stock. It's extremely difficult to find out anything about its finances.'

'But you did,' Henry said.

Tom's eyebrows went up. 'I beg your pardon?'

'Look,' said Henry, 'it's very late. Don't lie to me any more.'

'Lie to you?

'You told me when we first met that you weren't doing investigative reporting down here. You said you were a small cog in the machine, and that you were on a watching brief connected with Senator Olsen's murder. That wasn't true.'

'I hardly knew you then,' said Tom defensively.

Henry grinned. 'If you had,' he said, 'you'd have known that I didn't miss the fact that Margaret said you'd been here a fortnight when Emmy and I arrived. You didn't come here to report on Olsen's murder. You came to smell out this dirty laundry and you succeeded. How?'

'That, at least, is my business.'

Henry sighed. 'You journalists. All right, *what* did you find out?'

'Just that Huberman's stock in the company was being quietly sold, at a minimum price, to Olsen – who promptly resold it to other members at the going rate.'

'Just a minute,' Henry said. 'A share is worth what it's worth. It can't – '

'You're talking about shares in public companies, quoted on the Stock Exchange. A private company is . . . well, private. Especially in the British Seaward Islands. The price of shares can fluctuate wildly from day to day, and nobody is to know. Huberman always managed to sell to Olsen at the bottom of the market. Strange, wasn't it? Then a few days later, when the price had recovered dramatically, Olsen would sell. And curiously enough, if there were no other takers, Mr Albert Huberman would buy the shares back at a big loss. I'm not going to tell you how, but I could have gotten documentary proof of this. It was going to be one of Bill's block-buster columns – and then Olsen was murdered. Well, you can't run that sort of a story on a dead man. However, Olsen's death did seem curiously opportune, and Huberman was still here. I stayed on in the hope of getting something more on Huberman. Well, you know what happened. Bill called me back to Washington.'

'Because,' Henry said, 'he thought he had something which would lead further back than Huberman. Something that would break the relentlessly legal connection between Huberman's money and the CPF. Something leading back to Jackson Ledbetter.'

Tom held up a hand. 'Now, not so fast, Henry. When you're in the character-assassination business like we are, you have to tread carefully. Jackson Ledbetter and his Federation members are wealthy and influential men, and the first thing you learn working on Mawson's column is that you don't publish allegations against people of that calibre unless you can prove what you say.'

'And could you?'

Tom scowled, and took a drink of beer. 'I could have,' he said, 'if Huberman had stayed alive. Like I told you, the Justice people were into this thing even more than we were. They were out to get Ledbetter, and the only way they could do it was to put the fear of God into Huberman – not a difficult task, I may say – and then do some plea-bargaining. Huberman would have sold his grandmother down the river to save his own hide. But without Huberman – there's no case that would stand up in court against the sort of legal team that CPF could field.'

Henry said, 'Ledbetter telephoned Huberman from New York on Friday evening, and afterwards spoke to Mrs Chatsworth. As a result, Huberman booked himself on the night plane, packed his bags and made tracks for St Boniface. It doesn't take a detective of genius to make a pattern out of that. Ledbetter must have got a leak from the Justice Department, just as you did, and decided to call Huberman back for a conference.'

'But he never got there.'

'Exactly,' said Henry. 'That's the mystery. He arrived at St Boniface, checked his baggage and airline ticket, and went off to get some dinner. Then, for no apparent reason, he changed his mind and hired a boat back to St Matthew's – where he went into hiding in his cottage and was subsequently killed.'

Tom said, 'I suppose you searched the cottage?'

'The cottage and Huberman's clothes. There was no sign of a boarding pass or baggage checks. But remember, several people were in that cottage before I got there.'

'Supposing he was killed on St Boniface and then ferried back and dumped in the cottage?'

Henry shook his head. 'It's a nice theory,' he said, 'but if he'd been killed somewhere else, there couldn't have been that amount of blood in the room. No, he changed his mind and came back.'

'While his luggage went on to Washington and was claimed.'

'Maybe by a common thief, as you pointed out,' Henry said. 'You can't rule out coincidence in this business.' He paused, looking thoughtful. 'Except that . . . yes, it's an interesting idea . . .'

'And meanwhile,' Tom said, 'what in hell is going on up in the forest with Diamond and her boys and your Sergeant and Candy Stevenson and – '

'I told you, that's a sideshow.'

'Some sideshow. It's already wrecked tourism on this island, and that's the only – '

Henry stood up with disconcerting suddenness. 'I've been a

bloody fool, as usual,' he said. 'Don't you remember the other day Margaret saying that Priest Town was probably a corruption of Preston?'

'What on earth has that to do with it?'

'I'm going to bed,' said Henry. 'Got to be up early to catch him the moment he gets back.'

'Catch who?'

'The Governor, of course. Sir Geoffrey Patterson.'

The Governor of the British Seaward Islands was at the helm of his motor cruiser, *The Mermaid*, when she nosed into the jetty of the Golf Club shortly before eight o'clock on a brilliant breezy Monday morning. He was pleased to see somebody there to take his mooring line – the Club staff could be lax about early-morning duty – but his pleasure dimmed somewhat when he realized that it was the small, quiet man from Scotland Yard. However, he summoned up a smile.

'Morning, Tibbett. Lovely day.'

'Beautiful,' Henry agreed. He caught the deftly-thrown rope, and made it fast. Over the bay, a big grey pelican hovered, took aim with his body, and dived – to surface a moment later with a helpless fish struggling uselessly for life in the capacious pouch below his beak. The two men watched it for a moment, with mixed emotions. Then Henry said, 'Throw me your after line, sir.'

'Oh. Oh yes.' Sir Geoffrey removed his attention from the pelican and shouted into the boat's cabin. 'Darwin! the after line, if you please!'

A skinny black man dressed only in blue denim shorts and a canvas cap came scrambling up from below, and soon *The Mermaid* was tied up alongside the jetty.

Sir Geoffrey jumped ashore, took off his white linen hat and fanned himself with it. His tenure of office in the Caribbean had, for some reason, produced pinkness rather than tan in the Governor. His face was pink, and so were the portions of his plump arms and legs visible outside his spotlessly white shirt and shorts. He said, 'Up and about early, I see, Tibbett.'

'Yes,' said Henry. 'I was hoping to talk to you, sir.'

'Of course, a pleasure.' Sir Geoffrey did not sound particularly pleased. 'Perhaps we could take breakfast together. I believe the dining-room should be open.'

'I'd be delighted,' Henry said.

As they walked up through the fragrant gardens, the Governor said, 'Any new developments, Tibbett? Found that girl and her gang yet? Any more on the Huberman case?'

Henry said, 'I've a good idea where Diamond has her camp, but for several reasons we're playing it rather gently. As for the Huberman case — yes, I think you could say there are developments. Anything new from St Mark's?'

'I've been in touch with London,' said Sir Geoffrey. He puffed a little. 'It's an unhappy situation, Tibbett. Ah, here we are. Good morning to you, Parker. A table in the shade, if you please. Now, Tibbett, what will you have?'

When breakfast had been ordered and served, Sir Geoffrey said, 'Well, now, out with it, Tibbett. What do you want to talk to me about?'

'Sea Island cotton,' said Henry.

The Governor opened his protruding eyes even wider. 'Cotton?'

'That's right. The finest in the world, grown only in the Caribbean.'

'What do you know about it?'

'Not very much, sir.'

'Obviously,' said Sir Geoffrey. 'For a start, Sea Island isn't grown only in the Caribbean. In fact, it's hardly grown here at all any more. The original plants came from India some hundreds of years ago, and India still produces it.'

'All the same,' Henry said, 'I understand that the British Sea-wards — St Matthew's in particular — were once the world's biggest source of Sea Island. But the plantations have all disappeared now, and the only cotton trees one sees are growing wild.'

'That's perfectly correct.'

'I also understand,' Henry said, 'that there's a plan to revive the industry. Replant with new stock, and get the islands back into business again in a big way.' He ended on a slightly interrogatory note.

Sir Geoffrey took a mouthful of scrambled egg, shaking his

head as he did so. When he could decently speak, he said, 'There *was* such a plan. Indeed there was. Still is, I suppose, on paper. But it's ironic you should bring it up just now. I told you I'd been on to London yesterday. Well, I got the bad news that the House of Commons has voted overwhelmingly to suspend funding of the scheme indefinitely, in view of the disturbed political situation here. There's a great deal of money involved, you see. Well, can't blame London, I suppose. Next thing you know, we'll be in for independence here, like Tampica. No sense in throwing away taxpayers' money. Still, it's a disappointment. Can't deny it. A big disappointment.'

'And,' said Henry, 'a big relief to the United States cotton industry.'

Sir Geoffrey smiled, a little grimly. 'I should imagine so,' he said. 'The quality of West Indian cotton has always been the best in the world, and there's a definite movement in consumer demand away from synthetics and back to high-grade natural fabrics. That's why we worked out this scheme. We could have sold every ounce we produced, and more, I can assure you. It would have been the making of these islands.'

'I don't imagine,' Henry said, 'that the Golf Club was any more enthusiastic than the C P F.'

'Not enthusiastic, no – but it wouldn't really have affected them much one way or the other. They're only interested in St Matthew's, not in the other islands. We couldn't have touched their land, of course. It would simply have meant replacing a lot of useless scrub land in the interior of the island with plantations. Might have made it a bit harder to get staff, that's all.'

'It would have changed the image of the island,' Henry said.

Patterson laughed, wiping his mouth. 'You think the Golf Club cares about that? This is an ivory tower, my dear Tibbett, and so long as its battlements are intact, nobody inside cares about what goes on beyond the moat, if you follow me.'

'I wonder if that's quite accurate,' Henry said. 'You can see the effect that the riots have had on the Club.' He gestured at the empty tables.

'That's a different matter altogether, Tibbett. Civil disturbances and murders have nothing to do with cotton plantations.'

'I wonder,' said Henry.

9 a.m. 'Call it off?' said Owen Montague incredulously. 'Are you out of your mind? The island'll never get back to normal until we catch these dangerous criminals – '

'We'll catch them,' said Henry. 'All I'm asking is that you should call off your search party for the time being. Until ... well, for the time being.'

'I certainly can't do anything of the sort without consulting Commissioner Alcott,' said Montague snappishly.

'By all means consult him,' said Henry. 'I've already spoken to him, and he agrees.'

Montague shot him a look full of suspicion, and picked up the telephone. With the police station gutted, he had established uncomfortable headquarters in a small office at the back of the police garage, and this had done nothing to improve his opinion of life in general and interfering officers from Scotland Yard in particular.

'Commissioner Alcott? Good morning, sir. Tibbett is with me, and he tells me ... oh, did he? ... oh, I see ... well, I think I might have been informed ... yes, I know I've been informed now, but ... oh, very well ... sir ...'

He slammed down the receiver. 'It's extremely difficult to operate efficiently in a vacuum,' he said. 'If either you or Alcott would give me a good reason for this decision – ' He tapped his desk with a pencil, which promptly broke at the point. 'Did you know that the supermarket was broken into and looted last night?'

'Yes,' said Henry. 'I did.'

'Well, there you are. That sort of thing is going to go on and get worse, until we – '

'Look, Inspector Montague,' said Henry, 'I know where they are – or at least, how to trace them. They have supplies, which means they're not intending to move, at least for the moment.'

Montague was looking at him, with an almost comical expression of disbelief. 'You *know* where they are? Then, dear soul, why don't you tell us? What are you playing at?'

Henry grinned. 'I suppose you could call it politics,' he said. 'Or detection. Or preservation of the species. It doesn't really matter. Just call off your search party, there's a good fellow.'

'Since the Commissioner has ordered it, I have no choice. But I do it under protest, and I intend that fact to be recorded.' Montague put out his hand automatically to where the desk buzzer should be, but was not. Crossly, he got up, strode over to the door, and shouted, 'Geraldine!'

'Yes, Inspector?' A trim, attractive black policewoman appeared from the even more uncomfortable outer office, carrying a stenographer's notebook and pencil.

'Ah, Geraldine. Take a memo. To Sergeant Ingham. The search party detailed for this morning has been cancelled until further notice. Personnel to stand by. You'll have to run all the way with that one, dear, because they're assembling outside the station at this very moment. Then take another memo to Commissioner Alcott, copy to Chief Superintendent Tibbett. Search party cancelled according to instructions and under strong protest. I'll sign them both, and make sure they're delivered. Thank you, dear.' He gave Henry a furious look.

'Thank you, Inspector Montague,' said Henry. 'You won't regret it, I promise.'

'It's nothing to do with me, dear boy,' said Montague icily. 'Don't let me detain you.'

9.45 a.m. 'Ledbetter's telephone number? Sure, I can get it. What's all this in aid of?' Tom Bradley sat up in bed, blinking in the shafts of sunlight which came filtering through the shutters of his bedroom at the Anchorage. 'For Chrissakes, Henry, don't you ever sleep? We didn't get to bed till after five.'

'I'm sorry, Tom. There's so little time. Alcott is co-operating wonderfully, but I can't stall Montague for ever –'

'You're rambling, dear fellow,' said Tom. He stretched out a hand to his bedside table and, without looking, found a pack of cigarettes and a lighter. 'What's the idea? Are you intending to call Jackson Ledbetter and ask him, just as a favour to Scotland Yard, to admit he was paying off Brett Olsen via Albert Huberman to keep the Olsen Committee sweet?'

'No.'

'Now, you listen to me, Henry, and take my advice. All right, so Olsen and Huberman are dead. But the Olsen Committee is still alive, and so is the CPF, and so is the Justice Department. If there are any more tricks, Justice will be on to them like a raccoon on to a bag of garbage – but my guess is that there won't be. So, in a rough sort of way, justice will have been done. At least, the abuses will stop. Seems to me the best thing you can do is get after Sandy Robbins and clear up the murders, and get after Diamond and company and clear up this island, so that things can get back to normal. Don't go meddling with Ledbetter, he's too important.'

Henry said, 'Is that a warning?'

'A piece of friendly advice, pal. And believe me, I know of what I speak.'

'Yes,' said Henry. 'Yes, I think you do. I'd still like that telephone number.'

Tom took a puff at his cigarette and sighed. 'If you must, you must. Mind you, I don't know where he is right now. You'd best start at the CPF in Washington DC. If he's not there, try his home in Maclean – that's a plush suburb in Virginia. I can give you both numbers. If all else fails, there's his apartment in New York. You'll find my address book in the pocket of my blue suit in the closet. Take what you want and for God's sake let me get back to sleep.'

He stubbed out the cigarette and rolled over, pulling the sheet over his head. Henry found the small black book and copied two numbers. Then he said, 'I'll need the New York address.'

A muffled voice from under the sheet said, with a yawn, 'Should be in the book . . . no phone number though . . .'

'Ah, yes. Here it is. Thanks a lot, Tom.'

10 a.m. Henry was talking on the telephone to his old acquaintance, Officer Stanton of the District of Columbia Police Force in Washington.

He cut short Stanton's warm greetings. 'No . . . no, I'm not in DC . . . I'm in the Caribbean . . . no, not literally, worse luck . . . look, I'm here on a case and I need your help . . . You know Washington National Airport? . . . The shuttle service to New York?'

'Sure. Who doesn't?'

'What time does the last plane take off on a Friday night?'

'Nine o'clock,' replied Stanton promptly. 'I know. I was up in the big apple just last weekend.'

'And the first on Saturday morning?'

Stanton considered. 'Weekdays it's seven a.m.,' he said, 'but I've a feeling it's later on Saturday. Eight, or even nine. Eight, I think.'

'Good,' said Henry.

'What's good about it, for Chrissakes?'

'Never mind. Now, if somebody wanted to leave luggage at the airport overnight, what would he do?'

'Put it in a locker, I guess.'

Henry said, 'As I remember it, National doesn't have night flights, being so close to the city centre.'

'Right.'

'So how would anybody rent a locker after the last evening flight?'

Stanton laughed. 'You sure don't know the system, Tibbett. These lockers are pay-as-you-go.'

'Can you explain?'

'Sure. If the locker's not in use, it's open and the key is in the lock – but you can't move it, see? But you put your money in and – hey presto, the key's mobile. Put in your bags, close and lock the door and pocket the key. Once you open it again, you're back where you started. More money in the slot, or you can't relock it.'

'Supposing,' Henry said, 'That somebody deposits luggage, takes the key and simply walks off and doesn't come back?'

'What sort of a nut would do that?' Stanton demanded.

'Somebody who wants to dispose of something as unobtrusively as possible.'

There was a pause, then Officer Stanton said, 'OK. What are we looking for?'

'A matched set of luggage,' Henry said. 'I don't know how many pieces. Very expensive, black leather, monogrammed in gold with the letters A.G.H. Deposited late last Friday night or early Saturday morning.'

'And if we find it, what's in it that we're looking for?'

'Nothing.'

'Nothing! You crazy, or sump'n?' Henry could almost see the

rotating jaw as Officer Stanton demolished yet another stick of chewing gum.

'It's the luggage itself I'm after,' Henry explained. 'Not what's in it. Can you make ·a quick check and call me back at this number?'

'Sure, sure. Nice to hear from you, Mr Tibbett.'

'A pleasure, Mr Stanton.'

It was less than an hour later when Officer Stanton called the number of the Anchorage Inn from Washington National Airport.

'Well, we got it.'

Henry breathed a sigh of relief. 'Where was it?'

'In the unclaimed property department. The Agent Cashier – that's the guy with the master key – he checks the lockers about every twenty-four hours, and any unclaimed stuff is brought over here. They keep it about six months to see if anyone claims it.'

'I see. Well since you're on the spot, you might check for another unclaimed article.'

'What?' demanded Stanton, and when Henry told him, 'Aw, you're nuts. OK, I'll take a look.' A few moments later he was back. 'Well, I'll be darned. You're right, it's here ... no, not the same locker.'

'Hold it with the luggage,' Henry said. 'Test for fingerprints.'

'You going to send us some dabs for matching?'

'I hope so,' Henry said, 'but not immediately. The next thing is to get hold of one of those locker keys.'

'Look,' Stanton protested, 'those lockers didn't have keys. That's the whole point. The Agent Cashier opened them with his master key and –'

'I don't care which key or which locker,' Henry said. 'I just want a key to one of the baggage lockers at National. Can you get one?'

'Sure, but –'

'Can you give it to the pilot of the next plane taking off from Dulles for St Boniface? In an envelope addressed to me? I'll meet him there. Call me back and tell me when the plane's due.'

When Officer Stanton called back at one o'clock, he sounded as if life might be becoming too difficult for him. He prefaced his remarks by the word 'Jeez!' and a prayer that the Almighty would spare him from ever becoming involved with a British cop again as long as he lived. He added that a locker key from National Airport, in an envelope addressed to Henry, would be in the pocket of Captain Joe Stapleton of Trans-American Airlines, whose 707 was due to touch down in St Boniface at 4.30 that afternoon.

When Henry tried to thank him, he said, 'Aw, nuts!' and there was the sound of a deftly-spat gob of gum hitting the waste-paper basket. And then, 'It's been a real pleasure, Mr Tibbett.'

1.15 p.m. 'I honestly don't think I can do it, Henry,' said Emmy.

'It's our only hope. I hate asking you, but – think what's at stake.'

Emmy said nothing, but took a long drink of orange juice. The Tibbetts were the only occupants of the Anchorage bar at a time when it was usually alive with lunch-time custom. At last, Emmy said, 'It's not so much that I don't think I could pull it off – although it wouldn't be easy. It's ... well ... it doesn't seem ethical.'

'Ethical!' Henry was near the point of explosion.

Emmy said, 'Oh, I know. I don't want to go into the realms of philosophy, but I can't help it. You're saying that the end justifies the means.'

'In this case – yes, I am.'

'Well, I just can't accept that, Henry.'

'Look, Emmy – an innocent deception – '

'It's not an innocent deception. It's a double lie, and I can't do it.'

Henry gave an exasperated sigh. 'Well, obviously *I* can't, so I suppose I'd better forget the whole thing. And when a murderer gets off scot-free, and maybe a couple more people are killed, I hope you'll feel extremely proud of your high moral stand.'

'Henry!' Emmy was near tears. 'That isn't fair! You know I'd do anything to help you ... and the others ... that I didn't feel was positively wrong. I know that all you care about is getting to the bottom of the case. Like Lucy once said about you – '

'Lucy!' Henry stood up suddenly. 'Of course! Why didn't I think of her sooner? Lucy is the answer.'

Five minutes later, he was talking to Miss Lucy Pontefract-Deacon in Tampica. She was saying, 'Know him? Of course I know him, Henry. You ask the silliest questions sometimes ... never mind how ... yes ... yes ... that doesn't surprise me ... my goodness, yes, of course, you're right ... how extremely foolish we've all been, haven't we? ... Well, last time I did stumble to the right conclusion just before you did, but you've certainly beaten me to it this time ... Well, now, what do you propose to do? ... Yes ... yes, a splendid idea ... oh, won't she? Well, I applaud her for it, and you can tell her that I admire a woman with high principles. On the other hand, after eighty I feel one is allowed a little latitude ... yes, of course I will, it'll be a pleasure, Henry ... now, just a minute, the call should come from St Matthew's, should it not? ... Yes, of course, I visit there frequently ... let's see, what time is it now? ... I'll catch the two o'clock plane to St Mark's and hire a boat from there. Meet me at the quay and give Emmy my love.'

Henry was at the town wharf to welcome the small white launch which came scudding across the harbour. The boatman tied up alongside, and Henry leaned down to give his hand to the straight-backed, white-haired old lady who climbed with surprising agility on to the jetty, grasping a striped parasol in one hand and an enormous handbag in the other. She kissed Henry briefly, put up the parasol and walked ashore. Henry noticed with amusement that the Customs and Immigration Officers and the police reinforcements on the quay were lining up more as a guard of honour than an official screening barrier.

'Hi, there, Miz Lucy.'

'Nice day, Miz Lucy.'

'Haven't been to see us for a while, Miz Lucy.'

Lucy Pontefract-Deacon beamed. 'I always enjoy visiting St Matthew's,' she said. 'Such a pretty island. I imagine you will want to stamp my passport.'

The welcoming committee looked at its boots and mumbled something about that not being necessary.

'But I insist. These formalities are for our own protection, are they not?' She fumbled in her bag and produced a well-worn travel document. 'Do we go into the office? Ah, how very nice.

Thank you, Lemuel. You are looking very well. Give my love to your wife, won't you?'

A few moments later, willing hands assisted Lucy into the mini-moke beside Henry. As they drove away from the quayside, she looked at her passport complacently, and remarked, 'Nobody will be able to dispute that I was on St Matthew's today.' And then, 'Oh, dear. What a pity about the police station. Of course, it was an exceptionally ugly building, but wanton destruction is always distressing. You seem to be doing very well, Henry.'

'Don't talk too soon, Lucy.'

'Better too soon than too late. Now, let's go over this once more . . .'

At half past three, Lucy was sitting in the snug of the Anchorage with the telephone in her hand. She was saying, 'Cotton Producers' Federation? Mr Jackson Ledbetter, please . . . yes, it is very important . . . Mr Ledbetter's secretary? Good afternoon, dear . . . will you please tell Mr Ledbetter that Miss Lucy Pontefract-Deacon wishes to speak with him . . . and hurry, please, dear. I am talking from St Matthew's in the Caribbean . . .' She looked at Henry and winked. 'Thank you, dear . . . I thought he would . . . Hello? . . . ah, hello, Jackson . . .'

Chapter 14

Sebastian Chatsworth was delighted to put the *Island Eagle* at the disposal of Chief Superintendent Tibbett for the trip to St Boniface.

'How long will you need to stay there?' he asked.

'I'm not sure. Not long, I hope.'

'Well, it works out very well, because we've a member arriving on the flight from Washington at nine o'clock, so if you don't mind waiting till then, the launch can bring you both back here.'

'Business is picking up again, is it?' said Henry.

Chatsworth smiled ruefully. 'I wouldn't call Jackson Ledbetter on his own a big rush of business,' he said, 'but we can only hope that he's the first swallow of summer, as it were.'

Henry said, 'Ledbetter? That's Senator Olsen's pal, isn't it? He was here only a couple of weeks ago.'

'That's right. Had to get back to Washington when Olsen was killed – big C P F meeting – but now he's determined to come back and finish his holiday, riots or no riots.'

'I shall be interested to meet him,' Henry said. He did not add that there was little chance that he would do so before the next day.

The *Island Eagle* arrived at the airport quayside at twenty past four. Commissioner Alcott had alerted the United States Customs and Immigration authorities to Henry's visit, but all the same he was glad that he had made sure that his U S A visa was in order before leaving London. Once the formalities were over, Henry was escorted into a special crew-members' lounge to await the arrival of Captain Stapleton and his envelope.

The 707 touched down a mere ten minutes late, and soon afterwards Henry was shaking hands with a tall, slightly grizzled man who introduced himself as Joe Stapleton, conveyed Officer Stanton's best regards, and handed over a small envelope containing a locker key. He then excused himself, explaining that he had only a half-hour stopover before continuing the flight to Barbados.

Next, Henry made his way to the Trans-American desk and asked about flight times to New York. As he had hoped, it was possible to fly to the big city that evening, leaving at half past six, and to return in the early hours of the morning, getting to St Boniface at eight o'clock. Henry booked himself on these flights, giving his name as Mr Smith and his address as that of Jackson Ledbetter in New York – this being the only address in the city that came to his mind. Since this was a domestic flight within the United States, both name and address were accepted without demur. Henry paid his fare, checked in for the flight and re-ceived his boarding pass. Then he made his way to a public telephone and called Emmy.

'Look, darling, I'm going to New York ... don't squeak like that, I'll be back first thing in the morning, it's not so far, you know ... now, ring the Club and tell Major Chatsworth that I'm staying overnight on St Boniface, and that I'd like to be picked up by the first launch in the morning. And ring Commissioner Alcott – yes, he's at the Golf Club – and tell him we should be able to get the search party going around ten o'clock ... yes, I'll be going on it myself ... no, darling, there's nothing to worry about ... just following something up ...'

Henry cradled the telephone, and walked out into the blazing heat and sunshine of a West Indian afternoon.

He had not visited St Boniface before, and he was immediately struck by the hustle and bustle of the streets, the duty-free shops competing raucously for the custom of tourists in search of liquor, tobacco and perfume. Regretfully, he remembered that Tampica was well on the road to the same state of affairs; and yet, there was a colour and vitality in the narrow, crowded streets which was undeniably appealing. Henry allowed himself to be lured into the cool dimness of one of the shops, where he bought a bottle of Emmy's favourite scent and a silk scarf from Paris for a ridiculously low price. Then he made his way to the harbour.

Two big white cruise liners lay at anchor offshore, and many small launches were ferrying passengers to and from the quay. A few fishing boats huddled together at one end of the wharf, like survivors of an endangered species. Several large pleasure boats waited to set out on garishly-advertised trips to Tampica, St Thomas and St Mark's. Up at the far end of the quay, a cluster of little motor boats jostled each other like ducklings, while their black skippers lounged on the jetty, smoking and chatting. Henry made his way towards them.

As soon as they saw him coming, several men jumped to their feet and began asking Henry where he wanted to go, extolling the virtues of their boats. Henry mentioned St Matthew's Golf Club, and at once a gloomy silence descended.

A skinny, grey-haired man in tattered blue jeans – whom Henry recognized as the boatman who had brought Tom Bradley to St Matthew's – said, 'Sorry, man. We don't go there. Take you to Priest Town if you want,' he added, on a more cheerful note.

'Why don't you go to the Golf Club?'

The grizzled skipper shook his head. 'Golf Club's got its own boats,' he said. 'Don't allow nobody else to land at their jetty.'

The other men nodded and murmured agreement.

Henry said, 'Well, a non-Club boat landed there last Friday night.'

A chorus of dissent went up. 'No, man. No way. Couldn't be so.'

'This was late at night,' Henry said. 'Perhaps nobody noticed.'

This time, the dissent was even more vociferous. It emerged from the confused medley of sound that private boatmen did not operate after dark. Only a specially-ordered Club launch could possibly have conveyed a passenger back to St Matthew's at that hour.

'I was told,' Henry said, 'that some of you occasionally work at night.'

Looks were exchanged, and then the grey-haired man said, 'A few of us do, sure, man. But you said the Golf Club.'

'That's right.'

'Well, there's only two men in St Boniface can find that channel in the dark. One is my brother and he's been away in St Thomas for two weeks. The other is me, and I was home with my wife Friday.'

A round-faced young boatman piped up. 'It could have been the *Pelican*.'

'The *Pelican*?'

'Sure, man. That boat there, at the end of the trot. Mr Owen's boat.'

'Who's Mr Owen?'

'Very important man on St Matthew's, Mr Owen. Keeps the *Pelican* here for fishing trips and such. Fine man with a boat, Mr Owen. If any boat wasn't a Club launch gone there Friday night, it 'ud be the *Pelican*.'

The older man broke in. 'You crazy, Harvey. Mr Owen's not been here in a couple of weeks. Why, the last time he took the *Pelican* out was back in March. You remember, man. The day Senator Olsen got killed.'

Trying not to sound too eager, Henry said, 'You're sure about that?'

'Sure I'm sure, man. Mr Owen come down here jus' before lunch-time. Said he was goin' fishin', like he often does. He was back around half past four, and I remember because we was jus' listenin' to the radio and there was the fellow breakin' in to the regular programme to say as how Senator Olsen got murdered. That really shook Mr Owen up – seems he knew the Senator. White as a sheet, he went – said he must get back to St Matthew's in a hurry. But he didn't take the *Pelican*. He went off to pick up the Club launch.'

'With his fish?'

'He didn't have no fish. He'd catch big ones for sport, and throw 'em back.'

Henry said, 'Owen. That's a familiar name. I think I may know him. He's a tall, thin chap, isn't he?'

'Right, man.'

'And he's British.'

The boatmen exchanged glances. 'How's that?'

'Well – he talks the same way that I do.'

Heads were shaken. 'He talks like anybody else ... regular guy, Mr Owen ...'

'But he ain't been here, not since back in March,' added the older skipper.

'Oh, well,' Henry said, 'I must have been mistaken. It must have been a Club launch last Friday.' He walked slowly back to the airport.

Manhattan at half past nine on a spring evening glittered and snapped and crackled and lifted Henry's heart as it always had done since his very first visit. A ridiculous city, higher than it was broad, constantly on the brink of disaster, always throbbing with a special sort of magic. New York, New York, it's a wonderful town . . . ask any New Yorker, and hear him grumble. Then ask him if he'd live anywhere else in the world.

The address which Tom Bradley had given as Jackson Ledbetter's New York apartment turned out to be a mini-skyscraper, a mere thirty storeys high, located on a residential street in the east sixties. Around its ankles, a few brownstone houses still managed to cling to existence, but on every street corner a new building seemed to be under construction. Chic restaurants with blue-canopied entrances lined the north-south avenues, while on the east-west streets delicatessens offered delicious European carry-out foods. It was, Henry decided, a most desirable address.

Through the big plate-glass doors leading to the lobby, Henry could see a burly, red-faced doorman sitting at the desk, reading *Playboy*. Next door to the apartment building was the entrance to a small, elegant restaurant, and Henry was glad to find that he could give a good imitation of perusing the framed menu beside its door, while at the same time keeping an eye on the brightly-lit lobby. Sure enough, within a few minutes he saw his chance.

A middle-aged couple – the man in tuxedo and black tie, the woman in evening dress and mink – emerged from the elevator and spoke to the doorman, who hastily stashed his magazine under the desk and rose to his feet. He pulled on his cap, and a moment later was out in the street making for the corner of First Avenue, waving and whistling for a cab. Henry walked into the lobby, exchanged a nod and a smile with the couple, and made for the elevator. Soon he was on the seventeenth floor, and outside the apartment rented by Jackson Ledbetter.

Here, his actions would have surprised an onlooker – but fortunately there were none. He took a small knife from his pocket and made a little scratch on the door, near the lock. Then he wandered to the end of the corridor and for ten minutes enjoyed a magnificent view from the window over the lights of Manhattan, before riding the elevator down to the lobby again.

The doorman was back at his desk. He looked up in a bored way as Henry came out of the elevator – then did a double-take and scrambled to his feet.

'Hey, you. What you doing here?'

Henry stopped. He said, 'Visiting.'

'Visiting who?'

'Mr Jackson Ledbetter. Apartment 17B.'

The doorman was getting steadily more suspicious. He said, 'Now, just a minute. For one thing, Mr Ledbetter ain't here. And for another, I never seen you before. And for a third, don't you know it's not allowed for visitors to go up in the elevator till they've been announced?'

Henry smiled deprecatingly. 'I'm sorry,' he said. 'I'm from England, and I don't know the rules. Anyhow, there was nobody here when I came in, so I just went up.'

'I only been out a coupla minutes, getting a cab for ... here, Mr Ledbetter's not home, right?'

'Right,' said Henry.

'Well, it's near a quarter of an hour since I went out to fetch that cab. What you been doing up there all that time?'

'Writing him a note. When I found he wasn't there, I left a note for him by his front door.'

'The tenants' mail boxes is down here. Any notes, you leave with me.'

Henry said, 'Do you know when Mr Ledbetter will be back?'

'Naw. He's away for several days, that's for sure.'

'Any idea where he is?'

'Waal . . .' The doorman hesitated.

Henry's hand went to his pocket. He said, 'I'll be honest with you. I'm a detective. Just checking up on a few things for a client. If you could just tell me where Mr Ledbetter is . . .'

A green-backed note changed hands unobtrusively. The doorman said, 'No secret about that. He'll be in Washington DC. He's there more than he's here.'

'As a matter of fact,' Henry said, 'I'm really more interested in where he was last Friday night and Saturday morning.'

Another bill changed hands, and the doorman grinned. 'You're out of luck there. He was here.'

'On his own?'

'So that's how it is, is it? Well, he never brings no broads here, that's for sure. Kinda cold-blooded, if you ask me. No, sir – he was here and he was on his own.'

'How can you be certain?' Henry asked.

'Because I was on duty Friday evening when Mr Ledbetter came in, around half past five. He told me he had some telephone calls to make and work to do, and that he didn't want to be disturbed. Anyone asked for him, I was to say he was out.'

'And did anybody try to visit him?'

The doorman shook his head. 'Nobody. Not before I went off at midnight, anyways.'

'And Saturday morning?'

'I saw him again Saturday morning, I came on at nine o'clock, and not long after he came in from the street. I noticed he'd gone out early, and he said yes, he'd just stopped round the corner to get a newspaper.'

Henry said, 'That's very helpful. Thank you. Here's my card.'

'I bet,' said the doorman, 'you'd like it if I didn't mention to anybody that you were here.'

'On the contrary,' Henry said. 'By all means tell anybody who may ask.'

The doorman studied Henry's card, rubbing his forehead. At last he said, 'You say you're British?'

'That's right.'

'A British cop?'

'Yes.'

'Guess that accounts for it.'

Henry left the doorman shaking his head in bewilderment, and went out again into the invigorating Manhattan evening.

As a matter of fact, it was only about half an hour later that the telephone on the doorman's desk rang. He picked it up.

'Avenue Tower Apartments ... oh yes, sir ... good evening, sir ... well ... as a matter of fact, yes, sir ... some sort of an English cop, sir ... yes, he left a note ... well, it's a bit ... well, the fact is, sir, I'd have to go up and get it ... well, it was like this, sir. I was out for a minute or so, calling a cab for Mr Studmeyer, and this guy comes in and doesn't understand, being British . . . yes, went up in the elevator and left a note when he found nobody home . . . yes, sure, hold on, sir . . .'

A couple of minutes later, the doorman was back at the desk telephone. He seemed embarrassed and ill at ease. 'Well, sir, it's funny but there's no note that I can see . . . no, not very long . . . well, say ten minutes at the outside . . . or five . . . no, probably less than that . . . what's that? . . . Scratches or marks on the door? No, sir. No, certainly not . . . Well, a lot of the doors are old, aren't they, sir? Might easily have a little mark on 'em . . . wouldn't mean anything, would it, sir? . . . No, of course not, sir, but you know how it is if a tenant wants a cab . . . No, sir . . . yes, sir . . . good night, sir . . .'

The doorman rang off and mopped his brow. Then he began to mutter extremely uncomplimentary remarks about British policemen under his breath. Doormen's jobs were not all that easy to come by in New York.

Henry, meanwhile, was walking among the glitter and squalor of Broadway, wishing that Emmy was there to share it with him. A vaguely-remembered bell at the back of his mind sent him to Sardi's restaurant for a wildly expensive dinner, and to his delight he found himself mopped up by a slightly frenetic party of English actors and actresses – several of whom he had met in London – whose show had opened that evening, and who were carrying on the tradition of dining at Sardi's while waiting for the all-important *New York Times* review to roll off the presses. He left them with regret, to catch his plane from Kennedy Airport, and was pleased to see a few days later that Mr Barnes had been kind and even complimentary.

The flight back to St Boniface was uneventful. Henry dozed most of the way, opening his eyes only to take in the majesty of sunrise over the blue Atlantic Ocean. At five minutes to eight the plane touched down, slightly ahead of time owing to tailwinds. Formalities went smoothly and Henry had no baggage to claim, so he was waiting on the quayside by the airport when the *Island Eagle* came into sight, roaring across the bay and throwing up a fine plume of white spray. As the launch approached the jetty, Henry noticed that she carried a woman passenger. Another departing Club member, he supposed – must be almost the last. And then he saw that it was Teresa Chatsworth.

'Good morning, Mrs Chatsworth. Come over to do some shopping?'

'No,' said Teresa shortly.

'Why don't you come ashore before I get on board?' Henry extended his hand.

'Because I'm not going ashore, Mr Tibbett,' said Teresa. 'I came over so that we could have a talk on the way back. A private talk.'

Henry grinned. 'That's very flattering.'

'It wasn't meant to be. All right, Franklin, you can cast off. We're not expecting anybody else.'

As the launch headed out to sea again, Teresa led the way into the small forward cabin, where conversation could not be overheard by the crew. She sat down, motioned Henry to do the same, and lit a cigarette. Then she said, 'Now, Mr Tibbett, perhaps you'll do some explaining.'

'Explaining?'

'Please don't try to look innocent. For a start, what were you doing in New York last night?'

'Emmy told you, did she? Oh, just some business.'

'I wonder what business could take you snooping round Mr Ledbetter's apartment in the middle of the night?'

Henry nodded appreciatively. 'The grapevine is efficient,' he said. 'It was private business, Mrs Chatsworth.'

Teresa said angrily, 'You were brought here, Mr Tibbett, to solve the murder of Senator Olsen – in other words, to wrap up the case against Robbins and get the island back on an even keel. Instead, you have brought nothing but trouble. Robbins has escaped and murdered another innocent man, if not two, Diamond and her gang have used the whole thing as an excuse to stir up violence, and the Club is facing ruin. I'm putting it to you that you either do the job you were sent to do, or you get off St Matthew's, and fast.'

'Tell me, Mrs Chatsworth,' Henry said, 'does Owen Montague keep a motor boat on St Boniface?'

'Does – ? What on earth has that to do with it?'

'I just asked you – does he?'

There was a tiny pause. Then Teresa said, 'Not that I know of. It's possible, of course.'

'Or does your husband?'

'Certainly not. Could we get back to the point, Mr Tibbett?'

'If by the point you mean the framing of Sandy Robbins, I'm afraid it doesn't interest me at the moment.'

'How dare you use the word "framing"!'

Henry said, 'A lot of people on St Matthew's genuinely believe that Robbins is guilty, Mrs Chatsworth. Especially after Huberman's murder. But I don't think you are among them.'

'And what is that supposed to mean?'

'Jackson Ledbetter arrived safely last night, I gather?'

'Of course.'

'Why has he come back, Mrs Chatsworth?'

'To finish his holiday. Sebastian and I appreciate it, as a gesture of confidence in the Club. But then, Jackson is a close friend of ours.'

'Obviously,' said Henry, 'since he spoke to you on the telephone after he called Albert Huberman last Friday.'

'You are well-informed,' said Teresa. Suddenly she smiled. 'Of course, you want to know what was said. I'm afraid it wasn't at all sensational. Jackson simply wanted to assure me that he would come back as soon as he could. And, as you know, he has done just that.'

'You didn't talk about anything else?'

'Nothing. Oh, he asked me how the weather was down here. That's all.'

'I presume,' said Henry, 'that he has told you that he had a call from Lucy Pontefract-Deacon yesterday. Just before he decided to come and finish his holiday.'

For the first time, Teresa Chatsworth seemed to be caught off balance. In a small voice, she said, 'How do you know about that? You don't even know Lucy.'

'I have known her for a long time, Mrs Chatsworth.'

'But . . .' Teresa stopped. Then she said, 'I see it all now. You put her up to it.'

'Put her up to it?' echoed Henry innocently.

Teresa stood up. 'I refuse to continue this conversation any longer, Mr Tibbett.'

'You do? I thought you were the one who wanted to talk.'

'That's not funny, Mr Tibbett.' Teresa was seething.

Henry said, 'Mrs Chatsworth, I'm a professional policeman. You surely didn't think that I would come all this way to rubber-stamp a rather clumsy frame-up, did you?'

Teresa said nothing. Henry went on. 'There's one point on which I agree with you entirely.'

'I'm very surprised to hear it.'

'And that is the importance of getting St Matthew's back to normal as soon as possible – for everybody's sake.'

'Diamond and her people – ' Teresa began.

'Exactly,' Henry said. 'The search party should be waiting to go after them as soon as we get back. I'd appreciate your co-operation.'

'What does that mean?'

'Exactly what it says.'

'Oh, go to hell,' said Teresa Chatsworth.

Chapter 15

The Golf Club appeared to be just as usual, apart from the absence of guests. The Governor and Commissioner Alcott were breakfasting together, poring over a sketch-map of the island. Sebastian Chatsworth sat alone at another table, listlessly decapitating a soft-boiled egg. Two middle-aged American couples were all that remained of the members.

Henry refused an invitation to join Alcott and Patterson, saying he would be back at ten o'clock to join the search party. A short conversation with Major Chatsworth elicited the information that his car was waiting for him any time he wanted it, and that Jackson Ledbetter had ordered breakfast to be served in his cottage, number 105.

It was exactly like all the other cottages – stone-built and low-slung, tucked away for privacy among the flamboyant tropical trees and shrubs, presenting an unrevealing back to the pathway and a wide terrace to the sea. On the terrace, Jackson Ledbetter was sitting on a chaise-longue, wearing blue shorts and a gaudy shirt, and drinking coffee. He did not even look up as Henry approached.

Henry said, 'Mr Ledbetter?'

Ledbetter raised his head, confronting Henry with an enormous pair of dark glasses which completely masked any expression on his thin face. He said, 'I don't think we have – '

'I'm Chief Superintendent Tibbett of Scotland Yard, sir,' said Henry. 'I've been looking forward to meeting you.'

Ledbetter grunted, indicating that the sentiment was not mutual.

Henry went on, 'I expect you know that I'm investigating the murder of Senator Brett Olsen – and now, of course, of Albert Huberman as well. You knew them both well, I believe.'

'Sure. Fine men, both of them. I hope you catch that rat Robbins, Mr Tibbett.'

'The thing about catching rats,' said Henry cheerfully, 'is to have an efficient trap. Then, as I understand it, the world will beat a path to your door. Just as a matter of interest, when was the last time you saw Olsen, Mr Ledbetter?'

Ledbetter's face, behind the dark glasses, was expressionless. He said, 'The evening before he was killed. We had a drink in the bar.'

'He didn't mention a practical joke he intended to play on Huberman the next day?'

'He did not.'

'And of course you didn't suggest any such scheme to him?'

'Of course.'

'On the day of the murder,' Henry went on, 'I understand you were visiting St Boniface.'

'That's right. I had some shopping to do.'

'Shopping? Somebody told me you went fishing.'

'Then somebody told you wrong, Mr Tibbett.'

'You keep a boat on St Boniface, don't you?'

'I certainly do not.'

'Oh, well, I must have got my facts mixed up,' said Henry lightly. 'I've noticed West Indians tend to say what they think one wants to hear – very much like the Irish. Now, about this . . .' Henry took the National Airport locker key out of his pocket and threw it down on the marble-topped table. In the dead silence, it fell with a tinkling sound, and lay there between the two men, glinting in the sunshine.

Ledbetter said, 'What on earth is that?'

'Don't you recognize it? It's a key to a locker at Washington National Airport.'

'And what is that supposed to convey to me?'

'The interesting thing,' said Henry, 'is where I found it. There were two, you know. It's terribly easy to overlook a small thing like a key.'

There was another moment of dead silence. Then Ledbetter said, 'Mr Tibbett, naturally I want to co-operate in every possible way with your investigation – after all, both victims were friends of mine. But I must point out that I am on vacation and, I think I am entitled to a little privacy. This interview is quite unauthorized and unofficial, and I would appreciate it if you would confine your interrogations to a proper place and time.'

Henry grinned, picked up the key and put it back in his pocket. 'Of course, Mr Ledbetter. I'll be seeing you again . . . at the proper place and time.'

Teresa Chatsworth had left Henry at the jetty with a curt remark to the effect that she had already breakfasted and would go straight to the Club office. However, when Henry got there to pick up his car, there was no sign of her. The moke, however, was waiting – and soon Henry was eating breakfast under the arbour of potato-vines and goat's foot at the Anchorage Inn.

He was half-way through his scrambled egg and toast when Emmy came up from the beach, still in her wet swimsuit from an early dip. She kissed him, flopped into a chair and ordered orange juice. As she towelled the sea water from her short black hair, she said, 'And now, perhaps, you'll explain.'

'That's what Teresa Chatsworth keeps saying,' Henry remarked, between mouthfuls.

'Teresa? You've seen her already this morning?'

'She took the trouble to come all the way to St Boniface to meet me,' Henry said. 'First she wanted to have a private talk on the way back, and then she changed her mind. By the way, did you tell her I was going to New York last night?'

'Certainly not.' Emmy was indignant. 'I didn't tell anybody – not even John and Margaret. I told them all you were staying on St Boniface.'

'Good,' said Henry. He took a gulp of coffee and looked at his watch. 'I suppose we can be off fairly soon.'

'We?'

'The search party. Mustn't get there too soon.'

'What on earth do you mean?'

'Just playing a hunch,' Henry said. 'I hope to God I'm right. I must be right.' He hesitated. 'How would you feel about coming along with us?'

'On the search party? What possible use can I be?'

'I'm not sure. I just think it might be a good idea.' Henry spoke in the slightly vague, abstracted way that Emmy recognized as a sure sign that he was playing a situation by that strange instinct which he called his 'nose'.

She said, 'Can you tell me a little about . . . well, what you expect we'll find? Apart from Diamond and Sandy, that is.'

'Yes,' said Henry. 'We'll find a quite a lot of other people as well, including a murderer. Hello, Tom.'

Tom Bradley was coming down the staircase leading from the bedrooms to the terrace, wearing abbreviated orange shorts and a tee-shirt emblazoned with the patently untrue legend – 'St Matthew's – I'se born here'.

'Morning, Henry . . . Emmy . . . lovely day . . . didn't see you around last night, Henry . . .'

Emmy said, 'I told you, Tom – Henry spent the night on St Boniface.'

'Oh, well – *chacun à son goût*,' remarked Tom, with an execrable French accent. 'What about some breakfast, then? Where's the service around here?'

Henry said, 'To be strictly accurate, Tom, I spent last night in New York.'

Bradley did a small, involuntary double-take. Then he said, 'Oh, sure. And I nipped over to London to visit the Queen.'

'It's true, Tom,' Henry said. 'I went to New York, visited Jackson Ledbetter's apartment and flew back in the early hours of the morning. Did you know that Ledbetter is back at the Golf Club?'

'In person?'

'In person. And you'd better hurry up with your breakfast and then change into something more suitable for climbing in the rain forest, young Bradley. Unless you want to miss one of the better stories of your career.'

Tom was looking from Henry to Emmy, with an expression of comical incomprehension on his face. He said, 'What on earth do you mean?'

Henry said, 'You know perfectly well what I mean. You and Emmy are going to be the only civilians attached to the police search party going after Diamond Drake and Sandy Robbins. And, as I was just telling Emmy, we may find rather more than we bargained for.'

Derek Reynolds was suffering from an acute attack of inadequacy. He had been captured by Diamond and her men on Saturday, and now it was Tuesday morning. He had hoped that the dispersal of the group on Sunday evening, when Diamond and Candy raided Priest Town for supplies, might have given him a chance to escape or at least to communicate with the outside world. However, Diamond had shown her usual efficiency. Guard-to-prisoner ratio had never decreased below one-to-one – the guards armed and the prisoners shackled.

Monday had passed uncomfortably and uneasily. Diamond was clearly on edge, snapping out orders and lapsing into long periods of moody introspection. Several times during the day, she left the camp in the direction of the look-out tower, but returned taciturn and depressed.

Reynolds had done what he could in the way of gathering information. For one thing, he had formed a pretty accurate estimate of the size of the arms arsenal, and he was impressed. This was no mere amateur gang with home-made bombs. Which brought him to another question – who was financing and supplying the terrorists? Diamond had talked about outside support – but it seemed unlikely that any foreign power would take the trouble to intervene in a community as small and unproductive as St Matthew's.

Sergeant Reynolds was contemplating these problems when Brooks, who was on guard, suddenly said, 'Somebody coming.'

Diamond, Addison and Delaware were on their feet, guns at the ready. There was a sound of snapping twigs and rustling branches as somebody approached through the undergrowth. Then a woman's voice said softly, 'Diamond?'

Diamond relaxed. 'It's only Mrs Chatsworth,' she said. 'OK. Come right in.' Then, suddenly alert again, 'Who's that with you?'

'A friend,' said Teresa Chatsworth. 'Mr Owen.' She stepped into the clearing, followed by a tall, thin man with greying hair and a small moustache.

Teresa caught her breath in shocked surprise as she saw Candy and Reynolds, but before she could speak, Diamond said angrily, 'Where have you been? I've been waiting for orders since Saturday. When do we start?'

The tall man was staring furiously at Reynolds. 'Who in God's name is that?'

Diamond said, 'A crazy Englishman, member of the Club, came chasing after the white bitch. We had to take him.'

Owen rounded on Teresa. 'What is the meaning of this? My orders were to take Robbins and get rid of the girl.'

Diamond said, 'What was I expected to do? Let them go?'

Teresa ignored her. She said, 'Those were the orders I passed on. I never thought Addison would be so idiotic as to bring her up here.'

Diamond said, 'I can't see that it matters. Priest Town is just waiting to rise up and go into action. As soon as we get the signal to go, it'll be over in – '

The man said, 'I'm afraid you don't understand, Diamond. You have overstepped your orders catastrophically. You were never instructed to burn down the police station or murder an officer, let alone get involved in kidnapping. You have put yourself in a very serious position, and I don't know how I am going to help you.'

'I didn't burn down the police station,' said Diamond. 'I was inside, arrested, remember?'

'Please don't interrupt me. You were ordered to spring Robbins from the prison and bring him here. No more. Now police reinforcements have been brought in from all over the Caribbean, and there is a British destroyer standing offshore. You can give up all hope of an armed rising.'

Diamond faced him. She had torn off her sunglasses, and her single eye was blazing with fury. 'You filthy white pig!' she shouted. 'You never meant to go through with it, did you? You were just using us! I might have known the Chatsworth sow wouldn't – '

The man cut in, 'Please don't get hysterical. I have explained that our plans have had to be altered, thanks to your disregard of orders. If it were not for your unauthorized prisoners and the death of the policeman, I would simply arrange for you and your brother – ' he nodded curtly at Addison – 'and your friends to be taken to Tampica. Now that won't be possible. Murder is an extraditable offence. You would be brought back.'

'I've murdered nobody!' Diamond shouted. 'It was Sandy Robbins – '

'Exactly,' said the tall man softly. 'Once Sandy Robbins is unable to speak in his own defence, I think it will be possible to convince a court that he committed all three murders. As for the other prisoners – ' He broke off and turned to Teresa. 'There's nothing to keep you here any longer, Mrs Chatsworth. Thank you for showing me the way. I think you should get back to the Club now. And if you should happen to run into the police search party – just remember that I have some interesting tapes of telephone conversations.'

Teresa was looking at the tall man as if she had never seen him before. She swallowed, and said, 'What are you going to do?'

'That's no concern of yours, Teresa. Just remember, if we all keep our heads, nobody will get hurt.'

Shakily, Teresa said, 'I've never said anything on the telephone that could incriminate me. I agreed to help the CPF, for the sake of the Club, but – '

The tall man smiled. 'My dear, you are an accessory to murder, after the fact. I think that is the British legal term.'

'But – '

'Please go now. We haven't much time.'

Teresa did not answer. She turned and ran stumblingly back into the darkness of the woods. The tall man said, 'Please come with me, Diamond. I'll explain what I have in mind.'

Looking mutinous, Diamond walked slowly towards the tall man. He smiled, took her arm, and walked with her to the far side of the clearing, beyond the tents. Reynolds caught one phrase – 'The police will be armed, of course. Now, you have some police rifles here . . .' Then they were out of earshot.

Candy was whimpering. 'They're going to kill us . . . they're going to kill us . . .'

'Why should they kill you, Candy? Derek asked quietly.

Candy sniffed. 'That man's name isn't Owen,' she said. 'That's Jackson Ledbetter. I know him, and so he'll have to kill me . . .'

'Why do you think he ordered Mrs Chatsworth to get rid of you?'

'I don't know. Because of Al, I guess . . .'

'Mr Huberman?'

'Yes. I don't understand it, but . . . well, you heard what Diamond said. Somebody murdered Al, and they're trying to frame Sandy for it. Diamond said he was murdered at the Golf Club, so he never went back to the States after all. He came back to the Club, and if I'd been there I might have seen him . . . and I knew he was giving money to Senator Olsen ...' She began to cry again. 'Sandy, I'm scared ... I don't want to die ...'

Sandy Robbins looked at Derek Reynolds over Candy's blonde head, which was buried in his shirtfront. Since all three were bound hand and foot, movement was restricted to a minimum. He said, 'Mr Reynolds, they'll surely kill me and maybe you. But we've got to get Candy out of this. She's done nothing.'

'Neither have you, Robbins.'

Sandy's face lit up. 'You believe that? Man, I thank you.'

At that moment, Diamond shouted, 'Addie! Brooks! Del! Over here – we need to talk. Keep your guns trained on the prisoners.'

The three guards backed away towards Diamond and Ledbetter. When they were out of earshot, Reynolds whispered urgently, 'Listen, you two. I'm not a stamp collector. Well, only an amateur. I'm Chief Superintendent Tibbett's sergeant from Scotland Yard.'

'I don't see that helps any,' said Candy.

'Tibbett's sure to come with the search party. I sent him a note before I took off after Candy, and he'll have made sense of it by now. The only reason we haven't been found yet is that he's holding off deliberately.'

'Looks like he's held off too long,' Sandy remarked. 'If the police had gotten here yesterday – '

'You'd have gone straight back to prison, with a double murder charge, or even triple, just as Diamond said. Now, I'll tell you what I think they're planning over there, and what we must do ...'

The atmosphere in the encampment after the departure of Jackson Ledbetter was, to say the least, oppressive. Guards and prisoners formed two uneasy groups. Diamond scowled and fingered her gun. Addison had been sent to the tower as a lookout. Brooks and Delaware sat on the ground, elbows on knees and heads down, saying nothing and looking at nobody.

Suddenly there was a crashing in the undergrowth and Addison burst into the clearing. 'They're coming! They're on the trail to the tower! Listen, you can hear them!'

Diamond, Brooks and Delaware sprang into action. The prisoners were hustled behind the tents, accompanied by Brooks and

Delaware. Diamond and her brother went to the edge of the clearing and stood listening intently. Sure enough, before long came the sound of voices, of men moving through the forest. Diamond lifted her head, like an animal scenting prey. Then she said, 'Now!'

There was a deafening explosion of sound as Diamond and Addison sent a barrage of shots into the forest in the direction of the searchers. Then a brief silence, punctuated by shouts from the hunters. Diamond turned her head briefly and nodded to Brooks and Delaware, before loosing another volley of shots at the unseen targets.

At once, the machetes flashed from the belts of the two black men, and Candy screamed in terror – but this time the wickedly curved knives were not to be used for murder. Instead, the prisoners' bonds were quickly and neatly cut, as more shots rang out.

In the moment of silence that followed, Reynolds took a deep breath and shouted at the top of his lungs, 'Don't fire! Tibbett, don't fire! For God's sake, don't fire!'

The answer was another vicious burst of gunfire from Diamond and Addison, and a blow from a rifle butt that sent Reynolds sprawling to the ground with blood trickling from his mouth. Sandy took up the cry. 'Don't fire! Don't fire!'

Henry's voice, magnified by a loud-hailer, came out of the dark forest. 'I can hear you, Reynolds. Diamond, we are advancing on the encampment. We will not fire a single shot. You will be solely responsible for any casualties. Do you understand me?'

Brooks and Delaware stood with rifles trained on the three prisoners, immobile and questioning. Diamond turned and shook her head negatively. Then she called, 'What are your terms, Tibbett?'

'Release your prisoners. Send them out to us now. When they have reached us unharmed, we will move in. And when I say prisoners, I include Sandy Robbins. They will walk slowly. We will not fire.'

There was a moment of dead silence. Then Diamond laughed. 'Your terms are accepted.' She turned to the prisoners. 'Go on. Get out.'

Sandy and Candy looked at Reynolds as he struggled to his feet. He said, 'Follow me. Don't hurry. Don't look back.'

Slowly, the three walked across the clearing and into the woods. Once in their shelter, Candy broke into a run, but Sandy restrained her. Reynolds said, out of his shattered mouth, 'That's right. Slowly. A bargain has been struck. We must keep our side of it.'

So it was that several minutes passed before Henry was shaking Reynolds's hand and fixing him up with disinfectant for his bleeding jaw, and Candy was weeping with relief in Emmy's arms, and Tom Bradley was clapping Sandy Robbins on the back and laughing aloud and shouting congratulations. Then Sandy was surrounded by the policemen of St Matthew's, his erstwhile gaolers, who swept him up in a great explosion of joy and relief, while Owen Montague looked on with a tolerant smile. Needless to say, when the search party arrived at the encampment, it was deserted.

The police at once began collecting up the boxes of arms and ammunition. Henry took Emmy's arm and said, 'Let's go up to the tower. There may be something to see.'

From the platform of the tower, there was a clear view down to Jellyfish Bay. A white motor boat, looking like a toy, was anchored just off the beach, and a man was sitting in it.

'Mr Jackson Ledbetter,' said Henry. 'I wonder what Diamond will tell him. Presumably that the plan succeeded, that she and Addison provoked the police into firing and then dispatched the prisoners with police rifles. Shot by the police while trying to escape – quite an ingenious idea, considering the fix that Mr Ledbetter was in. I must consider recommending Sergeant Reynolds for promotion.'

'How could you possibly have known what was going to happen?' Emmy asked.

'I didn't, of course. I just had to make the best guesses I could. The first thing was to get Ledbetter down here, by Lucy's phone call. I'm glad now that you refused to do it yourself, impersonating Teresa. It was much better coming from Lucy, whom he knows. He never questioned it when she passed on as gossip from Teresa that Huberman's luggage had been found and fingerprinted. Of course, Ledbetter was the tall bearded man at the airport – Officer Stanton even found the false beard stashed in a second locker. He'd travelled as Huberman, on Huberman's boarding pass – that's why the airline swore that Huberman was on the plane. And then, of course, Lucy was able to elaborate on Diamond's activities, which the press has been playing down, on the Governor's orders. Ledbetter never intended things to get out of hand. He had to come down and ... ah, I think something is happening down there.'

As he spoke, four running figures broke out of the trees and on to the beach. In a moment they were in the boat, the anchor was up, and the small white hull was cutting a curved swathe of wash through the deep blue water, headed for Tampica.

'What will happen now?' Emmy asked.

'I don't know. There are several possibilities. Ledbetter may take them to Tampica, but it would be a big risk for him. To dispose of them would also be a risk – but if I were Diamond, I think I'd prefer to be in the hands of the police than where she is now. Of course, she may not know for certain that it was Ledbetter who killed Olsen and Huberman. Her part in the operation was merely to keep trouble simmering on the island in order to scotch the cotton-growing plan. Pity for Ledbetter that she got over-enthusiastic at the same time that the CPF was about to be investigated for bribery. As I said the other day, Diamond was never intended to be more than a diversion.'

'And Teresa?'

'She was the channel of communication. She passed orders and money from Ledbetter to Diamond – who knew him only as the mysterious Mr Owen. Ledbetter also undoubtedly told her that Huberman was going into hiding at the Club to avoid an embarrassing investigation – which is why Teresa arranged for his cottage not to be cleaned. I'm sure she didn't know about the murders. She thought Sandy was guilty. She just never connected the two operations.'

The boat was out of sight by now. Henry looked down at the shimmering sea, glinting with jewel colours. He said, 'Oh, well. One thing is certain. Ledbetter will come back to the Club, where I shall have the dubious pleasure of arresting him for murder. There's going to be quite an international furore, I'm afraid.'

But Henry was wrong. Mr Jackson Ledbetter did not return to

the Golf Club that evening, and it was not until late the following day that he was found. He was in his boat, the *Pelican*, which was picked up by some fishermen drifting off St Mark's island: and his skull had been split from behind by a machete, very neatly, like a coconut.

Epilogue

It was a relaxed, informal gathering at the Anchorage Inn. Sandy Robbins was back in his usual place behind the bar, his face one huge, perpetual grin. He was being assisted in his work by Candy Stevenson, who had moved to the Anchorage and was being employed by John and Margaret. Sandy's grandmother, a conservative matriarch, was alleged to be dubious about a mixed marriage, but no opposition was foreseen from any other quarter.

Across the bay, the lights of Priest Town glittered, and from a nearby bar the music of a steel band throbbed through the warm night air. Business at the Golf Club was still not brisk, but the *Island Eagle* had brought several members over that day, following the lifting of the curfew and the closing of the murder cases. The skipper who had helped Addison Drake in the abduction of Candy had slipped quietly home to Tampica and his absence was hardly noticed. Very conspicuous, however, was the surprise resignation of Major Chatsworth. He and Mrs Chatsworth had already left the island for England and the committee was busy trying to find a replacement. They had offered the job to John Colville, but he had turned it down, saying that he was happy in his own pub.

At the largest table in the bar, the Tibbetts, the Colvilles, Derek Reynolds, Sir Geoffrey Patterson, Owen Montague and Tom Bradley made up a lively, talkative party. Everybody seemed to be asking Henry questions, and nobody was giving him time to answer them.

At last, Henry said, 'Look, I can't lay this thing out for you precisely, because it's too complicated, and in any case . . . well, I was playing hunches. I'll try to put it as simply as I can. I started from the premiss that Sandy was innocent. Why? Several reasons, not least the faith that John and Margaret had in him. The fact that he had never been connected with the revolutionary movement. And, most important, the fact that he handles a machete better than anybody on the island. It's lucky for Sandy that he has an alibi for Ledbetter's murder, because that's the way he would have done it. Clean. One stroke. Like splitting a coconut.

'That being so, I had to consider who had actually killed Olsen, and the answer kept coming back to Ledbetter or somebody he'd hired. The cotton interests and the kick-back scandals all led in that direction – to Huberman or Ledbetter. But Sandy himself gave Huberman his alibi, and Ledbetter seemed to be right out of it. He was on St Boniface when Olsen was killed, and he was in New York at the time of Huberman's murder.

'It was an instructive experience – going to New York for the night and being back here for breakfast. It made me realize that Ledbetter could have done it in reverse. In fact, of course, he arranged to meet Huberman not in Washington or New York, but on St Boniface – a secret meeting prior to both of them returning to the States. Huberman was easily persuaded into a change of plan – that the best and most secure place to talk was, after all, the Golf Club, and Ledbetter could take them there in his boat, the *Pelican*. It was really very easy.

'But – how far can you stretch coincidence? Addison Drake happened to have given in his notice the previous evening, happened to be on duty that night, happened to leave on the first launch in the morning, happened not to have logged the arrival of the *Pelican*. All that had to be arranged – but by whom? Well, of course, by the person to whom Ledbetter spoke after he had spoken to Huberman – Teresa Chatsworth – who, incidentally, gave herself away by mentioning to me that Jackson Ledbetter was going to issue a rebuttal of the Mawson column on Monday. She couldn't have known that unless she had spoken either to Ledbetter or to one of Mawson's men.

'As for Olsen's murder – that was necessary because of the Justice Department inquiries, and to pin it on a native of St Matthew's was just what suited Ledbetter. Olsen had a reputation as a practical joker, and I've no doubt Ledbetter suggested the idea of hiring Sandy to make a fool out of Huberman. Then he took the launch to St Boniface, saying he was going shopping, and came back in his own boat. Sandy wouldn't have seen him lurking off Mango Trunk Bay, because he was swimming underwater. Once the little farce had been played out, Ledbetter had only to come ashore and attack Olsen from behind.'

Henry paused. Then he said, 'I'm morally certain that I'm telling it as it happened, but I'm glad I don't have to prove it in a court of law. As Tom remarked, Ledbetter and his Confederation are powerful people. I think I'd have got him for Huberman's murder, but it might have been harder to clear Sandy in the Olsen case. I don't know why it never occurred to me that Diamond would take care of the whole thing. Ledbetter cheated her, and that's something Diamond would never forgive.'

Emmy said, 'What are you going to do about Diamond, Henry? And her brother and the other two men?'

It was Sir Geoffrey Patterson who answered. He said, 'Dear Mrs Tibbett, we have talked long and hard over this matter. Diamond and her gang have disappeared. They are somewhere in the Caribbean, that is for sure, unless they are dead – we have no way of knowing. Only one thing is certain – none of them will ever set foot in the British Seaward Islands or Tampica again, because we have arrest warrants for murder out against three of them in the case of the police officer, and for kidnapping against all of them. Sooner than pursue the matter to its bitter conclusion, we have all decided that . . .' The Governor beamed and spread out his hands, embracing the lights of Priest Town, the steel band in the distance, the contented drinkers at the bar. 'St Matthew's is back to normal,' he said. 'That's what we think is important.'

It was just then that Sandy Robbins strolled over to the table, leaving Candy behind the bar. He said to Reynolds, 'Hey, Derek, man. Up there in the forest, you said something like you weren't a real stamp collector, only an amateur. Right?'

'Right, Sandy,' said Reynolds.

'Well, you did me a mighty good turn, man. So I wondered if this would have any interest for you. My father gave it to me before he died – said it might be worth something, but maybe he was just crazy. Anyhow, man, it's no use to me, so if you want it, it's yours.'

And he handed Derek Reynolds a yellowing envelope, with a Tampican postmark franking an oblong, purple fourpenny stamp.

Afterword

I hasten to point out that all characters, organizations and islands (except Antigua and St Thomas) in this book are pure fiction. I think everybody must be aware of the various corruption scandals which have recently erupted in Washington DC, but none of them has touched the cotton industry in any way. There is, of course, no such organization as the Cotton Producers' Federation – and if there were, I am sure its members would be the most blameless of citizens.

As a matter of interest, there is indeed some talk of reviving the cultivation of Sea Island cotton in the British Caribbean islands where it used to be raised extensively. If and when this scheme gets going, I am sure it will be with the good wishes and encouragement of the United States cotton industry.

I have to confess that the Anchorage Inn – but not its personnel – is based on an actual establishment. Those who know it will recognize it. Those who don't . . . don't expect me to identify it. It's much too precious.

More About Penguins and Pelicans

Penguinews, which appears every month, contains details of all the new books issued by Penguins as they are published. From time to time it is supplemented by our stocklist, which includes around 5,000 titles.

A specimen copy of *Penguinews* will be sent to you free on request. Please write to Dept EP, Penguin Books Ltd, Harmondsworth, Middlesex, for your copy.

In the U.S.A.: For a complete list of books available from Penguins in the United States write to Dept CS, Penguin Books, 625 Madison Avenue, New York, New York 10022.

In Canada: For a complete list of books available from Penguins in Canada write to Penguin Books Canada Ltd, 2801 John Street, Markham, Ontario L3R 1B4.